The Hearse

GandBPublishing@gmail.com

The Hearse

By R. L. Link

The Hearse
All Rights Reserved.
Copyright © 2023 Rollie Link

ISBN: 9798860268050

To Madeline Moscow

The Hearse

Just another February day in Omaha

Omaha, Nebraska sits on the west bank of the Missouri River directly across from Council Bluffs, Iowa, connected by the Aksarben Bridge — the new Aksarben Bridge, not the old one. The old one was torn down in 1968 to accommodate US Interstate 480 and a new bridge where it passes over the Missouri River. That bridge has no name, but everyone still refers to it as the Aksarben bridge. If one looks at the name "Aksarben," one will notice that it is Nebraska spelled backwards. It is not clear who actually came up with such a clever name, but it caught on and Omaha is filled with Aksarben this and Aksarben that.

Omaha is the Gateway to the West, and they have a museum there to prove it. To folks in Omaha, Council Bluffs is the end of the East. Omaha is where you see your first genuine cowboys, ask anybody. The cowboys you see in Council Bluffs are farmers in cowboy garb. That is the image, anyway. The reality is that cowboy country and real cowboys don't actually appear until one gets past North Platte, Nebraska, four hours and one minute west of Omaha by Interstate 80, which crosses into Omaha from Council Bluffs a few miles south of the Aksarben bridge. The cornfields and farms west of Omaha for 280 miles look much the same as the cornfields and farms one sees across the whole expanse of Iowa and

1

Illinois before Iowa. But if you ask anyone, Omaha is where the West begins.

This all has little to do with the story except it brings us to Carston Hancock III trudging up Harney Street against the wind, wearing his Tony Lama cowboy boots and his Stetson hat screwed down on his head, alternately clutching the collar of his western-styled winter coat and putting his hands over his ears to protect them from the minus-five-degree windchill brought down on him from the polar vortex that had held Omaha in its grip for ten days straight. He reached the door of the brick four-story edifice known as the old Hancock building in downtown Omaha just as he thought he could stand the frigid cold no longer and stepped into the warmth of the downstairs entry. He took a deep breath of warm air.

It wasn't just the relief from the freezing cold outside that Carston felt whenever he entered the old dilapidated building that had been constructed by his grandfather, Carston Hancock the First. It was the warmth of the building itself. A warmth he had felt since as early as he could remember. However, even though Carston the Third had an office on the third floor of the building, the building was no longer owned by the family. Carston Hancock II sold it years ago when property values were high and a fortune was to be made. A fortune which lamentably Carston the Third was not heir to and undoubtedly never would be. A few years after the sale his father passed and the fortune went to his stepmother, Pamala Fritz Blain Hancock Miller. Carston the Third had no idea where Pamala was living at the moment, evidence of the relationship with his

2

stepmother that was never going to result in Carston seeing any part of the inheritance. The building seemed deserted, and that was because it essentially was.

In the foyer, Carston dug the key to the mailbox from his pocket and checked the box nestled on the wall with a number of other boxes, many of which stood open and some with doors hanging by one hinge. He was surprised to find it empty. His office manager seldom checked the mail, even though the task was in her job description, which Carston had penned two years earlier in an unsuccessful attempt to establish just what her job was supposed to be. Carston trudged up the steps to the third floor and through the wooden door whose frosted glass windowpane read, "Carston Hancock III, Private Investigations." The office phone number and information about how to get ahold of him after office hours was posted on yellowed 5x7 card taped to the bottom right corner of the window.

"Whoa, it is fucking cold out there," Carston exclaimed to Stephanie, his office manager and receptionist, who was bent over the bottom drawer of a solid oak filing cabinet that had seen better days. The cabinet was part of the collection of once-elegant furniture from the office that his father had maintained after the sale of the building and that now housed Carston Hancock III, Private Investigations. Stephanie did not stand up. Carston admired her firm ass stretching the fabric of her navy blue skirt.

"What are you looking at?" Stephanie asked, not standing up or turning around. "Whatever it is, look at something else."

Carston diverted his gaze to Stephanie's desk and the mail stacked in a neat pile at the corner. He walked to the desk and started going through it.

"You got the mail today," Carston said in wonderment.

Stephanie stood and turned. "Just bills," she said.

"They keep coming," Carston exclaimed. "The whole world could crumble down around humanity and you would still get bills."

"Is that supposed to be some attempt at a profound statement on life, or what?" Stephanie asked sardonically.

Carston looked up from the stack of mail and smiled. Seeing Stephanie in the morning was the high point of his day, now that he wasn't seeing his wife Megan every morning anymore. Steph was gorgeous. She was five-foot-eight according to her driver's license, which Carston had a copy of. She was slim, thirty-one years old, with just the nicest ass and perkiest breasts imaginable, which she covered with a satin blouse and a professional-looking business suit that contrasted daily with Carston's western wear.

Stephanie had been working at Carston Hancock Investigations for two years. When his previous secretary and receptionist, who had also been Carston the Second's secretary and receptionist, finally retired at the age of 70, Carston had posted a help wanted ad online. Stephanie came in for an interview and he hired her on looks alone. Sadly, her work was competent but not much more. She was punctual, he could say that for her. Her first day on the job, she had changed her title from secretary/receptionist to office

4

manager to impress her friends who stopped in daily to chat, cultivating the impression that she was running the detective agency and that the whole place would go to hell in a handbasket if it weren't for her, which was hardly accurate. But he was fine with it. She looked good sitting there at her desk when potential clients came in, and first impressions were everything. She could call herself whatever she wanted, he didn't care.

"Listen up," Steph said in a serious tone. "You'll probably want to go in your office, clean yourself up, tuck in your shirt and find that sports coat you lost in there somewhere last summer so you look presentable. Pick up your office a little bit and clear off your desk. You got a client coming in."

Carston just stood there.

"Chop-chop," Steph said, motioning with the backs of her hands, shooing him toward his office door. "You need a case to work on. Those bills don't pay themselves. You need to make some money or you're going to lose that sweet ride you're so proud of. One of those bills is a past-due notice on your car payment."

Carston frowned at the envelopes in his hand.

"Move it," Steph said. "I'm calling the lady right now to tell her that you finally came in. She's been calling all morning. She wants to see you *tout de suite*."

"It's nine in the morning," Carston said. "You could have just told her I come in at nine."

Steph took a seat at her desk and leaned back, kicking off her shoes. "I'm calling her right now," she warned.

"What's it about?" Carston asked, halfheartedly turning toward his door.

"Wouldn't say. All I know is she sounded rich," Steph replied.

"Sounded rich?" Carston asked, raising his eyebrows.

"She didn't ask what you charge, she just said she wanted to hire you to do something for her. Exact words, 'do something for her.' Only rich people don't ask how much."

"If you say so." Carston raised his eyebrows again.

"Quit making faces." Steph turned her attention to the phone already in her hand. "Yes, Ms Thompson. This is Stephanie at Carston Hancock Investigations. Detective Hancock finally got in and he is anxious to meet with you. I'm sure that whatever you need done, he is up to it."

There was silence as Steph held the phone to her ear. "Yes, fifteen minutes."

She put down the phone. "She says to sit on you until she gets here. You got fifteen minutes to get your act together."

Carston turned and went into his office. It looked like someone had been living there, which was exactly what had been happening up until three weeks ago when Carston had moved into the Hotel LeVant, twelve blocks from the agency and just outside the Old Market district. Outside the district enough that the cost of a room was reasonable, especially if you were doing an extended stay and weren't paying for the room by the hour. Before the office, he had lived at a friend's house in West Omaha for two weeks after Megan kicked him out of their house out near Standing

Bear Lake. But then Steph had kicked him out of the office, telling him that he was starting to make it stink like some teenager's bedroom. That's how he ended up living in the Hotel LeVant, which wasn't too bad, really. It was better than living on the streets.

Carston had no idea where his sports coat was in the mess. He started picking up. A lot of the stuff laying around had found its way to the office when he was living there and had never found a place to reside in his new digs. There wasn't a lot of space in the room at the LeVant. He spent more time trying to decide where to put the stuff he picked up looking for the sports coat than he did actually looking for it.

"I don't hear a lot of cleaning going on in there," Steph called through the door.

"I'm looking for my sports coat," he called back.

Carston's detective agency had occupied this office for ten years. Before that, it had been his dad's office, even after he had sold the building. Carston the Third had always wondered why Carston the Second maintained an office there, when from what he could glean from the papers he found in the old file cabinet, his father made his fortune off the sale of the building and had no need to work at all. He had asked his landlord about it, but the landlord was just managing the property for some rich conglomerate and had no idea what his father had done there. It annoyed Carston that he was a private investigator and he couldn't even determine why his father kept an office in the old Hancock building and what he did there. And there was no one left to ask. Carston had no brothers or sisters, and his mother had passed away while he was in college. It was quick enough, she died of pneumonia. The doctors had said it was bronchitis and sent her home, but it wasn't, it was pneumonia. She died in her sleep, his father laying there listening to her raspy breathing until it stopped. But then it was too late and by the time the ambulance arrived she was dead.

When his mother died, Carston was attending the University of Nebraska, Omaha working on a degree in criminal justice, pretty much convinced that a graduate of the University of Nebraska, Omaha with a degree in criminal justice could get a job easy enough with the Omaha Police Department. He graduated in the upper middle of his class, applied to the Omaha Police Department and waited. During the wait he worked security at the Westroads Mall with four other guys and a woman who had all graduated from the University of Nebraska, Omaha with degrees in criminal justice and had put in applications at the Omaha Police Department. A year went by and the woman went across the river and applied to the Council Bluffs Police Department. She got hired. The other four ran across the river and put in their applications as well and waited. Six months later they decided to shotgun it and applied at every little suburb and small town in the greater Omaha area. Then they waited.

During the waiting time is when Carston's father passed away. Just a year after Carston's mother died he had married Pamala in Puerto Vallarta, Mexico. For some reason Carston had not been invited. His father told him it was a whirlwind romance that ended there. From what

Carston could tell, it did truly end there. Pamala took off with the Hancock fortune the morning after Carston II's funeral. At least she had paid for the cremation. She did not say goodbye, she didn't say see you later, nice knowing you or *adios*. She said nothing to him. She just left. A week or two later, a realtor contacted Carston to inform him that his father's house, which the realtor referred to as his stepmother's house, was for sale and any stuff that he still had left there would need to be moved out right away, as the house was priced to sell and it would go fast. Carston moved what was there to a storage shed.

One morning a few months later, the property management company that was managing the old Hancock building contacted him to ask what he wanted to do about his father's office. At the time Carston was not aware that his father even had an office in the old Hancock building. That very afternoon he met with the building manager to look at his father's office. Walking in, he felt the warmth that he felt every time he entered the building. He had grown up in the Hancock building, and even though the place had seen better days, by the time he left that day, Carston had signed a lease to take over his father's office. For two months he used his office to study for his Nebraska private investigator's license. When he passed the exam, the background check and the interview with the Sheriff, he got bonded, rehired his father's old receptionist Aggie and opened his agency.

Business had gone reasonably well for close to a decade. Carston learned his trade, made some money, mostly working for insurance companies as a contract investigator. He and Megan had met in college and reconnected when she moved back to Omaha between jobs to live with her parents. They married and bought one of the least prestigious houses on the fringes of a prestigious neighborhood out by Standing Bear Lake. Everything was going well for him, living paycheck to paycheck but still making ends meet, until it all fell apart over one little indiscretion.

On second thought, it wasn't just that one small indiscretion. There were other things leading up to it, but the one small indiscretion was the tipping point. That one small indiscretion landed Carston in the Hotel LeVant and found him late with his rent at the old Hancock building and late on his car payment. And to make matters worse, it had been a long cold winter and his insurance gigs had dried up during the holidays. And now it was February and Carston was broke. Everything he made went toward payroll. Megan's father was bankrolling her, he never liked Carston anyway, and his marriage was a war of attrition that he was losing. Carston was ready to surrender, but so far there had been no terms for it. Carston was waiting. It was out of his hands.

"What are you thinking about?" he heard Steph at the door.

"Wondering how the hell I got myself in this predicament," Carston answered.

"I think we know how you got yourself in this predicament," Steph answered.

"I guess," Carston replied thoughtfully.

"You want me to talk to Megan, see what I can do? Put in a good word for you?"

"I really don't think she wants to talk about it," Carston replied after a moment of thought.

"I could do that," Steph said.

"I don't think so," Carston replied.

"Okay, I'll just let you take care of it," Steph said. "You've been doing so well so far. It's your marriage."

Neither spoke for a minute.

"You got five minutes to get your shit together," Steph broke the silence. "So listen up, just so we're on the same page: if the new client asks, I'm telling her we get five bills a day plus expenses."

"Five hundred a day?" Carston commented, raising his eyebrows again.

"Five hundred a day, plus expenses," Steph corrected. "That's what we soak the insurance companies for."

"This isn't an insurance company," Carston replied. "We can't afford to chase away business right now. How about we shoot her a deal."

"One, you don't even know what she wants you to do yet," Steph exclaimed. "Two, this bitch is rich, mark my words."

"You're the boss," Carston panned.

"Don't you forget it," Steph laughed and left the doorway. "Get that office presentable. You wanna look like you're worth five hundred a day."

"Plus expenses," Carston shot back. "Hey, what's her name?" he called out after a moment.

"Glenn Thompson," Stephanie shouted back.

Glenda

Carston was seated in his partially picked-up office behind his partially-cleared desk when he heard the door to the agency open and the unmistakable sound of high-heeled shoes.

"May I take your coat and gloves?" he heard Stephanie ask pleasantly.

He heard the woman mumble a thank you and the sound of her taking off her coat. A moment later a tall, slim woman, blond hair with subtle grey streaks, elegantly dressed for almost nine-thirty in the morning and very much Carston's type, sashayed her shoes into his office.

Carston stood up. "Ms. Thompson, please take a seat," he said, sweeping his hand toward the chair on the opposite side of the desk.

Glenn Thompson looked around the room, not interested at all in the chair that Carston was gesturing toward. She spotted a couch on the back wall beside the door, turned and flounced to the couch, flopping down not quite elegantly into the cushion and making herself at home.

"Can I call you Glenn?" Carston sat down himself, behind his desk.

"My friends call me Glenn," she said nonchalantly. "You can call me Glenda."

Glenda was watching Carston get an eyeful of her. She was used to that. She was getting an eyeful of him at the same time. He wasn't quite what she expected, although she wasn't sure what she had expected. First of all, Carston was tall and looked quite fit and quite attractive. He had thick black wavy hair that made him look like a private detective right out of one of those old black and white movies they used to make about private detectives. He had wide shoulders and no gut. He looked like he wasn't a stranger at the gym. He had a bit of a stubble going. Obviously, he was going for a look. There was a coat rack on the wall behind him with a Stetson cowboy hat hanging from one hook, a wool mackinaw on another. Glenda bent down and looked under his desk. He was wearing pointed-toe cowboy boots, not those square-toe boots that were the fashion nowadays.

"So, he's a cowboy," Glenda thought. Half of Omaha thought that they were cowboys. That was alright. She was looking for a cowboy sort.

Carston was watching Glenda scope him out. She was giving him the onceover twice. She bent down and looked under his desk. He wiggled his feet, wondering what else she would be looking for. She looked up.

"What can I do for you?" Carston asked.

Glenda leaned back on the couch, getting comfortable. "I need you to locate a missing hearse."

"You want me to find a missing hearse?" Carston always answered with a repeat question when he didn't know what else to say.

"That's what I just said," Glenda replied. "I want you to locate a missing hearse. That's what you do, right? Locate missing things?"

Carston took a second to answer. She was right, that's what he did. He didn't know why he was trying to be coy. It was just something about her. "Okay, I get five hundred a day for finding hearses," he said flippantly without getting any details whatsoever and just as suddenly feeling like a rookie taking on his first case.

"Fine," she replied just as quickly. "And I'll give you a five grand bonus if you find it before the cops." She could see that she had his attention.

"Okay, let's start from the beginning." Carston sat up straight, pulled a notebook in front of him and took a pen out of the cup on his desk with the words "Aksarben Rodeo 2002" emblazoned around it such that one could only read a part of it without turning the cup.

"My uncle Thomas, from Montreal, passed away last week. He moved to Montreal from Omaha some time ago. He grew up here though. His whole family is here. He wanted to be buried in the family plot." Glenda stopped speaking for a moment.

"Okay," Carston responded to the pause.

"The funeral home in Montreal put his casket on a plane to Omaha yesterday morning with an arrival time of noon. He arrived at Eppley a half-hour early. A hearse from the funeral home in Council Bluffs was there to pick up the casket and deliver it back. But then the hearse was stolen between Eppley and the funeral home. So now we don't know where Uncle Thomas is. I want you to find him."

"So Uncle Thomas lives in Montreal but he wants to be buried here, he gets a flight into Omaha, he gets picked up at Eppley around 11:30 in the morning by a funeral home in Council Bluffs, then somehow the hearse with the body in it gets stolen between Eppley and the funeral home."

"Isn't that what I just said?" Glenda asked.

14

"Yes, you did, but there's a lot missing in the narrative. Did the hearse with the drivers in it just disappear driving across the Aksarben bridge?"

"No," Glenda replied. "Just the hearse was stolen, with Uncle Thomas in it. The drivers decided to lunch at Spaghetti Works in the Old Market district before they went back to the funeral home." Glenda was already getting a little tired of having to explain everything to Carston.

"Right down the street here? In broad daylight? Did they leave it running while they were in there or something?" Carston asked.

"I don't know what they did," Glenda replied. "When you take the case then maybe you can go over to the funeral home and ask them all your questions. Or call them up, or whatever it is you do. If I had all of these answers to your questions I wouldn't need you, now would I?"

"Do you have the name of the funeral home?" Carston asked, ignoring the tart response.

"Harmon and Mott." Glenda took a business card from her purse and held it out. "I have their card."

Carston waited a moment for her to get up and bring him the card, but she sat where she was on the couch holding it toward him. He got up, went around the desk, walked the three steps to the couch, and took the card from her outstretched hand.

"Nice boots," she commented. "Tony Lamas?"

"Yep," Carston answered as he turned and walked back to his desk. He sat down, looked at the business card, put it aside and picked up his pen.

15

"Just a few more questions if you will indulge me," Carston said patronizingly. "I need a phone number where I can get ahold of you if I have any—," Carston stopped himself. "If I want to report anything to you. And an email address. And where I can find you if I need to talk to you face to face."

Glenda dug into her purse and came out with another business card. She extended it toward Carston, who sighed as he got up from his desk and came around it to retrieve the card from her.

"My card," she said as he took it from her hand.

Carston went back to his desk and looked at the card. "Flingnasties?" he commented.

"My bar," Glenda answered. "I'll save you asking me: I inherited it from my late husband Jerry."

Carston was reading the card.

"That's where you can find me," Glenda continued. My work number on the front, my mobile number on the back. You should have no trouble getting ahold of me when you have something to report."

Carston flipped the card over.

"Is there anything else?" Glenda asked. "If not, I think it is important that you get right on this. Time's wasting."

Carston looked up quizzically. "Why is it so important to find the hearse and Uncle Thomas before the cops do?"

"I don't think that has any bearing on the case, Detective Hancock. You locate it, tell me where it is, and I'll take it from there. You don't even have to recover it, just let me know where it is. When I

16

get my hands on Uncle Thomas, you get your fee plus your bonus."

"So to make things clear: you don't care about the hearse, you just want Uncle Thomas?"

"Uncle Thomas is in the hearse," Glenda replied.

"This all sounds a little shady," Carston commented as Glenda stood up. "Why is it so important to find Uncle Thomas and his ride before the cops do?" he asked again.

"Evidently you don't take a hint," Glenda replied. "That's none of your business."

"I have my standards," Carston said seriously. "I don't want to get dragged into anything that isn't above board."

She turned to him and stood for a moment. "I've been in the bar business since I was ten years old. Every bar that ever opened, the owner planned to open an upscale establishment and cater to upper-crust clientele. That's when they open. They have all these high standards. But the last thing they do before they get closed down, they turn themselves into a titty bar. All those high falutin' ideals go out the door and the strippers come in. I think your detective business is at the titty-bar stage." She shrugged. "Sometimes being a titty bar is a better fit, sometimes it is the last dying gasp before they go belly up. Either you want the case or you don't."

"I want the case," Carston replied. "I just want you to know that I'm not going to do anything illegal or unethical if it comes to that."

"Let's hope that it doesn't come to that." She smiled, turned and walked out the door and into the reception area where Stephanie was holding her coat and gloves. She took the coat, donned it, took the gloves, thanked Stephanie and went out the door. As soon as she left, Stephanie came into Carston's office and sat on the recently vacated couch that was still warm from the previous occupant.

"Well," she said.

"What do you think?" Carston asked.

"I think it was a lot of show," Stephanie replied. "She was jerking you around."

"For what reason?" Carston asked.

"'Cause she's a bitch," Stephanie remarked.

"I'm glad you said that; I'm not allowed to," Carston responded.

"It was a lot of bullshit," Stephanie replied. "I liked the titty bar analogy and all; it sort of fits right now."

"It was titillating," Carston snarked.

Stephanie laughed. "What do you think is going on?" she asked. "I'm talking about the bonus for finding Uncle Thomas before the cops. No doubt there is something going on. I mean, who pays a detective five bills a day and a five grand bonus to find something the cops are already looking for?"

"No idea," Carston replied. "It's none of my business, isn't that what she said?"

Stephanie shrugged her shoulders. "When you think about it, considering we're taking this case so that we can pay the overdue bills this month and hopefully have enough leftover to pay me, maybe it is better if we don't know why she wants to find him before the cops. All she wants you to do is locate the hearse with her uncle in it, let her know where it is and sit on it until she shows

18

up. 'Your honor, that's all I had to do with it. I found the hearse and collected my check.'"

"Probably right," Carston said. "I'm going to start off over to the police station and see what police records has on it, then I'm going to prowl around a little. I'll end up over at the funeral home in Council Bluffs eventually and find the hearse drivers, try to get a feel for this thing."

"Sounds like a plan," Stephanie agreed.

"I'll call you with a status report when I have a status to report," Carston said.

"I'm going out for lunch with an old friend who just blew into town, it might be a long one. Lots of catching up to do. If you call, just leave me a message and I'll get right on it when I get back," she replied.

Carston got up from his desk and took his coat from the rack. Stephanie remained seated. "Have you heard what the weather is supposed to do?" he asked as he put on the coat.

"Supposed to warm up a little later," she answered.

"About time," Carston remarked, taking the Stetson from the hook where it hung. "My lucky day: I get a big case and it warms up for me to work it. Can't beat that."

"Can't beat that," Stephanie repeated, still not getting up from the couch. "Anything you need me to do before I head out for lunch?"

Carston stood for a moment. "I don't know of anything at the moment, but we'll see what happens. Something comes up, I'll probably need you to get on it. As soon as I know where we are going on this I'll let you know. I'll leave you a message if you aren't here."

"I'll be back as soon as I can get away," Stephanie smiled. "You know how it is, old friends you haven't seen for a while."

As Carston went toward the door, Stetson in hand, Stephanie held up a slip of paper. He stopped and took it from her.

"Address of Harmon and Mott Funeral Home and Crematorium in Council Bluffs," she said before he could look at it. He stuck it in his coat pocket without comment and continued out of the office.

Stephanie tried to relax on the couch. There was nothing she could do but wait for something to come up, just like Carston said. They didn't work a lot of cases like this one. No one did. It cost a lot to hire a private detective and there weren't that many individuals who were willing to shell out that kind of money. Mostly Carston Hancock Investigations worked insurance cases, picked up the overflow that the companies' own adjustors didn't have time for. Insurance companies had the dough. The cost didn't make any difference to them; they made it up in premiums. Stephanie would have liked to see the cash flow for someplace like Mutual of Omaha. And Omaha was the center of insurance companies for the US. Insurance companies built the Omaha skyline. There had always been plenty of insurance work to keep a private eye busy in Omaha, but since the first of the year they had gotten nothing. It was a mystery to them both. Carston did a yeoman's job on the investigations, never a complaint. Stephanie submitted the reports without delay. They were a team. They never gouged the insurance companies, they never padded the bills. Carston was not a greedy man. They charged the insurance companies five hundred a day plus expenses.

Now it was the end of February. They'd had nothing but nickel-dime cases for two months. Carston had taken to chasing runaway foster kids for the Douglas County Department of Human Services and that didn't even pay their overhead. Stephanie took a deep breath. She prayed to God that Carston found that hearse with Uncle Thomas in it fast and collected that bonus. She had her own rent to pay.

Just a Routine Investigation

Carston walked the four blocks to where he had parked his Escalade earlier so that he wouldn't have to pay parking fees or plug a meter. It was only eight blocks from the parking lot connected to the LeVant to his office, but he had driven half of it to save the frigid walk. It was already starting to warm up, especially now that he was walking with the wind, not bucking it as he had on his way in to the office. It would have been a shorter walk to begin his investigation at Spaghetti Works, but he decided instead to see what he could find out at the police station first, hoping there was an incident report filed already that would lead him to the stolen hearse and an easy and quick paycheck. Stranger things had happened in his ten years as a private detective. It was surprising sometimes how much information a reporting officer didn't follow up on, preferring to pass the case on to someone else rather than put in the legwork themselves. Then there was always lag time between the filing of the report and when it arrived on someone else's desk in investigations to follow up on it. Carston could count on twenty-four hours at the least before anyone even looked at the case, and if the reporting officer was a master procrastinator and didn't file his incident report promptly, forty-eight.

He got to his car and drove directly to the police station, his tires crunching over the chunks of dirty snow and ice that were freed from the undercarriages of cars when they hit the potholes in the pavement that formed an obstacle course as they travelled the same route before him. He arrived in the parking lot to find an open spot in one of the four fifteen-minute visitor parking spaces right outside the door. The day was starting out well: first a case, and now rock star parking. If there hadn't been an open visitor's space he would have had to park in the ramp and pay. He walked quickly across the parking lot, through the double doors into the warm building and directly to police records. He knew the way. When he got to the window he was greeted less than enthusiastically by one of the three women behind the counter. The other two looked up briefly and went back to their work. The woman who greeted him did not get up from her desk. She was an average looking woman, average height and weight, dressed in an average looking skirt and blouse. Her most distinguishing feature was her voluminous black hair streaked with gray that cascaded over her shoulders. She was making the most of it. Carston thought that if she were a criminal instead of a police records clerk that the hair would give her up every time.

"What can I get you today Mr. Hancock?" she asked pleasantly enough, tossing her head back swishing the hair back and forth in the way that women with voluminous hair do subconsciously.

"I need whatever you've got on a motor vehicle theft yesterday around noon at Spaghetti Works in Old Market. It was a hearse."

The woman was typing into her computer while Carston was talking. He waited for her to finish.

"It have a body in it?" she asked.

"Yes, as a matter of fact it did, not to be confused with all the hearses that were stolen around noon outside the Spaghetti Works in Old Market that didn't have bodies in them," Carston teased.

"Smart-assery does not help me find the information you are looking for, Mr. Hancock. You should be aware of that, considering the number of times you've been in here looking for information," the records clerk deadpanned without looking up.

"Sorry, I just couldn't help myself," Carston said good-naturedly, hoping that the records clerk was sharing the levity of the moment.

"I have the call and the responding officer's disposition, no incident report yet."

"When do you think you will get the incident report?" Carston asked.

"When the officer dictates it and when one of us decides to type it in," the records clerk replied.

Carston waited for her to say something more. The printer just inside the window and on the right behind the counter began to make a whirring sound. The woman got up from behind her desk and crossed the room to it. She stood for a few seconds until the whirring stopped, followed by a click as the printer spit the paper report into a tray. The woman took it from the tray and slid it across the counter to Carston.

"Ten bucks if you want to take it with you. You get to look for free."

"I know," Carston acknowledged, turning the paper right side up and reading it. He pulled a small spiral notebook from his coat pocket and started jotting down information, case number, date, time, location, the names of the two funeral home employees, make, model, year and license plate number of the vehicle. A short narrative that said nothing more than the two employees left the hearse with the engine running and the doors locked parked a block from Spaghetti Works in the Old Market district while they went in to have lunch. They came out approximately forty-five minutes later and the hearse was gone. There was nothing more. The officer referred the case to investigations. In a note at the bottom, almost an afterthought, the responding officer reported that there was a body in a casket in the back of the hearse. That was the extent of the report.

Carston looked up. The woman had returned to her desk.

"What do you do with these reports if I don't pay for them, if I just jot down the info and leave?" he asked.

"I put it through the shredder," the woman replied.

"That's kind of a waste, isn't it? What would happen if I just grabbed it and ran?" Carston said, raising his eyebrows.

"I would jump that counter, run you down and beat you to within an inch of your life." She smiled but did not look up from her computer screen.

He stood grinning at her and pulling the report slowly across the counter toward himself with his index finger, keeping his eyes on the woman who still was not looking up.

"Same thing I tell you every time you come in here and ask me that question," she said, making no effort to get up from the desk.

"Can I take a picture of it?" Carston asked suddenly.

"I don't care," the woman replied.

Carston thought for a moment. There wasn't anything in the report other than, "got a missing vehicle call, investigated and found vehicle missing, casket with a body in the back." Carston pushed the report back to the center of the counter. "Thanks, and have a nice rest of your day. It's warming up out there today."

"You too." The woman still did not look up.

Carston hesitated a moment, then decided to ask what he really wanted to know. "So the officer referred the case to motor vehicle theft. But if he hasn't done an incident report..." Carston trailed off.

"They aren't actively working it," the woman finished for him, looking up this time. "They will assign it to a detective when they get the report. Until then, no one is working it. So whoever you are working for, tell them not to expect the detectives to jump right up and run out to find their hearse for them."

"Thanks," Carston said, turned and left down the hall, happy with that bit of information.

Carston made his way to the parking lot. He drove out of the lot and headed back the way he had come, past his office to the Old Market district. The Old Market in Omaha was situated just south of Dodge Street and a few blocks west of the Missouri River. Traffic was light and he drove into the district and parked close to the Spaghetti Works. He debated whether to plug the meter or not. It wasn't cheap to park in the Old Market district. He didn't plan to be in there long, just long enough to get some info, if there was even anyone working who had been around the day before. It could be no one there knew anything about it. He looked around and didn't see any cops or parking enforcement officers. He decided to screw it, he would take his chances. If he got a parking ticket, he would charge it back to the client.

Carston walked through the front door and was met by a receptionist with a clipboard in her hand. It was early and there were only a few customers scattered about.

"Number in your party?" the woman asked. She was a tall thin woman, blondish short hair, mid thirties and a little older than the waitresses that worked in the restaurant, he thought. She also was not in uniform. A tag on her breast read Alice.

"Alice, I'm Carston Hancock, Hancock Investigations." Carston dug out the little leather wallet that contained the gold badge that he had bought at the uniform and law enforcement supply store in Bellevue. Opposite the badge was his official Nebraska Private Investigator identification. He held it open so that she could see it, giving her all the time she needed. He had found that people loosened up if he didn't hurry them by flashing his badge and ID and pulling it away.

"What can I do for you?" she asked. "You're not here to eat?"

"No, I'm not." Carston no sooner got it out of his mouth before she looked past him at a couple coming through the door.

"Two today?" Alice asked them.

"Two," the man held up two fingers.

"Just a minute," Alice said to Carston. "Follow me please," she said to the couple, leading

27

them into the dining area. Carston returned the wallet with his badge and ID to the inside pocket of his coat, banging his knuckles on the pistol that rode in a shoulder holster below his left armpit.

Alice returned momentarily. "What do you need?" she asked, not particularly pleasantly.

"I'm investigating the theft of a motor vehicle yesterday. The driver and a coworker came in for lunch and the vehicle was stolen while they were in here," Carston explained. "They left it running."

"Vince and Bill," Alice said. "They got their hearse stolen."

"You know them?" Carston asked.

"Sure, they come in every time they're on this side of the river picking up a body. Nice guys, a little morbid if you know what I mean."

"Morbid?" Carston asked. "In what way?"

Alice laughed a little. "Not creepy in that sense. They work for the funeral home, they come in, park the hearse outside, sometimes there's a body in it. They always like to tell me if there is a body in it. Kind of teasing, you know. But they're good guys."

Alice turned her attention past Carston again.

"How many in your party today?" she said to someone behind him. Carston turned and saw three men in suits with overcoats.

"Four," one of the men answered. "We're waiting for one."

"I'll seat you," Alice grabbed four menus from a stand next to her and led the three to the dining area.

"Could you just tell me how it all went down?" Carston asked when Alice returned.

"They came in, I seated them right over there." Alice stopped to speak to someone behind him and pointed to the three businessmen who she had just seated. A man dressed much the same came past him and went to the table.

"Vince and Bill came in. They said they had picked up a body at Eppley. Told me it was parked right outside if I wanted to take a look, kind of teasing like I told you. They're always like that. They stopped in for lunch, like usual," Alice related. "They got done and Vince stayed here while Bill went to get the car. Evidently it wasn't parked right outside, it must have been parked a ways away because Bill came back a while later and he is freaking out. 'The hearse is gone!'" Alice said in a low voice, mimicking the voice of a male freaking out. "Then they called 911 and a cop came over. Pretty quick response, actually. He gave them hell for calling it in on the emergency number, took a statement and then left. Bill and Vince called a taxi to take them back to the funeral home." Alice was laughing and snorting toward the end of her story.

"I'm sorry," Alice said, getting control of herself. "I know it isn't funny, but it was. You gotta know those two to appreciate it."

"Anything else?" Carston asked. He had gotten out his notebook but had not written anything on the page.

"Nope, cop left, Vince and Bill called a cab and tried to come up with a good story to tell their boss while they waited. That's it."

Carston was looking at the blank page, his pen poised. He wrote "Alice" at the top.

"So Harmon and Mott hire you?" Alice asked. "Because I don't think the cops are doing much about it."

Carston looked up. "Why's that?"

"It's the middle of the winter. Cars get stolen down here every week. People leave them running and other people take them. Happens all the time when it's cold."

Carston didn't comment.

"There's all kinds of people roaming around here. They're all handy with a slim jim," Alice continued.

"Slim jim?" Carston said.

"Yeah, a slim jim. Flat piece of metal thing that they slip in the door and pop the lock," Alice said.

"I know what it is, it just surprised me—" Carston stopped.

"That I know what a slim jim is," Alice said, giving him a somewhat exasperated look. "There's all kinds of stuff going on in the Old Market, homeless people, weird people, crazy people, people peddling drugs, people panhandling, people walking around looking for a hearse to steal. Not a lot of violent crime, though, that's good."

"My office is a few blocks away, I know about the Old Market," Carston said defensively, resenting it a bit that he was getting a lecture from the girl who sat customers at the Spaghetti Works.

"I'm just telling you." Alice recognized the defensiveness in his voice.

"What kind of excuses were they coming up with while they waited for the taxi?" Carston moved on.

"Nothing really. Crazy stuff, some of it they were joking around, like an alien spacecraft took it. It sounded to me in the end like they were just going to 'fess up to it."

"I suppose that would be best, considering the cop just took a report and they probably didn't want to venture far from it with their story," Carston mused. "Anything else you can think of that would help me on this, you being such an expert on crime in the Old Market?" Carston put just a hint of sarcasm in his tone.

"It's probably on the other side of the river," Alice said without hesitation.

"I know that," Carston replied defensively again. He had done enough theft investigations for insurance companies to know that a lot of stolen goods on the Omaha side often ended up going across the river to Council Bluffs. The two jurisdictions were slow to communicate.

"You asked," Alice shot back.

Carston took the small wallet with his badge back out of his pocket again and found a business card tucked behind the ID. He handed it to Alice.

"Give me a call if you come by anything that might help me locate the hearse," Carston said as Alice took the card.

"Even if you already know it?"

Carston laughed at Alice's spunk. "Even if I already know it," he said. "You've been a lot of help, thanks."

Alice held out her hand and Carston took it. "Appreciate the time." He shook her hand and let go.

"My pleasure," she replied. "You said your office isn't far from here, but I haven't seen you come in before, I don't think."

"I don't get out to eat a lot," Carston said. "I'll try to make it in a little more in the future."

"That would be nice," Alice replied and smiled.

Another couple entered and Alice turned her attention to them. Carston walked out onto the sidewalk and the slightly less than frigid February air. He was standing in the shade of the building, which subtracted ten degrees from a temperature that was still far from balmy. He walked to his car. As soon as it came into sight he saw the parking ticket stuck under his windshield wiper.

Harmon and Mott Funeral Home and Crematorium

It was a short drive back to his office. As Carston drove past the Hancock building he counted himself lucky to spot a parking space right outside the front doors. He pulled in forward to get it before he got robbed by someone else in traffic instead of driving past and backing in as he had been taught in drivers' ed. He had to maneuver back and forth between the car parked in front and the one behind to get close enough to the curb, a job in itself with a vehicle as large as his Escalade. He jumped out of the car and locked the doors, leaving it running so that it would warm up. He ran into the building and up to his office, taking two steps at a time.

"Here, can you pay this?" Carston tossed the parking ticket on Stephanie's desk as he went past to his office.

"Where did you get this?" Stephanie asked, examining the ticket.

"Old Market," Carston replied from his office.

"What are you looking for?" she called back.

"Nothing, I'm using the potty," Carston yelled. "I just stopped in to see what you've come up with and then I'm heading over to Council Bluffs." His voice faded as he closed the door to the restroom that was connected to his office.

Stephanie was always a little put off that Carston had a restroom attached to his office and she had to use the one down the hall when he was working there. Usually, Carston was not in his office and she was free to use it if she wanted. He still referred to it as his bathroom though and that did not sit well with Stephanie. He often told her that she could still use his bathroom when he was working there, that it wouldn't bother him. But when he was in it was awkward for Stephanie to tinkle with Carston sitting six feet away and on the other side of the door. She heard the toilet flush and a minute later Carston was standing in front of her desk.

"So, what do you got?" he asked.

"I don't have anything," Stephanie replied. "What was I supposed to get?"

"I thought that you would be on the internet doing some research," Carston replied.

"Is there something in particular you want researched?" Stephanie shot back.

"Maybe thefts of hearses?" Carston suggested.

"How did you get a parking ticket?" Stephanie asked.

"I stopped by Spaghetti Works and talked to the lady there. She happened to remember the guys who were driving the hearse coming in. They're regulars. She said they came in for lunch, left the hearse running while they ate, and when they were done eating and went out to leave, someone had taken it."

"Okay, and what part of that involves you getting a parking ticket?" Stephanie asked.

"I thought I would only be in there a minute, so I didn't plug the meter," Carston replied.

"Was the gal working in Spaghetti Works kind of cute?" Stephanie asked.

"Not bad," Carston replied. "Older and more mature-looking lady."

"It took you more than just a minute to talk to her? You maybe had to joke around a little, sweet talk her, get to know her a little better?" Stephanie asked snidely.

"It took more than a minute because she had a lot of info," Carston replied. "Plus, we kept getting interrupted by customers coming in."

"You didn't plug the meter so you could save fifty cents, and now it's going to cost us sixteen bucks that we don't have in the budget."

Carston shrugged his shoulders. "We'll charge it back to the client. No biggie."

"Right, it's just sixteen bucks, no biggie. We're high rollers here in the Hancock building," Stephanie chided.

"Okay." Carston was tiring of the accusations. "I need to get going. I left my car running right out front. I'm heading over to Council Bluffs."

"Did you plug the meter?" Stephanie wouldn't give it up.

"No, that's why I need to get going," Carston turned to the door. "By the way, I don't think the officer who did the initial on the theft has put in his report yet. No report, no investigation. It buys us some time. Let's hope he is one of those cops that puts things off, which will buy us even more time. We could use the bonus."

"No kidding," Stephanie responded. "We have parking tickets to pay."

Carston went out the door and Stephanie could hear his footsteps as he went down the stairs.

She got on her computer, typed "hearse thefts" into Google and hit enter. She immediately got four pages of sites reporting on the same hearse with a body in it that was stolen from outside a church in Los Angeles three years before. She started reading.

Carston was relieved that his car had not been ticketed again. A car was waiting to take his parking space as soon as he pulled out. He turned toward Dodge Street and the Aksarben bridge that would take him over the frozen Missouri River into Council Bluffs, Iowa. Carston always thought of his father when he crossed the bridge. As a young man, his father had flown a Piper Super Cub under the old Aksarben Bridge, south to north. Radar at the Eppley airport tracked him all the way to the little grass strip in Crescent, Iowa where he hangared his airplane. The Iowa State Patrol and the Nebraska State Police arrived at the airport before his father got the plane into the hangar and the door pulled closed. The stunt caused his father to lose his private pilot license for a year. His father sold the cub and never flew again, but he told the story to the day he died. Carston looked out over the Missouri river as he drove over the modern, six-lane bridge, imagining what it would have looked like to see a little yellow airplane heading directly for traffic, only to disappear from sight and come out the other side. It made him smile every time. Carston Hancock the Second had a spirit for adventure, something that Carston Hancock the Third did not.

Carston knew exactly where the Harmon and Mott Funeral Home was from the map that he had pulled up on his computer back in the office. He was familiar with Council Bluffs. When he was fresh out of high school he used to drive over every Friday night. There was a small two-year college there, Iowa Western Community College, so there were parties every weekend. Those Iowa Western kids knew how to do it up. Some slickers from Omaha showing up at their parties was a big deal, and the Council Bluffs girls were easy. Carston and his buddies from Omaha were regulars.

Carston parked in one of the spaces in the small parking lot to the side of the mortuary's main doors and went in. The place looked and smelled like he expected, dark and musty. It was an old, one story brick building. Not as old as the Hancock building, though. The architecture suggested early sixties, with furnishings from the same era. Like the Hancock building, it was past its prime. A tall, thin, balding man who looked to be in his early fifties, wearing a dark suit, emerged from an office to one side of the entry.

"Good morning, can I help you?" he asked. "Henry Mott," he introduced himself and held out his hand.

"You must be one of the owners," Carston remarked as he shook Henry's hand.

"I am," Henry replied.

"I'm Carston Hancock, Hancock investigations."

Carston took his wallet from the inside of his coat and opened it, giving Henry time to see the badge and read the ID. When Henry turned his eyes away, Carston took a business card from the wallet and handed it to Henry, then returned the wallet to his coat pocket.

"Are you here about the hearse?" Henry asked.

"I am," Carston replied. "I was hired by Glenda Thompson. I believe it was her uncle riding in the back when it was stolen."

"Yes, very embarrassing," Henry said in that sincere and distant way that funeral home people talk.

"I'm wondering if Bill Harper or Vince Barker are still employed here after the unfortunate incident and if so, might I have a word with them?" Carston tried to lighten up the moment a little with his question.

"Yes, Vince and Bill still work here for us. They went to an early lunch. This afternoon they are scheduled to pick up a body in Missouri Valley," Henry deadpanned. "They are taking our other hearse, and we certainly hope that they do not lose that one as well. It's the only one we have left."

Carston realized that Henry was trying to make a joke about the hearse as well. He laughed appropriately.

"As long as we're on the subject and I've got you here, what's your take on all this?" Carston asked.

Henry looked Carston in the face for a full fifteen seconds before responding. Carston was starting to think he was some sort of robot maybe, left to mind the store while the ghouls were out collecting bodies.

"It was an unexpected turn of events," Henry started speaking as if the conversation had not been on pause. "It was a routine trip: drive to

Eppley, pick up the deceased, bring him back for burial. We do it all the time."

"What about stopping at Spaghetti Works, is that routine?" Carston asked.

"Yes, it is," Henry replied. "I certainly wish that they had not left the hearse running so someone could make off with it, but they usually make it an outing when they are on the Omaha side of the river."

Carston gave Henry a questioning look.

"Bill and Vince have been with us a long time. It is hard to find responsible people in this business. People with the proper decorum to do their job. Sometimes a little laxity is awarded to make the job of driving dead people around a bit more palatable."

"Leaving a hearse running with a body in it while they go in to eat isn't what I consider responsible," Carston commented.

"People make mistakes," Henry replied.

Carston thought for a moment. He should ask Henry more questions, but he was having trouble coming up with anything to ask.

"Do you have any idea where Vince and Bill might be dining at the moment? I would sure like to talk to them before they run up to Missouri Valley. Ms. Thompson would like to find her uncle quickly, before the police find him."

"I believe they will probably be at Marzoe's Bar and Grill, just down the block on the corner with Broadway." Henry nodded toward the street that Carston had driven to the mortuary.

"Thanks," Carston said and waited.

Henry did not respond. Carston was more convinced that he was a robot.

"As I said, Ms. Thompson wants me to find her uncle before the cops do. What do you think is up with that?" Carston asked.

"I don't know," Henry replied. "I'm sure she has her reasons."

"I'm sure she does," Carston responded.

"People always have their reasons," Henry replied. "A lot of times they are personal and they don't want to share them. Sometimes they do. We in this business are good listeners. Otherwise we respect their wishes and do as they ask if we can accommodate them, and it is not often that we can't."

"Yep," Carston replied and turned to leave, then turned back. "What were Ms. Thompson's wishes?"

"Actually, it wasn't Ms. Thompson we talked to," Henry replied. "It was the funeral home in Montreal who made the arrangements. They relayed the family's request for a small, private memorial with just a few family members present. Closed door, no staff, no interruptions, just a quiet time to reminisce, to say farewell. Followed by cremation."

Carston pondered this information. "Was there any mention at all of Ms. Thompson?" he asked.

"No," Henry answered without comment.

"Sounds simple enough, I guess," Carston remarked. "I'm going to go look for Bill and Vince. If I happen to miss them, will you ask them to give me a call when they return? I'll make the trip over from Omaha again if they do. I would really like to talk to them."

"I will do that," Henry replied.

Carston was fully convinced that Henry was a robot. "Hopefully, they'll still be at Marzoe's."

Henry nodded and Carston turned to leave. Just as he got to the door, Henry called out to him, "Mr. Hancock."

Carston turned, hand on the doorknob.

"Did your father happen to fly an airplane under the Aksarben Bridge years ago?" Henry asked.

"Yes, he did," Carston grinned.

"That was quite the stunt," Henry smiled back.

"Before I was born," Carston remarked. "But I heard about it, that's for sure. He was famous for it."

"Quite the stunt," Henry repeated. "I was just a teenager. There was an amusement park right there, before you cross the bridge. I was on the Farris Wheel with a girl when he did it. It was early evening. I saw it. A lot of people saw it, but we were at the very top of the Ferris Wheel and had the best seat in the house. I thought he was going to crash into the bridge, everybody did, but then he went right under it, his wheels almost skimming the river. It was as smooth a maneuver as I have ever seen an airplane do. He made front page news on both sides of the river, you know."

Carston laughed, waved, then went out the door, leaving Henry standing and watching him. Perhaps Henry wasn't a robot after all.

Marzoe's

Carston got into his car and started it up. It was still warm from the drive over and hot air blew on his feet from the heater vent. He pulled his phone from his pocket to check for any messages or emails. There was a text from Stephanie telling him that someone had left a message for him to call a number. Stephanie thought that maybe it was a divorce lawyer. Carston had a moment of panic. Things had been rough between him and Megan for the last month and a half. Carston was in the wrong, he knew that, and he couldn't take it back, but he had counted on time being on his side. So far it had not been. Megan's anger was growing daily and Carston was at a loss how to stem it and turn it around. And he did want to turn it around. But nothing was working. He went from reasoning to begging and from begging to resignation, then back to reasoning. But Megan was not in a mood for reason, she turned her back on his begging, and at the moment Carston was in a state of resignation. He put his phone back in his pocket and drove out of the lot.

It took only a few minutes for him to find Marzoe's. It looked like a dive bar that might have at one time been a chain restaurant and then gone through at least a couple of transformations before it became Marzoe's. It sat right off Broadway in the parking lot of a strip mall that had also seen better days. He scanned the lot for a hearse and did not see one. He parked but left the engine running. He doubted that Vince Barker and Bill Harper were still there, unless someone had stolen their hearse again. Carston chuckled at that thought. He locked the doors with his key fob and went into the establishment to ask if the two funeral home employees had even been there. Maybe they went somewhere else. Like back to Spaghetti Works.

Marzoe's was dark and it took a moment for Carston's eyes to adapt from the bright February sunlight reflecting off the snow outside. From the inside it was obvious that during one of the building's transformations from chain restaurant to downscale bar, someone had removed the windows and boarded up the holes. His eyes scanned each one in a subconscious search for a glimmer of daylight sneaking through. Each one-time window now sported a neon beer sign. When his eyes adjusted to the dark interior, he saw a bar on the back wall, a dozen or more tables in the center, a small dance floor and a step-up stage area on the right. Three pool tables occupied the area on the left. A few patrons were scattered about eating or drinking their lunch. A tall gangly fellow wearing a blue flannel shirt, sporting long hair and a beard stood behind the bar, eying him eying the room. Carston made for the bar and climbed up on a stool.

"What ya hungry for?" The bartender approached from the other side of the bar across from Carston, absently wiping a glass with a towel that was either stained or dirty, Carston couldn't tell.

"Looking for a couple of fellows. They work for the funeral home down the street. Their boss said they came here for lunch," Carston replied.

"We don't have any of that," the bartender pointed up at the menu written in chalk on a blackboard on the wall behind the bar. "Special today is meatloaf."

Carston looked at the menu. "How about a burger and fries?"

"Cheese?" the bartender asked.

"Sure," Carston replied.

"American, cheddar, Swiss or provolone?" the bartender asked.

"Provolone," Carston replied.

The bartender turned to a register on the back wall and put in the order. "Anything to drink?" he asked without turning around.

"Got a Fat Tire?" Carston deadpanned.

"Draw or bottle?" The bartender was starting to get on his nerves.

"Draw," Carston said with exasperation in his voice.

The bartender punched the screen with his index finger a couple more times for good measure, then took the glass that he had been wiping with the stained or dirty dishrag and filled it from a tap that carried the Fat Tire logo. He placed it on a coaster in front of Carston. Carston was wishing he had ordered the bottle.

"Bill and Vince," the bartender said. "You just missed them. They're headed up to Missouri Valley to pick up a body and bring it back down."

"You know them pretty well?" Carston asked.

"Come in here all the time," the bartender said.

Carston had fished out a business card from his wallet and placed it on the counter in front of the bartender. "Carston Hancock Investigations,"

Carston introduced himself. "I'm investigating the theft of a hearse from the Old Market yesterday. Vince and Bill were driving it."

"Oh yeah," the bartender laughed. "I heard all about it."

"What did they tell you?" Carston inquired.

"All about them going to lunch over there and leaving the hearse running. How Vince went out and it wasn't there anymore." The bartender laughed again.

"I think it was Bill went out and found it missing," Carston corrected.

"What the fuck difference does it make?" the bartender scoffed. "One of them went out and the hearse was gone." He laughed again.

"Did they say anything in particular that you think might help me to find it while they were telling you all about it?" Carston asked, agreeing that who went out and found the hearse gone probably had no bearing on the case.

"Nope," the bartender said. "Said the cop was an asshole and didn't seem very interested in the fact that someone stole their hearse and the body in it during broad daylight sitting right outside a fancy restaurant with a half a dozen of them moping around the district mooching free donuts."

"They said that?" Carston asked.

"No, I'm saying that," the bartender grinned. "You weren't a cop or something before you become a private dick? You're not touchy about the donut thing?"

"Never been a cop," Carston reassured him. "I've never been anything but a private detective."

A bell rang from a window at the far end of the bar. The bartender threw his dirty dishcloth down and went to the window. The dishcloth fell to the floor. He returned with a plate that held a rather delicious looking cheeseburger and a pile of waffle fries on the side. He placed it on the bar in front of Carston and then went to fetch a bottle of catsup.

"Need utensils?" he asked.

"Napkin would be nice," Carston replied.

"The bartender found a napkin behind the bar and put it next to Carston's plate.

"This is really good," Carston said, his mouth full of burger and bun. He took the napkin and wiped the grease dribbling down his chin.

"Should have tried the meatloaf," the bartender replied. "It's our specialty."

"I'll come back next time I'm over here." Carston took another bite. "You got a pretty good business here?" he asked.

"Goes in spurts," the bartender replied. He had found another glass to dry with the dirty dishcloth. He looked around for it and spotted it on the floor where it had fallen. He picked it up and shook it before he started polishing the glass. "We get the lunch crowd, then it dies down a little. Then around three we get the Iowa Western kids, they come in with their fake IDs after class. We get a lot of them on Fridays," he commented. "Most of them get out of here before things get really hopping. Later in the evening we get a weird mix of bikers and cowboys. We have live music sometimes when we can get someone in here. We don't pay them much, you know. Most of them are bands coming through. But we keep busy, especially on the weekends."

"Have any trouble between the bikers and the cowboys?" Carston asked between bites.

"Not much," the bartender replied. "We got the Hell Fighters over here. Pretty tame compared to the other side of the river. They're loud. The cowboys are loud. Worst thing, some band comes through and the bikers and the cowboys try to see who can be the loudest. Bunch of fucking idiots. It's like they're trying to impress the band, showing off. The only thing more obnoxious than a bunch of girls trying to get in the back room to diddle with the band members during the breaks is a bar full of cowboys and bikers trying to put on a show. They're all weird."

Carston was laughing out loud at the bartender's animations as he waved the dirty rag and the glass that he was cleaning with it while he railed on about the bikers and the cowboys and the girls diddling with the band members backstage.

"Only time I have trouble is if a girl band comes through, then things go to hell in a handbasket every fucking time."

"Have any trouble with the cops over here?" Carston asked. He was wiping up the last of the catsup with a waffle fry.

"They come through about every night on the weekends, sometimes twice a night if we have a girl band. I don't have trouble from them. Sometimes some Iowa Western kids overstay and the cops come in and catch them drinking under age, but not a big deal."

"They bust your ass for that?" Carston asked.

"I check IDs. The cops know that. They pretty much just write 'em a ticket and kick them out.

Only problem is if they find too many of them, then they get pissy about it."

Carston gave him a questioning look.

"The kids, their IDs are crap. But no one says I have to be good at spotting the fakes, the law says 'any reasonable person.' I mean, I'm a reasonable person. Not my fault I'm not an expert at spotting fake IDs. I'm a bartender. Spotting fakes is the cop's job. The kids show me something that says they are of age, I'm not going to give them grief. It's not my place to tell them their ID is shit." The bartender pointed toward a lit sign on the wall that had a date on it. Below the date it said, "If you were born after this date you will not be served alcohol in this establishment."

"Convenient," Carston nodded toward the sign.

"Got it from the beer distributer. The date changes on its own."

"Double convenient," Carston remarked.

"Tell you the truth," the bartender said, "Writing tickets so that the cops can show that they aren't just out here fucking the dog all night, I'm doing them a favor, and they know it. Just got to be smart enough to know how much they're going to let you get away with and not go too far."

"You know your business," Carston replied.

"Damn right," the bartender answered.

"I'll pay up," Carston said, ending the conversation.

"Twelve twenty-two," the bartender said without hesitation.

Carston got a ten and a five out of his wallet and put it on the counter.

"You need change?" the bartender asked.

"Nope," replied Carston. "You got my card there. If Vince and Bill come back in here and happen to regale you with anything you think that I might like to know…" Carston trailed off.

"I'll give you a call," the bartender replied.

"What's your name, by the way?" Carston asked.

"Martin." The bartender reached across the counter to shake hands.

Carston shook hands with him.

"I'm the owner, me and my wife. I'm Martin and she's Zoe."

"Makes sense," Carston said. "Pretty clever. I thought it was a catchy name."

"Yep, been here fifteen years now," Martin remarked.

Carston was about to leave, but he turned back as he had a thought. "You ever hear of a bar called Flingnasties?"

"Over in West Omaha?" Martin replied.

Carston shrugged his shoulders. "I guess so, I've never been there."

"Stripper bar," Martin remarked. "Three stages. Kind of a rough place. I heard some things about it."

"What have you heard?" Carston asked.

"Just that there might be some mob connections with it."

Carston didn't comment. He dismissed the mob connection idea out of hand. People in Council Bluffs were always saying that there were mob connections to the bars and meatpacking plants in Omaha. People in Omaha always said that there was a big mob underworld laying low in Council Bluffs. The same people who told him about mob connections usually had a few other conspiracy theories that they liked to clue him into as well. In all his travels and all the investigations he had done on both sides of the river, he had never run into anyone with real mob connections. Bikers and street gangs, sure, but never the mob.

"Okay, I'll get over here again and try the meatloaf one day. Give me a call if you catch wind of my missing hearse." Carston left the bar and went out into the bright afternoon sunlight. His car was still parked and running. He had another panic attack. He had totally forgotten that he had left it running. He was glad that no one had slim-jimmed it and taken it. He hit the button on the key fob and heard the click of the lock. He opened the door and got in.

Carston decided to hang around for a while on the Council Bluffs side in case Vince and Bill got back and called. It shouldn't be too long, he thought; it wasn't that far to Missouri Valley and back. There were a few places he knew where cars stolen out of Omaha had been recovered around Council Bluffs in the past. He would check them out in the meantime. He also knew a fellow who had some connections, not to the mob, but connections nonetheless, and who had given him some tips that had panned out for him in the past. It would cost him a few bucks, but a tip for a tip, that was the way it worked. He would charge it back to the client.

Carston worked his way down Broadway, through the historic business district and then south toward the train yards. It was the industrial gut of Council Bluffs. Easy access to the trains that funneled through going east and west, and not too far from the river and the barge traffic. I-80 came through just south of the yards. It was a hub, which made the area attractive to criminals trying to move stolen goods and drugs. There were parking lots and loading docks on every block where a stolen car could be dumped or a deal could be made without drawing much attention. A stolen hearse was another thing, though. The Omaha Police might not be looking for it, but a hearse abandoned in a parking lot, no matter where it was, was sure to draw some attention. Carston was aware that he had to find the hearse before someone else found it and called it in to the police. The urgency of the case and Carston's total lack of direction were already wearing on him and he had only been on the case a few hours.

Smart Auto Body and Repair

Carston pulled into the parking lot next to Smart Auto Body and Repair and looked around behind the seat for his thermo insulated coffee cup. Smart Auto Body and Repair was a rundown business that had seen better days on a street that dead-ended at the Union Pacific railroad tracks. Kenny Smart started the business in his thirties when he thought that he could do it better than the guy he was working for at the time. Kenny had to be in his seventies now. For forty years he had been there on that dead-end street, through the good years, and now through the bad years. His son-in-law David had been carrying the workload for the last ten years, but Kenny still came in every day. He didn't know anything else. He sat in his office holding court over his old cronies, who had been coming in for decades because they didn't know anything else either. When Kenny wasn't holding court he was out in the shop piddling around with one project or another and supervising David, which inevitably got on David's nerves and resulted in a fight that only ended when someone came in to jaw with Kenny. This was what Carston walked into, cup in hand. He could hear the yelling before he even opened the heavy steel door. It did not deter him for a moment. He pretty much walked into the same scene every time he came to visit Kenny.

It took a few seconds for David to notice that Carston had come in. He had already come

52

through the door and was walking across the shop to check out the commotion, only his Stetson bobbing above the roofs of the cars packed into the shop, craning his head to see what the two were at each other over. It was always entertaining to watch.

"Your fucking detective buddy from over in Omaha is here," David interrupted Kenny's diatribe.

Kenny turned around. "What brings you over here to God's country?" Kenny turned and asked as if there had not been any conflict between him and his son-in-law moments earlier. David went back to what he had been working on when Kenny stuck his nose into his business and started lecturing him on how to do his job.

"Take him to his cage, will you?" David said over his shoulder. "Lock the door when you leave so he can't get out."

Kenny was already on his way. By the time Carston followed him into the filthy office, Kenny had picked up a filthy coffee cup that said Union Pacific on it and was filling it from the pot that sat in the filthy Mr. Coffee machine.

'Want a cup?" Kenny asked.

"As long as you didn't make it out of water from the toilet," Carston commented.

"Nope, not today," Kenny poured the coffee into the cup that Carston held out. "Never going to let me live that down, are you?" Kenny said, taking a seat in the swivel chair in front of the filthy desk covered with parts and repair manuals that probably dated back to the shop's grand opening.

One day a few years before, Carston had come to visit Kenny. Kenny poured him up a cup of coffee, as usual. After a few sips Kenny asked him how it tasted and Carston told him that it tasted fine. Then Kenny proceeded to tell him how he came to work and the water was out, so he had to take some water out of the toilet for his morning brew. Carston had thrown what remained in his cup on the floor before Kenny could explain that the water didn't come out of the bowl, it came out of the tank. He admonished Carston for getting so uppity about it. Since then Carston asked first.

Carston sat in one of the broken-down chairs reserved for Kenny's guests. Kenny hitched up his overalls and took the swivel chair at the desk. He was a skinny, bent-over man, who probably stood six foot if he stood up straight. His long stringy hair stuck out from under the blue ball cap with the Smart Auto Body and Repair logo stenciled on the front of it. He leaned back and eyed Carston.

"So, what you looking for today?" Kenny asked.

"A stolen hearse," Carston said.

"A hearse?" Kenny repeated. "A hearse is pretty hard to move. You wouldn't think that would stay under the radar long."

"I don't know what to think," Carston replied. "Some funeral home guys picked up a body at Eppley yesterday and then stopped by Spaghetti Works in the Old Market for lunch. Left the hearse running and locked the doors. Came out when they were done eating and the hearse was gone."

"What, they didn't want the dead guy to get cold so they left it running?" Kenny snorted.

"I don't know. I haven't had a chance to talk to the two guys," Carston replied.

"Where they from?" Kenny asked.

"A place here in Council Bluffs, Harmon and Mott Funeral Home," Carston replied.

Kenny was thinking. "Gotta be someone who thought it would be fun to drive a hearse. I can't see anyone taking it thinking that they could turn it over quick," he reflected.

"You think it was a joyrider?" Carston asked.

"You steal a car because you think that you can make a quick turnover. You run it across the bridge and you peddle it around. You want a soft target, something easy to make off with, something you can get rid of quick and something that isn't going to draw attention to you while you're doing it. A hearse don't fit the bill."

"You don't think maybe someone over here would see a hearse as a good business opportunity? I mean, gotta be a shortage of used hearse parts out there. Supply and demand," Carston said.

"Exactly, supply and demand," Kenny remarked. "Not a whole lot of hearses getting in wrecks. No demand for parts. Sure, I suppose the parts bring good money, but you're talking about a pretty specialized market. You're going to be sitting on them parts for a long time, maybe some of them you never sell. A lot of risk for the return."

Carston was thinking. When he didn't say anything, Kenny continued. "Besides, the cops are out there looking. Not a whole lot of people peddling hearse parts. If a hearse gets stolen, chopped, and a week later pieces are showing up on the used parts market, it doesn't take a lot of detective work to figure out that one. Might as well put an ad on Craigslist: 'I have that hearse you're looking for.'"

It took Carston another moment to respond. Kenny took a drink of coffee and let him ponder.

"So let's say it was a joyride. Someone saw a hearse parked and running. They thought it would be fun to take it for a ride. I mean, the doors are locked. Someone is just roaming around Old Market and happens to have a door opening kit, so they pop the door and take it for a ride? That doesn't seem any more likely."

"Who said the doors were locked?" Kenny asked.

"It was in the police report," Carston replied.

"I thought you was a private detective," Kenny said. "You ever work a stolen car case where the victim said they left it running and didn't lock the doors? Come on. You know they left the damned thing running without locking it up. Probably weren't even thinking."

"Point taken," Carston said. "Anyway, I got nothing to go on right now. I really need to find this hearse quick and all I can do is drive around to every parking lot in every part of town that joyriders dump cars and hope that I spot it."

"I'll keep an eye out and my ear to the ground," Kenny said. "But it's a needle in a haystack."

"I know," Carston said.

"Is this an insurance gig? You're getting paid by the hour, what's the hurry finding it?"

"It isn't an insurance gig," Carston replied. "The niece of the body in the casket hired me to find it before the cops do."

Kenny raised his eyebrows. "Before the cops do?"

"Yep, and a big bonus if I do," Carston replied.

"You saying that I might have a piece of that bonus should I point you to that hearse?" Kenny asked slyly.

"Yep," Carston said. "That's why I'm sitting here talking to you."

"Here I thought it's because I'm such good company," Kenny chided.

"That too," Carston winked.

"You hitting on me?" Kenny asked

"No," Carston said. "Purely a business proposition."

"Oh, we're in this together," Kenny snickered.

"Right," Carston replied.

"Right," Kenny said back to him.

Carston grinned.

"I suppose now you're going to just take off and leave me here with that lazy ass David, now that you're done with your business proposition," Kenny said.

Carston pulled out his phone to check for messages, hoping that there was something from the funeral home, but there was nothing.

"Maybe I'll just stick around here while you make some calls, see what you can find out." Carston got up and refilled his cup from the pot of coffee. "I'm waiting for the two guys who were driving the hearse to get back to the funeral home from picking up a body in Missouri Valley. I haven't even talked to them yet."

"Pin them down on the locked door bullshit," Kenny nodded. He was reaching for the phone on his desk. "I'll lay you odds that they didn't lock the doors."

"What difference would it make at this juncture?" Carston asked. "If they did or they didn't, it isn't going to change anything to help me find the hearse."

"Principle of the thing," Kenny replied.

"Well, maybe they think they locked them, but didn't get them all locked," Carston suggested.

"You are one naive son of a bitch for a private eye. If I ever need to hire you, you better give me a god-damned good deal, considering."

"You find me that hearse, I'll give you a card for a free one," Carston replied.

Kenny turned his attention the phone and was not listening to Carston. "Hey, I got a good one here, you'll like this," he said into the mouthpiece. The detective got up with his cup and walked out to the shop.

"What's going on?" David asked when Carston walked up to where he was bent over the engine of a ten-year-old Ford F-250. David looked very much like his father-in-law probably looked at his age, both in stature, dress, and in his bearing, right down to the blue ball cap. He was even starting to get that same stooped stance. "They say that girls like to marry their fathers," Carston thought.

"Looking for a stolen hearse."

"I'll bet you don't get a lot of those cases," David remarked.

"First ever," Carston replied. "Had a body in it, too."

"No shit?" David exclaimed. He stood up and turned to face Carston.

"Do you think Kenny can help you find it?" David asked.

58

"You know something? I was dead in the water from the git-go with on this one," Carston admitted. "I don't even know where to start looking. I only hope Kenny can point me in a direction."

"Who does the hearse belong to?" David asked.

"Harmon and Mott, here in Council Bluffs," Carston answered.

"Yep," David was bobbing his head up and down. "And I bet ol' Vince Barker was driving it."

"You know Vince Barker who works at Harmon and Mott?" Carston was thinking it was good that he had come out to talk with David.

"I went to high school with his kid," David replied. "Hell of a baseball player. The kid, I mean."

"No kidding? Tell me about it." Carston wanted to encourage David to keep talking.

"Just I played baseball for Abraham Lincoln and so did he. He was a year ahead of me. Played shortstop. His old man came to every game."

"Interesting, what kind of guy was the dad?" Carston replied, urging David on.

"Nice guy, creepy," David said. "He drove the hearse to games. I think he worked late, but he would show up at every game driving the hearse. It's interesting that you say there was a body in it when it was stolen. We always wondered if there was a body in the back when he came to the games. He had a buddy with him most of the time. One thing, they both loved baseball."

"Bill Harper," Carston said.

"Who's Bill Harper?" David asked, confused.

"Probably Vince's buddy," Carston explained. "That was who was with him when the hearse got stolen."

"That was a long time ago. I haven't seen him since," David commented. "Vince has worked at the funeral home forever, I think."

Carston didn't comment. He was thinking where he wanted to take the conversation.

"How did it get stolen?" David asked.

"They left it running while they were at lunch and someone took it," Carston answered.

"Probably Gavin, Vince's kid," David remarked. "He was a sneaky little thief. He would steal anything you left laying out, and you didn't want to let your bag out of your sight when he was around. Probably even had a set of keys to the hearse."

Carston filed that little bit of information in his head before he responded. "I doubt it, they parked the hearse outside Spaghetti Works over in Old Market."

"Just saying," David remarked. "He's good for it."

"I guess that's a start, an angle to look at," Carston commented. "You think that this Gavin might have had a hunch his dad was going to pick up a body at the airport, stop off at the Spaghetti Works in the Old Market and he makes his way over there so that he can steal the hearse his dad is driving with the body in it? What for? It seems like a stretch."

"Don't take no what for when it comes to Gavin." David was nodding his head to emphasize his comment.

Carston laughed. "Well, good as I've heard so far. I don't have anything else to follow up on right now."

"Yep," David remarked.

No one said anything for a moment. Kenny was banging around on the other side of the garage. Carston thought that he must have gotten off the phone.

"You know if this Gavin is still around?" Carston asked.

"He's still around. I see him once in a while," David answered. "Haven't talked to him in years, though."

"Possible he's living with his dad?" Carston asked.

"Don't know," David replied. "I don't think it would be hard to find him, though. For a detective, I mean."

"Yeah," Carston agreed.

Kenny came up and leaned on the workbench. David looked like he wanted to go back to work on the F-250.

"I'm going to take off, then," Carston announced. "Maybe check some lots. I'm hoping those guys get back from Missouri Valley and I can talk to them today."

"I made a few calls, nothing. Give it some time. I'll put some feelers out. You might want to check down around Lake Manawa and down along the river," Kenny suggested.

"Been some stolen cars dumped down there recently?" Carston asked.

"Not that I'm aware of, but that's where I would dump one if I was out joyriding. Especially a hearse. Not much going on down there this time of year."

Carston acknowledged with a tilt of his head and turned toward the door. It was getting late and it would be starting to get cold again. He had been at Kenny's garage for almost an hour. Days were short this time of year. Carston was thinking about Gavin Barker and someone dumping a stolen car down by Lake Manawa or along the river in the middle of February. Neither idea was fitting into his investigation. First of all, it made no sense that Vince Barker's grown son would go over to Omaha to steal his dad's hearse while he was having lunch. Carston could not imagine a motive for doing that. And who dumps a stolen hearse at Lake Manawa when it is ten degrees above zero with a ten-below windchill, then hikes out of there? Lake Manawa was in the middle of nowhere. Same with along the river.

Carston left the shop and drove around the railyards and parking lots, aimlessly looking for a stolen hearse and wishing that either Bill Harper or Vince Barker would call him. The sun was nearly set, and Carston was working his way down to Lake Manawa. He had pretty much exhausted everywhere else he could think of and resigned himself to the fact that no one from Harmon and Mott was going to call. From Lake Manawa he could hop on Interstate 80 and cross back over to Omaha. Carston was depressed. A lot was riding on this case and after a day at it he had nothing to go on.

Barbie

Carston pulled into the Ameristar Casino and Dog Track before he hopped on I-80 to cross over to Omaha. He had heard nothing from anyone at Harmon and Mott, which was aggravating him enough that he decided to give them a call, see if they were still there and why they weren't calling him. He parked his car and pulled his phone out of his pocket. He had missed a call from Stephanie. She hadn't left a message. He brought up the number to his office and hit call. It was late and Stephanie might have already left. She left early a lot, especially if it looked like Carston wasn't coming back, but he thought he would try.

"Hancock Investigations." He was surprised to hear her voice and not a message.

"What did you call me about earlier?" Carston asked.

"Some lawyer wants to talk to you. He didn't leave his name, just a number. I looked it up and it comes back to Barton Law Offices. I didn't know what you wanted to do. It doesn't sound good. They specialize in divorce cases. I'll text you the number. I'm going home. Talk to you tomorrow. Ta-ta."

A moment of panic came over Carston. He didn't say anything.

"I'm bugging out of here," she repeated. "Nothing going on and I want to stop in at that new boutique down the street before they close. They have some interesting outfits." Carston's silence was causing her to ramble. She didn't like it when he didn't say anything. She couldn't tell what he was thinking.

"Sure," Carston said absently. "I'll talk to you tomorrow."

A few seconds after he ended the call his phone chimed. Steph had sent him the text with the number for Barton Law Offices. He hesitated. This had come with no warning. Megan had not said anything about a lawyer. He had talked to her just the day before, checking in, seeing if there was anything she needed. She had been short with him, but not in a mean way, just like he was interrupting something. He looked at the time on his dash: it was ten to five. He was tempted to make the call, hope that he caught someone there, see what was going on, but his better judgement told him to hold off. He needed time to think. He was caught totally unaware.

Carston got out the piece of paper that Steph had given him earlier with the phone number and address of Harmon and Mott. He called the number. It rang six times before someone picked up.

"Harmon and Mott Funeral Home and Crematorium, Henry Mott speaking."

"Henry, this is Carston Hancock, I talked to you earlier. I'm wondering, did Vince Barker and Bill Harper ever come back from Missouri Valley, or did they disappear this time too?" Carston did not hide the aggravation in his voice.

"Oh," Henry said. "They did come back. I just assumed that you had already talked to them at Marzoe's. They didn't mention anything, and neither did I."

Carston pulled the phone away from his face and turned toward the window. "Fucking hell," he mouthed to the window, fogging it.

"Are they still around?" Carston turned back to his phone.

"You just missed them," Henry replied. "But they usually stop in at Marzoe's after work for a beer or two before they go home. I'm sure if you hurry you can catch them there." Carston ended the call without a word to Henry, threw his car into drive and tore out of the parking lot toward Broadway.

Carston made short work of getting himself through the Council Bluffs traffic to Broadway and then to Marzoe's. It was rush hour, but most of the traffic in the afternoon went from Omaha to Council Bluffs, not the other way around. He made good time. There were more cars in the Marzoe's parking lot than there had been when he was there earlier. He found a parking space and went inside. This time he turned off the ignition. Martin was still working, and Carston called to him like they were old friends.

Martin walked over to where Carston had taken a stool at the bar. It appeared that he was polishing the same glass with the same dirty dishtowel. "What ya having?" he asked.

"Looking for Vince and Bill," Carston was scanning the crowd. Most of them were young people, a mixed crowd of boys and girls sitting at the tables laughing and having a good time. He didn't see anyone over twenty-five, and certainly no one who looked like they just came from a funeral home.

"What ya drinking?" Martin asked again.

"Fat Tire," Carston turned to him. "In a bottle," he added quickly as Martin was placing the glass that he had been wiping under the tap.

"Just missed them," Martin said. He reached into the cooler, pulled two bottles of beer from it with one hand and pulled a bottle opener from his pocket with the other. He deftly popped the caps off the bottles and placed one in front of Carston. He took a sip from the other.

"God damn it," Carston exclaimed, exasperated. "I just want to talk to them for ten minutes."

"Sorry," Martin said, taking another sip.

"You work here all day and all night?" Carston asked.

"Pretty much," Martin said. "Keeps the overhead down."

Carston took a sip from the bottle.

"Sit up straight and look sober," Martin said abruptly.

"I am sober," Carston responded.

"The cops just came in," Martin warned.

Carston turned to see two uniformed police officers bundled against the cold coming through the door. One male and one female. They quickly scanned the room and both seemed to spot one table in particular at the same time. They walked briskly to the table and said something to the occupants, who were visibly nervous. Carston couldn't hear what was being said, but the occupants of the table reached in unison for their wallets or purses, pulled out IDs and held them out to the officers who took them individually and scrutinized them. The male officer placed one of them in his back pocket and continued to check others. After they had checked them all the male officer spoke to the young man whose ID he had removed from his back pocket and was inspecting again. He got on his radio and called in some information, waited and then talked to the young man again. He stood up and went with the officer to an empty table in the corner.

"Shit," Martin said under his breath.

"What's up with that?" Carston asked.

"Underager," Martin said. "No biggie, I checked IDs on all of them when they came in. The one that kid has was shit, but what the heck, I'm no ID expert, I checked it. That's all that counts."

The woman officer turned and scanned the bar. Her eyes fell on Carston. He waved and she waved back. She called something to the officer at the table with the young man, pointed toward Carston and Martin, then proceeded in their direction.

"Carston Hancock the Third," she announced when she got close.

"Barbie Rimes," Carston responded.

"What brings your scrawny ass over to this side of the river?" Barbie held out her hand.

"Working a case," Carston took her hand and shook it. "We used to work security together over at the Westroads, what, twenty years ago?" Carston explained to Martin.

"Twelve years ago," Barbie corrected him.

"Feels like twenty," Carston said.

"Are you saying I've aged prematurely?" Barbie chided.

"No, not saying that at all," Carston backpedaled.

"Besides, I saw you two years ago," Barbie remarked. "You were working a stolen car case for Allstate."

"I know," Carston replied. "Just making conversation for Martin's sake."

"Are you over here looking for another stolen car?" she asked.

"I'm trying to locate a stolen hearse," Carston told her after a moment of thought. He had gotten nowhere in his investigation thus far. It was time to up the ante. "It was stolen while parked down the street from Spaghetti Works in the Old Market at lunchtime yesterday, belongs to a funeral home here in Council Bluffs."

"Harmon and Mott?" Barbie asked.

"Yep," Carston replied. "You get something from Omaha PD on it?"

"Nope," Barbie answered. "Just guessing."

"Had a body in it," Carston said in a conspiring voice.

"Oh, no shit?" Barbie snorted. "That's got to suck for ol' Henry Mott."

"Yeah," Carston said. "It sucks for more than Mott."

"They hire you to find it before we do?" Barbie asked.

"As a matter of fact," Carston began slowly, surprised that Barbie immediately suspected that particular request, but happy to let her assume that the funeral home was his client.

"No doubt," Barbie continued. "I'm pretty sure Henry does not want that hearse to sit in impound for a week while the dicks process it. Not to mention a corpse stinking up the evidence vault while they hold it as stolen property until they get a disposition on the case," she laughed.

The three remaining kids from the table followed the one that was ticketed out of the bar. The other officer came up and stood beside Barbie. He was a big guy, made bigger by his heavy coat and the gear that he had strapped around his waist. He folded the ticket he had written for possession of alcohol under age and slipped it into the breast pocket of his uniform, then threw a poor facsimile of a Nebraska driver's license on the bar in front of Martin. Even Carston could see it was a laminated photocopy.

"Just for the future," the officer said sarcastically, "this is shit."

Martin glanced down at it. "Looked genuine to me when I checked it," he said defiantly. "Besides, I didn't serve him, one of the other kids came up and got a pitcher."

"And four glasses." The officer picked up the ID and put it in the same pocket as the ticket. "You're responsible for what happens in this bar."

Martin shrugged his shoulders. "Like I said, I checked them when they came in," he mumbled.

"This is Detective Carston Hancock the Third," Barbie nodded toward Carston.

The officer did not proffer his hand. "Omaha PD?" he asked.

"Private Detective Carston Hancock the Third," Barbie clarified. "We worked security at the Westroads back in the day, before I got hired on here."

The officer didn't say anything for an awkward moment, then he turned and walked toward the door without a word and waited there for his partner.

"Friendly sort," Carston commented.

"He's an asshole." Barbie raised her eyebrows. "A loveable asshole though, once you get to know him."

"I'm sure," Carston said.

"He just doesn't have a personality," Barbie said in his defense. "Other than that, he's fine."

"That's the truth," Martin added.

"Right, Martin," Barbie said. "Like you're Mr. Congeniality. You two should get together and hold a grump fest. You could get the rest of the grumps in here and sell them a lot of beer. Great Grumpy over there could sit at the door and collect the cover. You'd both make a killing."

Carston laughed. Martin didn't respond.

"I suppose I better get back on the street." Barbie held out her hand and Carston shook it again. "The sergeant gets pissy if we aren't on the street. God forbid he might have to actually take a call for us. Or worse yet, have to do an accident report."

"Beings you don't have a case from Omaha on the hearse yet, if you hear anything, you want to give me a call?" Carston asked.

"We just haven't gotten anything official asking us to be on the lookout for it," Barbie said. "But I'm sure they've put it in NCIC as a stolen vehicle already."

"Just asking," Carston smiled. "For old times' sake? If you see a hearse parked unattended somewhere, like a parking lot, you could just not run the plate and let me know."

"If I hear anything, I'll pass it on, for old times' sake," Barbie said. "But if I actually I see it, I'm running it through NCIC and taking the stat. Isn't every day you get a stolen hearse on your plus side."

"Fair enough," Carston said.

Barbie turned and walked out. Her partner was already out the door when she got there, leaving it open for her and letting a frigid February wind come through the interior of the bar.

"Asshole," Martin said as the door closed behind Barbie.

"But a loveable asshole," Carston remarked.

"Yeah, right," Martin retorted. "Your buddy there is an asshole too, she's just better at hiding it. And it is kind of coincidental that you come in here and the next thing your little cop buddy out of the past comes in here with loveable asshole and cites one of my customers."

"What?" Carston said incredulously. "You think that I'm working with the cops, that's why I'm here?"

"Wouldn't put it past them," Martin said.

"Well, I'm not working for the cops. I worked with Barbie a dozen years ago as mall security. That's it."

Martin didn't reply. Carston couldn't tell if he bought it or not.

"Her partner got a name?" Carston asked.

"Hank Goss," Martin said. "He comes in here about once a week and grabs some Iowa Western kid up and writes a ticket. Sometimes he brings Barbie with him, most of the time he's by himself."

"So he comes in and writes kids every week, but I happen to coincidentally be here tonight and that makes you suspicious of me?" Carston remarked.

Martin shrugged his shoulders. "Just saying, you happen to be here and all."

Carston let it go.

"I was hoping to catch Barker and Harper here," Carston took a sip from the bottle.

"Well you're shit out of luck, because they left." Martin picked up the glass and started polishing it again.

"What do you know about those guys?" Carston asked, hoping for something he could use.

"They come in here most every day, sometimes twice a day," Martin replied. "They work three blocks down the street at the funeral home. Barker gets the special, Harper a burger or a slice of peperoni pizza."

"You're not helping," Carston said half seriously.

"They are customers, not friends," Martin said.

"They married, got kids, got wives? They talk to you, don't they?" Carston asked.

"Harper is a bachelor and as far as I know always has been. Barker was married at one time. His wife is gone. He has a grown-up kid who works over in Omaha," Martin rattled off.

"Barker's wife passed?" Carston asked.

"Don't know," Martin replied. "He doesn't have a wife anymore. That's all I know."

"What about his kid?" Carston asked.

"Don't know," Martin said. "I just know he has one."

"He doesn't brag about his kid, like what a great baseball player he was in high school, nothing?" Carston pushed.

"Nope," was all Martin said. "I know what he looks like. Barker brought him in a few times. Never introduced me. Like a said, I'm a bartender, not their friend. People talk to me when they got no one else to talk to."

Carston drained the bottle, placed it on the bar and stood up. "Give me a call if you happen to hear anything," he said, putting on his coat.

"Will do," Martin replied, polishing his glass.

Gavin goes on the run

Gavin Barker had not slept well. His girlfriend Wendy and he were on the outs again, at least for the time being, and that was working out pretty well for Gavin, considering his circumstances. She told Gavin that she needed a break from him and that she was staying at her apartment in Omaha that she shared with her friend. He wondered what she was up to. He hadn't heard from her for a couple of days. He wondered if taking a break meant that she was sharing herself with someone else. Gavin didn't care if that was the case, he wasn't the kind to try to keep a short rein on someone. He could share, just so long as she came back to him. He liked her a lot.

Gavin lived in his sprawling ranch house nestled on an acreage high in the bluffs of the Missouri River valley north of Crescent, IA. He liked it out there. The house sat on a hundred and sixty acres of bluffs and rolling woodlands. A half mile by a half mile. He probably owned a third again that much surface area as the land behind his house took a steep slope up for a quarter mile before it leveled off. His property line was at the top of the bluff. His house sat four hundred yards from the road into Crescent. It was his kingdom. Beyond the house were three outbuildings, a machine shed, a second garage and an old barn that Gavin had been trying to fix up off and on since he had moved there six years before.

Gavin was awake at seven that morning. He lay in his bed while he thought about getting up and dressed to go to work at his office in Omaha. He heard a car door slam from the direction of his machine shed. He jumped out of bed and went to the spare bedroom that had a window that faced toward the bluffs. He looked out to see a red Dodge Ram four-wheel-drive pickup parked just in front of the unattached garage and two men walking around his outbuildings. He hadn't heard them drive in. One of the men was trying the door to the machine shed while the other was looking straight toward the house. Gavin ducked down and scampered to his bedroom for the Colt forty-five semi auto that his father had loaned him a long time back and he had never returned. The gun was loaded.

Gavin crawled back to the window in the spare bedroom on his hands and knees and peered over the windowsill. Both men were now walking toward the old barn. Gavin ran into his room and started to dress quickly. In less than a minute he was sporting a pair of Lee Rider jeans, a long-sleeved chambray shirt and a pair of rugged Frye harness boots. He was not dressed for work. Going to work was no longer on his mind. He had more urgent concerns at the moment. He pushed the pistol into the waist of his jeans and went quickly to his attached garage, looking out the sliding glass door on the way that led to the patio behind the house and gave him a clear view of the machine shed, the unattached garage, the old barn and the bluffs beyond. There was no sign of the two men.

There were two vehicles parked in his attached garage, an Audi R8 coupe and a BMW X7.

75

The BMW was built like a tank. If he had to ram his way out, it would do the job. Gavin got in, started the engine and hit the door remote at the same time. It took an excruciating amount of time for the door to come up. Gavin's heart was beating so hard he could feel it. He watched the door in his rearview mirror, knowing that the door had to reach its complete height for the BMW to make it out. He listened to the drone of the opener. He put the BMW into reverse and as soon as the sound of the door opener stopped, he nailed it. The BMW lurched out of the garage. Gavin did not look around. He made a bootleg into the snow piled alongside his driveway, threw the vehicle into drive and made a break for the road. Only then did he look back to see if anyone was following him, and he was not surprised to see the Ram coming around from the back of the house in pursuit as he turned onto the road. For just a brief moment, Gavin thought that perhaps he should have closed the garage door. Whoever it was prowling his outbuildings now had full access to his house through the open garage. He put it out of his mind as quickly as it had come into it and concentrated on escaping into the bluffs that he knew so well, hoping that he would lose his pursuers. The Ram had not come to the end of the driveway when Gavin turned left onto a gravel road that would take him up into the bluffs and come out in a maze of farm fields and back roads.

When he came out onto flat land Gavin drove furiously into the countryside, making sure that he kept moving and that he wasn't being followed. When he felt it safe to slow down he fished his phone out of his pocket and called into work to tell his receptionist that he would not be in, family emergency. He asked her to reschedule any appointments that he had for the day. She told him that it would be no problem. Gavin had easily shaken the two men in the Ram. He had grown up roaming the hills and bluffs between Missouri Valley and Council Bluffs. Now he worked his way around to the east and south of Council Bluffs as he realized he was hungry. He took the old Bellevue bridge across the Missouri River into Nebraska to get a bite to eat. He was sure no one had been trailing him for a long time. He also needed gas. He pulled into a Casey's convenience store and up to the pumps. He was putting the nozzle into the tank when his phone rang. He took it out of his coat pocket and looked at it. The number was blocked. He almost let it go to voice mail, but then just before the sixth ring that would send it there, he accepted the call.

"Where are you?" a familiar husky voice asked.

"Should I be talking to you, Harvey?" Gavin asked.

"Why wouldn't you?" Harvey replied. "You were talking to me yesterday."

"I had a couple of visitors out at the place this morning," Gavin said. "Early visitors."

"Is this some kind of guessing game? Because if it is, I need to know how to play," Harvey remarked. "What kind of visitors did you have?"

"Guys like you," Gavin replied.

"Guys like me?" Harvey laughed out loud over the phone. "What kind of guy am I?"

"The kind of guy that wants to hurt somebody."

"We've been buds since high school. I'm not going to try to hurt you," Harvey replied calmly.

"I didn't say you want to hurt me." Gavin was getting into his BMW to stay warm while the gas was being pumped into the tank. "I said someone like you. Some guys who looked like they didn't really want to talk to me."

"I'm not the one you need to be afraid of," the voice on the other end sounded exasperated. "I'm trying to help."

"Are you?" Gavin replied.

"Where are you?" Harvey asked.

"Somewhere north of Omaha," Gavin lied.

"No, you aren't," Harvey replied.

Gavin didn't answer. The pump clicked off.

"Where's the hearse?" Harvey asked.

"I wondered when you would get to that," Gavin replied.

"Everyone is looking for you," Harvey said patiently. "All they want is the hearse. No one wants to hurt you. You need to trust me."

"That's all?" Gavin replied. "And that's the problem. Someone told me I'm expendable."

"I don't think anyone said you were expendable, that's not the case at all," Harvey responded.

"I do think that's the case," Gavin replied. "I'm a little spooked right now."

"I think that you should be, considering Glenn wants the hearse and you don't seem to be holding up your end of the deal," Harvey replied. "Now she doesn't trust you, and that's your fault. You brought that on yourself. So I'm trying to help you out. You need to wiggle out from under this, and I think I know how you can do it. Glenn hired a private detective to find you and the hearse. Right now, that is all she's thinking about, getting the hearse. You call this detective up, tell him where the hearse is. He tells her. You are out of the loop. You go home, get your shit together, give her a few days to calm down, then you and Glenn kiss and make up."

Gavin thought for a moment. "I know an awful lot about her."

"And that is why when she realizes how valuable you are to her, she'll—" Harvey paused. "She'll realize how valuable you are to her and everything goes back to the way it was."

"You sound so reassuring," Gavin replied sarcastically.

Harvey didn't answer.

"Look, you are the one who told me to watch my ass. I know what 'watch your ass' means," Gavin said.

"I told you to watch your ass," Harvey replied. "I didn't say to go rogue weird on us."

"On us?" Gavin commented. "On us?"

"Christ," Harvey's voice sounded exasperated again.

Neither spoke for a minute.

"Look," Harvey said. "I call up my friend and tell him to watch his ass, that's all, nothing more. Somehow he spirals out of control and falls into a ravine. Just call the private detective. Carston Hancock is his name. Quit being stupid about it."

Gavin didn't answer.

"Got something to write on?"

Gavin dug into the console between the seats and found a pen and the envelope that his registration came in. "Go," he said.

Gavin wrote down the name and phone number.

"Got it?" Harvey asked.

"Got it," Gavin replied.

"You got yourself into this mess," Harvey remarked. "All you had to do is what Glenn asked you to do. Nothing more. Everything would have been fine if you had just done that. Now it isn't fine."

"You said to watch my ass," Gavin retorted.

"All you had to do was what she asked you to do and watch your ass while you did it. Everything would have been fine. You fucked this up, not me."

Gavin didn't reply.

"Call the detective and tell him where the hearse is." The call went dead.

Gavin threw his phone in the passenger seat and got out of his vehicle to remove the nozzle and put it back into the pump. When he got back in the vehicle he pulled forward and parked in front of the convenience store. The sign in the window said that they sold pizza by the slice. He left the BMW parked and running while he went inside. When he came back out, he had made up his mind to go into the office. He couldn't just keep driving around and he would be relatively safe in the office with everyone around. For the moment it was his best move. He also did not want to call the detective from his cell phone. It would be better to call from the office phone. He was thinking that there might be a bit more anonymity calling from there. He pulled out of the convenience store and onto the highway, making his way north past the Offutt Airforce base toward Omaha. A half hour later he parked the BMW in his assigned space on the third level of the parking ramp next to the building that housed Barton Law Offices where Gavin was a junior partner.

Susan, Gavin's receptionist, was visibly surprised to see him come in. He was not dressed for work, wearing blue jeans and a Carhartt work jacket. Not the usual attire at Barton Law Offices, and Gavin was usually particularly particular about how he dressed. Gavin was tall, slim and handsome with an athletic build. Susan had always found him quite attractive. In the office he always wore tailored suits and not a hair stood out of place. At the moment, his hair looked like he had just gotten out of bed. She had never seen him in such a casual and rumpled state. He looked like a farmhand. She did notice that the jacket was particularly clean. She didn't know why she would think that it wouldn't be, but Susan was raised on a farm and she was unaccustomed to seeing farmhands with clean coats. It was the one thing that didn't fit in his appearance.

"I just stopped in to pick up some stuff and make a few calls. If anyone calls or comes in looking for me, I'm not in," Gavin told her as he walked past. She just nodded and watched him go into his office, shut his door and pull the shades.

Gavin pulled the envelope out of his pocket and sat at his desk. He punched one of the buttons for a line out and dialed the number he had written on the envelope. The phone rang twice.

"Carston Hancock Investigations," a pleasant voice answered. "Stephanie speaking."

"Stephanie, I need to talk to Detective Hancock," Gavin said in a businesslike tone.

81

"Detective Hancock is not in at the moment; can I have him call you?"

Gavin thought for a moment. "Yes, he can call me at this number," Gavin read off the number to the office phone. "It is important that he gets back to me as soon as possible," he added.

Stephanie wrote the number on a notepad. "Can I get your name and what this is in reference to?" she asked.

"I'll tell him what it is about when he calls."

"Can I give him a name to ask for when he calls?" Stephanie tried again.

"I'll be here at this number," Gavin answered.

"I will let him know," Stephanie replied.

Gavin hung up.

As soon as Gavin ended the call, Stephanie punched the phone number into her computer search; the result came up at the top of the page. "Barton Law Offices," she read aloud. She clicked on the link and their website came up. It was very well done. It looked like someplace that she wouldn't mind working. The website looked much trendier than Carston Hancock Investigations. There were nine lawyers listed. Her eyes went to a list of lawyers in the firm that specialized in divorce. Immediately Stephanie had an anxiety attack. She got up to get a drink of water and collect her thoughts. She had not thought that Megan would take things that far. She had hoped that Megan wouldn't take it that far. Carston would be crushed. Stephanie sat for a moment, trying to decide what to do. She could hear the clock on the wall ticking. Stephanie picked up the phone and punched in Carston's mobile number. It rang three times without an answer. She hung up.

She would wait, treat it like any other call she took. She didn't want to get something started. She would wait for him to call and then give him the information. No big deal. Just like any other call that she took in the course of a day that he had to return.

Gavin sat back in his chair and waited. He had no idea how long it would take for Hancock to get back to him, but he felt relatively safe in his office. He picked up his phone and pushed the button for his receptionist.

"Yes," she answered. "You need something?"

"If anyone comes in, I'm not here," Gavin instructed her. "I will just take phone calls."

"Okay," Susan replied. It was the second time that he had instructed her that he did not want to talk to anyone except whoever it was he was waiting for a call from. She wondered what the problem was. It was unusual for him to lock himself in his office like that and close his blinds when he didn't have a high profile client. "Anything else?"

"Nope," Gavin said. "I'm waiting for an important call. I just don't want to be disturbed otherwise."

"Someone in particular you are waiting for a call from?" Susan asked.

"Yes," Gavin replied.

Susan waited for a moment, but Gavin didn't say anything more.

"If someone calls, I'll put them through."

"Thanks," Gavin replied, knowing that she was confused and that he was not helping, but he wanted to say as little as possible to as few people as he could until he got this mess sorted out. He ended the call, sat back in his chair and closed his eyes. He got himself into this mess and he didn't even know what mess he had gotten himself into. All he knew was that he was working with some very dangerous people. People who wouldn't think twice. Gavin was scared.

Flingnasties

Carston came out of Marzoe's, got into his car and fired it up. He took out his notebook and checked the address of Flingnasties. He was familiar with most of Omaha and he knew right where it was. It was not one of the best parts of town to be caught out in, but it was cold and Carston figured that it was too cold for ne'er-do-wells to be hanging around waiting for a target to come by. Besides, he had his gun and his work had taken him to worse parts of town. He wasn't a greenhorn. He knew, though, that the best way to avoid getting carjacked, mugged and beaten was to avoid those parts of town where his chances of getting carjacked, mugged and beaten were good. Carston was not a tough guy. He had nothing to prove.

Carston pulled into the lot at Flingnasties. The building was a huge expanse. Definitely not the neighborhood hangout, like Marzoe's. It was after eight, dark. The parking lot was well-lit and big, half full of cars, all of them parked as close to the door as they could get. Across the front of the building was the name Flingnasties spelled out in bright red florescent letters. Below that and to the left was a pink neon sign in the shape of a naked, long-haired woman with letters that promised "Exotic Dancers." To the right was an equally obnoxious-looking sign—this time in green—that showed the same naked neon woman hanging on a pole with letters that announced "Pole Dancers."

85

"A titty bar," Carston muttered to himself. He wondered which had a higher status in stripper society, exotic dancers or pole dancers. He parked as close to the door as he could find a spot, turned off the engine and waited. During the day it had warmed up considerably from the last couple of frigid weeks while the polar express came through, but when the sun went down it went from bearable back to damned cold. He didn't want to get out of the warm car. At least it wasn't windy, he thought. Carston jumped out of the car and sprinted to the door.

Just past the door was a vestibule where a bar chair sat below a sign proclaiming that all patrons would be IDed without exception. The chair was empty. The noise of the crowd and the even louder sound of music blared from the bar area beyond the vestibule. Carston proceeded in the direction of the music. The inside of the building was spacious, with a shotgun layout. There appeared to be several rooms connected to each other extending in a row to the back of the building, and each one seemed to have a stage with at least one, sometimes two, half-naked women undulating against a pole for a crowd of screaming men who were running up to put dollar bills in their G-strings.

Carston spotted Glenn sitting at the end of the bar in the first room talking to the bartender. The bartender spotted Carston making his way there and alerted her. She turned and without any expression watched him approach.

"Take a seat," she patted the stool next to her when he got there.

Xavier + Dimp (dead) killed while looking for hearse. Members of motorcycle gang.

Zee called Dimp's phone, X answered was told to keep looking for contraban in hearse.

Susan - Gavin's reception

Plaza Bar - Martin bartender
Kenny Smart - owner Body Shop
David - Kenny's son-in-law
Gavin - son of Vince + lawyer
Barbie Rime - cop, she worked
security at West Rd with PI.
Hank Gross - Barbie's partner
Barker + Harper = Vince + Bill
Wenay - Gavin's girlfriend
Harvey - working with Glenn

Carson Hancock - P.I.

Stephanie - Office mgr

Glenda (Glenn) Thompson niece
to dead uncle Thomas Dunn

Alice - Spagetti work posters

Vance + Bill - hearse drivers

Harmon + Matt - Funeral Home

Jerry Thompson - Glenn's husband. Was her uncle's right hand man. Also presumed to be dead.

Klingenstein - Ship bar

Mona + Tip - hotel de Vent employees

Sylvia - hooker

Carston climbed onto the barstool, hooked the heels of his Tony Lamas over the rail and situated himself.

"Have you come to tell me that you found my hearse?" she asked expectantly.

"Not yet," Carston replied.

The brief expression left her face. "Any leads?" she asked hopefully.

"Nothing that I can work on yet," Carston replied. "I spent most of the day trying to run down the two guys who were driving the hearse when it was stolen. I keep missing them. I checked all the usual dumping grounds over in Council Bluffs, too, and nothing. I put out some feelers. Talked to a couple of people who usually have inside contacts, asked them to check around. I'm hoping someone gives me a call."

"Expedience is of utmost importance," Glenn reminded him sternly.

"I know that," Carston replied. "I'm doing everything that I can at the moment."

There was an empty chair on the other side of Glenn. While they talked a huge bear of a man pulled it away from the bar and sat in it. He had to stand at least six foot five. Even in his winter clothing, the muscles of his legs bulged tightly against the denim of his jeans and his biceps stretched the knit of his sweater. His chest looked like a brick wall. He had a mop of curly black hair and an equally dense beard. He took the seat casually and leaned around Glenn to listen to the conversation. He unnerved Carston.

Glenn felt the man's presence and glanced back at him for a moment, then back to Carston.

"Harvey," Glenn announced to Carston, tipping her head toward the bear. The man nodded a greeting of sorts. Carston got the impression that the nod might be the extent of Harvey's conversational skills.

"Harvey is security here. He is supposed to be watching the door," Glenn said.

Harvey made no movement that indicated he had any intention of leaving.

"This is Detective Carston Hancock the Third," she explained to Harvey. "He's supposed to be locating our hearse for us."

Harvey nodded. The two sat looking at Carston, waiting for him to say something.

Carston decided his best bet was to continue his report. "The good news is that, as of this morning when I was at the records office investigating what information the Omaha PD has on the theft, the cop who took the stolen vehicle call hasn't filed a report," he said somewhat triumphantly, as if that revelation was the most important element in the search.

Neither Glenn nor Harvey responded.

"If the cop doesn't file a report, no one is looking for the hearse," Carston explained. "A lot of times cops are lazy. They don't like to write up reports, they like to drink coffee and regale people with their exploits as cops. So they let their reports stack up until they get called out by the command staff on them." He looked at the two looking at him. "And if there isn't a report, the vehicle theft division doesn't do anything. They wait for the report. The longer the cop doesn't do the report, the longer we have to work on it ourselves and the cops aren't doing anything," he explained further, thinking that it should be getting through, at least to Glenn, that time was on their side.

"So, you are hinging your own investigation on the supposition that a lazy cop isn't going to file a timely report?" the giant broke the silence.

Carston was taken by surprise. He hadn't expected the big man to speak, especially in such an articulate manner. His voice was as low and ominous as his appearance.

"No, just saying," Carston said defensively.

"And I'm 'just saying' that maybe the report has been filed by now and you don't have as much time to sit on your ass as you think you do," Harvey challenged.

"You're right," Carston agreed, hoping that Harvey would let it drop. He looked at Glenn, hoping she would intercede. "I don't have a lot to work with here, all I'm hoping is to buy a little time."

"With what?" Harvey asked.

Carston gave him a confused look.

"What kind of collateral you got to buy time? Sounds like you're counting on dumb luck. You're not buying anything."

Glenn sat quietly, listening to the two go back and forth. Carston gave her another pleading look.

"Harvey's my head of security," she replied to the look.

"Right now, I'm working with what I've got," Carston replied, hoping to turn the conversation.

No one said anything. Carston felt his phone vibrate in his pocket. He pulled it out and looked at the number. He didn't recognize it. He was afraid it might be the lawyer that Stephanie said was looking for him, and he didn't want to talk to a divorce lawyer at that particular moment, but he told himself that he better take it, it could be anybody. He swiped the answer icon. A muffled voice came over the phone that he barely recognized as Martin from Marzoe's.

"Hang on a minute, I can't hear. I need to go somewhere quieter," Carston looked up at Glenn and Harvey. "I've got a call I need to take."

Harvey was back to nodding. Carston got up and went to the vestibule where it was still loud, but he could hear Martin.

"What's up?" Carston asked into the phone.

"Just now I had a couple of bikers come in here asking about Vince and Harper. I asked why they were looking for them and they told me that they was just looking for those two and wanted to ask them some questions," Martin paused for a moment. "Just like that, they are looking for those two, same as you," he paused again. "I'm just thinking, probably they're looking for the same hearse you're looking for, too."

"You think that?" Carston said sarcastically.

"You don't have to take an attitude," Martin replied. "You wanted me to call you."

"You're right, Martin," Carston replied quickly. "I did, and I appreciate the call. What did these guys look like?"

"They looked like bikers," Martin said.

"Generic Harley-rider type bikers, or the real thing?" Carston questioned.

"Hell Fighters," Martin answered.

"Okay, semi-bad asses, then," Carston remarked.

"These two looked to me like semi-bad asses looking for someone to kill so that they can be

90

major bad asses," Martin said. "I get a lot of local wanna-be bikers in here, and I've never seen these two before. They most assuredly are scary bikers."

"Anything else about what they said that might be useful?" Carston asked.

"Actually, thinking about it, they just said that they were looking for Vince, not Bill. You were the one looking for both of them. They was also asking if anyone else had been around asking about Vince."

"What did you tell them?" Carston asked the question with trepidation.

"I told them that you had been in earlier asking and talking about the same thing."

"Why would you tell them that?" Carston shouted into the phone.

"Because they didn't look like the sort that took kindly on someone lying to them," Martin shouted back.

Carston was thinking what the ramifications of Martin's revelation might be to his own investigation when Martin spoke up again. "I gave them your card. They might be giving you a call."

Carston took a deep breath. He was not dealing with a normal thinking person. There might be a reason why Martin was working in a dive bar and grill all day and all night, and it might be that Martin was not particularly bright. There are people like that, you talk to them and at first they seem normal, but then after a while you figure out that they just aren't keeping up. Carston told himself that in the future he needed to be more careful with Martin.

"Okay," Carston said. "All that is good to know. Thank you, Martin. Is there anything else I might want to know?"

"Can't think of anything," Martin replied.

"Call me if something else comes up," Carston said.

"Sure thing." Martin didn't end the call.

"You got something else?" Carston asked.

"Nope," Martin replied.

"I'm going to go ahead and hang up if you don't have anything else," Carston said into the phone and ended the call.

Carston went back to the bar and took his place on the stool that he had left. Glenn and Harvey were in a conversation that abruptly stopped when Carston got close.

"Did that call have anything to do with our missing hearse?" Glenn asked.

"No, actually it had to do with something else." Carston decided that he wasn't going to show his hand so quickly.

"I was hoping it might be a lead or something," Glenn said.

"That would be nice, but it wasn't."

Harvey was nodding to punctuate everything Glenn said.

"I'm going to get out of here and go home," Carston said. "I got those feelers out and hopefully someone will give me a call soon. Until then, not much I can do."

"Not much to show today for your five hundred bucks," Harvey spoke up.

"Hopefully tomorrow I earn that and the bonus," Carston replied. "I'm optimistic that by then I'll have some good leads to follow up on."

Harvey started to say something, but Glenn touched his arm and he nodded twice.

"Talk to you tomorrow." Carston got up and went for the door. He could feel their eyes drilling into his back as he walked away. He was wondering just what Stephanie had gotten him into. There was a lot more to this one than his usual stolen vehicle case. Maybe there was even more to this one than a stolen hearse with dear old Uncle Thomas in it. Carston was starting to wonder what would happen if the cops got to the hearse before he did. He suspected he could lose more than his bonus. He needed to go home, get some rest and bust this case tomorrow. There was a lot more at stake than he was being told.

Carston drove his car to the parking lot behind the Hotel LeVant and found a space. Oftentimes when he came home all of the spaces were taken by people who were wining and dining at the Old Market. There was a sign warning drivers that the parking lot was private parking for Hotel LeVant patrons only and that violators would be ticketed and towed, but the warning was seldom enforced. He was feeling lucky as he pulled in and parked. It made him hopeful that he would get a break soon. Hope was all he had at the moment. Carston locked his car and sprinted to the door of the hotel.

Anyone who spent any time at the Hotel LeVant knew that it was a flophouse. Rooms by the hour, by the night, by the week or by the month. But the hotel was old and stately and it looked good in pictures. It still had a dusty and worn elegance. There were always people visiting Omaha and looking for someplace to stay close to the Old Market who were attracted by the low rates and the close proximity to the area. None of them were repeat customers. A group of four such visitors sat in the lobby with drinks from the bar, looking around somewhat dubiously, trying to figure out exactly what felt wrong about the place. Carston nodded to them on his way to the elevator.

Carston rode the elevator to the sixth and top floor. He had a suite there. It was actually a nice place, a little dated, a little worn, but at least it was not one of the rooms like those on the second floor that might see three or more separate tenants a night. Carston threw his coat on a chair by the door, his sports coat on top of that. He shrugged out of the JackAss shoulder holster, feeling the weight of the Smith and Wesson 686 .357 magnum revolver and the twelve extra rounds in his hand. He tossed it on the chair and went to mix himself a drink. He was irked that Glenn had not even offered him a drink in her bar. His cell phone started to ring from somewhere in the pile of clothes and armament on the chair. He dug it out on the fifth ring and quickly swiped the screen before it went to voicemail, recognizing the number.

"Martin," he said into the phone.

"Yeah, you told me to call you if anything else came up."

"I did," Carston said encouragingly. "What do you have?"

"You know those bikers I was talking about?" Martin asked.

"Yes," Carston replied. "I don't know them personally, but I remember you talking about them."

94

"Do you want to hear what I have to say?" Martin asked after a beat.

"Yes, I do," Carston said seriously.

"Well, one of them is dead," Martin said matter-of-factly.

Carston did not know how to respond.

"Someone killed him," Martin responded to the silence.

"Killed him?" Carston said.

"Yep, someone shot him," Martin replied.

"When?" Carston asked.

"Between the time they was in here and the time that Augie came in and told me about it," Martin answered.

"Who is Augie?" Carston asked.

"Lives over by the funeral home," Martin said. "It sounds like Augie found him in the parking lot of the funeral home, dead."

"The biker?" Carston asked.

"No Augie, Augie came in here to tell me that they found Augie shot dead in the parking lot of the funeral home," Martin said sarcastically. "One of those bikers that I was telling you about a little while ago was found shot dead in the parking lot of the Harmon and Mott Funeral Home." Martin accentuated the words as he said them.

"Okay, okay," Carston said. "Anything else?"

"Nope," said Martin.

"Nothing else?" Carston asked.

"Are you dense?" Martin replied.

"Okay, thanks for that info. I'm heading over there to the funeral home right now to see what I can find out. I'll stop in after that. Keep Augie there if you can. His drinks are on me," Carston said, ending the call and pulling the JackAss shoulder holster back on, the heavy Smith swinging into place under his arm.

Xavier Warner

Xavier Matthew Warner sat in his Dodge Ram four-wheel-drive king cab pickup truck in the parking lot of the Kum and Go convenience store a block down the street from the Harmon and Mott funeral home. He could not make out clearly what was going on, he was too far away. But this was as close as he dared get to the crime scene without being conspicuous. He was nervous as it was. Didn't they say that murderers always return to the scene of the crime? But Xavier wasn't the murderer. He was just there when the murder occurred. All the same, he felt guilty and he had no desire to draw attention to himself. He could see two marked Council Bluffs patrol cars, a Pottawattamie County sheriff's car, a van and an ambulance in the parking lot. He assumed the van was some crime lab vehicle that they had brought in to process the scene. He had watched enough TV to lead him to that conclusion, anyway. Xavier watched the coming and going of cars and people from a distance, his lights off and his engine idling. His truck's radio was barely audible. It was cold outside and even though it was toasty warm inside the cab of his pickup, Xavier fell under a wave of shivering periodically while he kept his vigil.

Xavier was born and raised in Council Bluffs. His family home was on Kimberly Drive. He attended Abraham Lincoln High School, where he had been a linebacker on the football team, the Lynx. Since he could remember, Xavier had wanted to be an Iowa State Cyclone. His senior year of high school he applied to get into Iowa State University on a football scholarship. When he failed to get a scholarship, he enrolled in ISU anyway, determined to win a position on the team as a walk-on. That didn't happen, either. He did succeed in landing a scholarship as a discus thrower and a hammer thrower on the Cyclone track team. Xavier was a 'Clone, through and through. His Dodge Ram four by four pickup was cardinal with gold highlights, as close to a 'Clonemobile as he could get. The words "Iowa State University" were displayed across the back window.

Xavier majored in Physical Education at ISU, Leisure Studies in particular. He did well enough academically, graduated in four years, a true accomplishment for a guy who came from a family that thought anything beyond a high school education was a waste of time and money better spent getting experience in the real working world. Unless, of course, one could secure a spot on the football or basketball team, then it was a steppingstone to greatness. Xavier knew that under his father's show of pride on graduation day, there was a little bit of disappointment that Xavier was not destined for the NFL. No one makes a career of throwing a discus, as his father had told him on a number of occasions.

When he graduated from university, Xavier landed a job with the Council Bluffs Parks and Recreations department as an event coordinator. It was a good job. It was a job that his father told him was probably as good as he was going to get, considering he wasn't NFL material. But a good job nonetheless. Xavier thrived and prospered at Parks and Rec for five years. He got good evaluations and some decent raises. He bought a little house with a one-car garage, he was dating an elementary school teacher; everything was going smoothly for him. Then he got the Harley bug. Two of his friends had bought new Harley Davidson motorcycles. Xavier found the boom-putt-putt of the engine like music to his ears. And his friends each got five hundred Harley dollars in the deal, to buy whatever they wanted in accessories and clothing. They came by his house on their bikes, dressed from head to toe in Harley boots, Harley pants, Harley shirts and Harley jackets. They just looked so biker. Xavier headed straight to the Harley motorcycle shop with his friends following on their new Harleys to help him buy one of his own. And he used his own Harley bucks to buy five hundred dollars' worth of bad boy from the Harley boutique.

While Xavier's two friends remained weekend rabblerousers and went back to their respectable day jobs on Mondays, Xavier got caught up in trying to live up to the Harley image. He got shaggy, although that in itself was not his downfall. But soon, even though his city uniform was a yellow polo with CBPR embroidered on the right breast, his Harley wear became his true uniform, and he showed up to work every day looking more and more and more like someone who parents didn't want their kids around. His supervisors talked to him about his appearance. Xavier got surly, which also fit his new and developing persona, and before the summer of his sixth year at Council Bluffs Parks and Recreations

Xavier had a new job at Handy Auto Parts and Speed Shop that paid half what he had been making, with no benefits.

Xavier fell deeper and deeper into the biker lifestyle. He hung out in biker bars and on the fringes of a biker gang, the Hell Fighters. It was just a matter of time before he fell in with them, served his apprenticeship as a prospect, then became a full-fledged Hell Fighter, replete with colors flying on the back of his leather vest, which at that very moment was hidden beneath his wool winter coat.

A burgundy-colored Cadillac Escalade pulled up to the curb and illegally parked on the wrong side of the street in front of the Harmon and Mott funeral home. A man who looked like he might be a detective got out of it and ran to one of the patrol cars. Xavier had a hard time seeing any detail in the dim light of the streetlights, but he could tell that whoever was in the patrol car wouldn't let the man get in the front passenger seat. He watched the man climb into the back.

Other than the detective showing up, nothing else had occurred in almost an hour. Just the patrol vehicles, the van and the ambulance idling in the parking lot. Xavier let his mind go over the events of the past few days. He needed to make sense of what had happened.

Three days before, Xavier had met with the vice president of the Council Bluffs chapter of the Hell Fighters. The VP said he had something he wanted Xavier to do. It might be risky, but he thought that Xavier was a smart guy, someone who could very well move up in the ranks if he proved himself up to the task. Xavier was excited. He was ready for anything.

Yesterday, Xavier drove to the Eppley airport and waited as instructed, wearing his Hell Fighter colors prominently to identify himself. There he waited for the arrival of another Hell Fighter from Montreal, Canada to get through customs. When they finally met, the Hell Fighter from Montreal introduced himself as Gimp, a name that fit him: he had a slight limp when he walked. Xavier introduced himself simply as X. Hell Fighters had one name, a nickname, so they were Gimp and X. Members guarded their real names, so should anything go down, should one Hell Fighter get arrested and turn, should an undercover agent or member of a rival gang somehow infiltrate the club, everyone knew everyone else only by their nicknames. Only a select few knew any member's given name.

The first thing that Xavier noticed was the "Nomad" patch on Gimp's vest. It meant that Gimp didn't belong to the Montreal chapter. It meant that he didn't belong to any chapter. As a nomad, Gimp did the business of the club, and he had the authority to use whatever and whoever he needed from any chapter where he was doing the club's business. Xavier was at Gimp's service. That was the only orders he had gotten from his VP, and Xavier was determined that whatever Gimp needed from him, he would provide it.

What should apparently have been a simple and routine mission for Gimp went awry from the very beginning. First off, Gimp was late in locating Xavier. As they hustled from the terminal building to the parking ramp where Xavier had parked his truck, Gimp filled him in with what he needed to know. A hearse would pick up a body from the very plane he had flown in from Montreal. There was not going to be any finesse involved: as soon as they spotted the hearse leaving the cargo area, Xavier would run it off the road, ram it if need be, Gimp would jack it, force the driver out and take the hearse. That was it, nothing more. All Xavier needed to do to prove himself was to force the hearse to a stop so that Gimp could accomplish what he had come to accomplish, and that was to jack the hearse.

The problem was that it took Gimp forever to get through customs. When he did, they hurriedly stationed themselves where they could see the tarmac gate, but they were already over a half hour past when the plane landed. No hearse ever came out of the cargo area. They waited an hour and a half. Finally they realized that the hearse had gotten past them. Xavier felt an attack of anxiety that he was responsible for some unfathomable reason for missing the hearse, but Gimp was cool about the whole thing. He asked Xavier if he knew where the Harmon and Mott funeral home was. Xavier took him straight there. They made three or four passes by the funeral home so that Gimp could get a good look at all sides of it. Then they settled themselves in the parking lot of the Kum and Go convenience store where Xavier was sitting at that moment and waited. Gimp was good at waiting; Xavier not so much. He wanted to keep moving, look for the hearse, but Gimp told him to be patient, let the hearse come to them. It had to come home sooner or later. They spent the whole afternoon patiently waiting. A taxi came in and dumped two passengers off. The hearse never did come home. When it got dark, the two men who had arrived by taxi left in a car and drove past the Kum and Go where X and Gimp watched them go by, noting the make, model and license number of the car. A third man came out of the building fifteen minutes later and drove out the other direction. The place was dark. Xavier drove Gimp to the Holiday Inn Express on Broadway, where he got a room. While Gimp made some calls on his cell phone, Xavier watched Wheel of Fortune on the TV with the sound turned down, reading the closed captions so as to not disturb Gimp's conversations. Xavier knew that his duty was to mind his own business and wait for Gimp to tell him what came next.

Right around nine they left and walked to the Village Inn restaurant adjacent to the hotel. Xavier ate a combo of eggs, bacon and pancakes. Gimp had a tenderloin. They both had a slice of pie for dessert. Gimp picked up the bill. Xavier thought that he was a pretty decent guy and most likely someone whose recommendation would be quite helpful in moving up the ladder of the Hell Fighters organization.

After they were done eating, Gimp had Xavier drive him around. They did some reconnoitering and Gimp got the lay of the land. Gimp directed him to turn here, turn there. Gimp was not much for small talk and Xavier did as he was instructed and let the man think. Once they drove into the parking lot at the Harmon and Mott funeral home briefly and looked around. Gimp left Xavier in the truck while he walked around the building, peering through the windows and shaking all the doors. He came back and they drove over the bridge to Omaha and drove around the Old Market district. At eleven Gimp called it quits and told Xavier to take him back to the hotel. They went to his room and while Gimp made more phone calls Xavier watched some more TV, this time an old black and white rerun of Gunsmoke. When Gimp was done with his calls he went to the bathroom, stripped down to his jeans and a tee shirt and went to sleep on the bed. Xavier slept on a chair in the corner of the room. Gimp gave him the comforter off the bed for a cover.

Gimp got up at six o'clock and dressed. He asked Xavier if he knew where Crescent, Iowa was. He had a rural address that he wanted to check out. Xavier told him that he was sure he could find it. He was up to the task and drove right to it. It was a nice place, a dozen miles north of Council Bluffs, a few miles north of the little town of Crescent, on the road that went from Council Bluffs up to Missouri Valley. Gimp told him to pull into the long drive. The place was quiet. The house was a modern two story with an attached two car garage that looked to be fairly new. There was a machine shed, a three-car unattached garage and an old barn behind the house, the bluffs beyond that. The two got out and Xavier followed Gimp, trying doors and looking through windows. They saw no signs of a hearse. Gimp suggested the barn and the two proceeded that direction. Just before they got there, they heard a vehicle come out from the garage attached to the house. They both turned to see a white BMW X2 SUV make a bootleg turn in the driveway and fly down the rutted drive toward the highway. Both he and Gimp ran for the Ram to

104

pursue it, but by the time they got to the road there was no sign of the BMW. They drove south at a good clip toward Crescent but the BMW had disappeared.

Xavier and Gimp spent most of the day going from one small town to another small town with names like Neola, Shelby, Avoca, Underwood and Oakland in search of the white BMW. Later in the afternoon they drove around Council Bluffs, then Omaha. Finally, back to Council Bluffs, the Village Inn, and then to the room at the Holiday Inn. Gimp made some more calls. Xavier watched TV. Abruptly Gimp ended a call, asked Xavier if he knew a dive called Marzoe's, and when Xavier told him it was only a few blocks away, Gimp made haste to the Ram. The urgency was not lost on Xavier and he got them there within minutes.

When they went inside they found the bar filled with patrons. A few wannabe bikers dressed in their Harley gear were playing pool and giving the two Hell Fighters a veiled eye. Most of the tables were filled with just regular Council Bluffs blue collar workers and in the corner a guy with a western shirt and a cowboy hat strummed an acoustic guitar and wailed a country western cover. Gimp went straight to the bartender and with no introduction whatsoever asked him pointedly if he had seen Vince Barker and if he knew where he was. The bartender did not hesitate to say that Vince had been in earlier and had left. The bartender also asked Gimp if this was about the stolen hearse, which caught both Gimp and Xavier off guard. Gimp asked him why, and the bartender explained that there had been a private detective looking for Vince all day about a hearse with a body in it stolen over in Omaha at the Spaghetti Works in the Old Market district. He offered a business card to Gimp. It was obvious to Xavier that the bartender was going to give Gimp whatever he wanted to get him out of there. Gimp took the card and stood glaring at the bartender.

"That it?" Gimp asked him.

The bartender nodded and Gimp turned on his heel to leave. Xavier followed. When they got outside and back in the truck, Gimp pulled out his phone in one hand and balanced the business card on his knee. He called the number on the back of the card and waited. It rang six times and went to voicemail.

"You have reached the voicemail of Carston Hancock the Third, private investigator. Please leave a message at the tone and I will return the call as soon as I can." There was a beep. Gimp ended the call. He made another call. "The law office of Gavin Barker, Barton Law Offices. Please leave a message at the tone." Another beep and Gimp ended the call. He instructed Xavier to drive to Omaha and gave him the address from the business card. Xavier drove him across the river, through the Old Market district and past the Hancock building. He asked Gimp if he wanted to get out, but Gimp said no. Then they drove by the building that housed Barton Law Offices. Gimp did want to get out there. He left Xavier in the truck to wait. He came back fifteen minutes later and instructed Xavier to take him back to Harmon and Mott.

Xavier had been an exemplary chauffeur. He had kept to himself, minded his own business, not asked any questions. Gimp had hardly spoken to

Xavier for two days. On the way back across the river Gimp finally opened up to him. A casket containing a body and some valuable contraband had come from Montreal. The plan had been designed to slip the contraband through customs. Clearly whatever was in the casket was illegal contraband, although Gimp didn't explain and Xavier didn't ask. But it was valuable. The contraband had been stolen from the Hell Fighters in Montreal, and they wanted it back. They were not concerned about any collateral damage in the process; in fact, the more the better. Show people what happened when they tried to double-cross the Hell Fighters. The plan had been simple. Ram the hearse that picked up the body. Take it to some location where they could open the casket and remove the contraband. That would have been where Xavier proved his worth to the Hell Fighters. Then Gimp would head cross country to a place where he could smuggle the contraband back across the porous border between the U.S. and Canada, then to Montreal. Xavier noticed that Gimp also did not explain what vehicle he was going to drive cross country with the contraband, or where he was going to get it. Xavier knew better than to question him.

When they neared Harmon and Mott, Gimp instructed Xavier to park at the Kum and Go, telling him that they would walk to the funeral home. Gimp asked Xavier if he had a tire iron. Xavier parked and retrieved the iron from under the seat. The two set off on foot. Gimp walked around the building with Xavier following dutifully behind. He found a back door that was in the shadows and couldn't be seen clearly from the street. He shook the door handle. It was a heavy door, set solid in the frame. He told Xavier to pry the door and stepped back. That was when it happened. Everything had been going fine until then. But just as Gimp stepped back and Xavier stepped forward, the quiet frigid winter darkness was rudely interrupted by the sound of two explosions. At the same moment Xavier heard two heavy thuds and knew exactly what had happened. As Gimp began to slump toward the ground, Xavier was on a dead run. He knew better than to stand around waiting to see who was next.

Shot in the back

Carston did a drive-by of Harmon and Mott Funeral Home and Crematorium, went around the block, then pulled to the curb and parked just past the drive that was closed off by yellow crime scene tape. There was that silence that the frigid night air brought to the Midwest. Carston could not hear anything outside his vehicle, and inside the only sound came from the heater fan that was one notch down from full blast. The whole scene was dimly lit by the streetlights and the lights from the funeral home, giving everything a yellow tint. Steam rose from the exhaust of the police and emergency vehicles parked in the lot, adding to the eeriness. He could see Barbie working on something in the patrol car closest to him, lit by the dome light. Carston left his vehicle running as he sprinted around the front of the patrol car and frantically pulled on the passenger side door handle to open the door and get in out of the cold. It was locked. Barbie saw him come around the front of the car and peered out the passenger side window at him.

"Back seat," she yelled through the closed window.

Carston heard the click of the lock and pulled the passenger door open. He stood looking in. There were paper and evidence bags scattered on the passenger seat and the floorboard of the front seat of the car.

"I said get in the back seat," Barbie shouted harshly. "I got my shit all laid out up here."

Carston slammed the door shut, opened the back door of the patrol car and slid in. The back of the car smelled like sweat and puke. He did not close the door all the way. He knew that if he did, he would be locked in, like a rat in the trap.

"What's going on?" he asked as he settled in and tried not to think about who the last person to sit back there was and why.

'What do you know about it?" Barbie asked.

"I don't know anything," Carston replied innocently. "I just came over to see what is going on."

"What, you think I'm a dumb ass?" Barbie said. "You just happen to come by my murder scene and decide to stop by and have a chat? What do you know about the guy laying on the ground over there with two bullets in his back?"

"Two bullets in the back?" Carston repeated.

"Quit fucking around, I'm not in the mood," Barbie said. "Start talking or get out of my car so that I can get my report written."

Carston paused for just a moment and then spoke up. "I'm working this stolen hearse case. We talked about it earlier. I think that this guy that got shot might have something to do with it."

"And what makes you think that?" Barbie prodded.

Carston was thinking.

"Spill it," Barbie prodded again. "This is serious. I got a dead guy laying in the parking lot not ten yards from me and I'm not in the mood for games."

"Martin from Marzoe's called me up earlier and said that after I left, two Hell Fighters came in asking the same questions I was asking, how to get hold of Vince Barker and Bill Harper. He told them where they work." Carston paused. "I guess he did. He didn't say that exactly, but he must have. He told them everything else. Then he called me again a little while ago to tell me that some guy came into the bar and said that a biker got shot and killed in the parking lot at Harmon and Mott. Martin thought probably it was one of the same ones who were in his place earlier. So here I am."

"And?" Barbie asked when Carston quit talking. "Why do you think Martin was so forthcoming with information?"

"Because he also told them I was looking into the theft as well, and he gave them my business card that I left with him," Carston replied. "I think that they got everything he had to give. I don't think that he wanted them coming back."

Barbie was mulling it over.

"Your turn," Carston said.

"A call came in that there was a body in the parking lot of Harmon and Mott. I drive over here and I find one Augie Neilson standing in the lot freezing his ass off in a jean jacket and a pair of cowboy boots, a body laying on the pavement with a stream of frozen blood coming out from under it. Augie tells me that he lives three houses over and was getting ready to go to Marzoe's on foot when he heard two distinct shots from a gun. He knows guns, and they were gunshots. Under the circumstances he decides to sit tight for a while and not venture out. About ten or fifteen minutes later his thirst gets the best of him and he hasn't heard anything else. He decides it is safe to head out and he cuts through the parking lot, first because it is a shorter route, and second, he's wondering what all the shooting was about. Short story short, he stumbled over our body over there."

"Got an ID on the body?" Carston asked.

"Nope," Barbie answered. "Nothing. No ID, no nothing."

"Hell Fighter?" Carston followed up.

"Yep, he's wearing his colors under his coat." Barbie left out that he had a Montreal rocker on the back and a Nomad patch on the front.

"Martin told me that there were two of them in Marzoe's earlier. Got any idea who the other one is?" Carston inquired.

"Not a clue," Barbie replied. "First I heard of the other one."

"You know what he was doing here?" Carston asked.

"According to you, they were looking for Bill Harper and Vince Barker," Barbie answered.

Carston was lost in thought.

"You carry, don't you?" Barbie asked.

"Yes," Carston replied.

Barbie didn't say anything in response.

"You think I'm in danger?" he asked.

"I don't know," Barbie said. "Do you think you are in danger?"

It was Carston's turn not to respond.

"Who hired you?" Barbie asked.

Carston thought for a moment. "I've given you what I have on the case, but honestly Barbie, professionally I can't give you that information. Just can't do it."

Barbie thought for a moment. "Fair enough."

Carston was surprised that she let it go so easily. "What's with the van?" He was looking at a plain white van that was idling on the other side of the parking lot, well away from the body. "CSI?"

"No," Barbie replied off-handedly. "I don't know what it is." She had gone back to filling in blanks on an official looking form.

"An unmarked van is sitting inside your crime scene and you don't know what it is?" Carston asked, giving the van a better look.

"Been sitting here since I got here. No one in it," Barbie replied without looking up.

"It's running," Carston remarked.

"Is it?" Barbie said, not sounding concerned.

Carston continued to eyeball the van.

"You can take off, you got what I got." Barbie was dismissing him. "I'll let you know if anything comes up that ties into your stolen hearse."

"I think it is pretty clear that it does," Carston remarked.

"I'll wait and see where the evidence points before I start jumping to conclusions," Barbie replied. "You can take off. I got to finish this paperwork up."

"I think I'll go check that van out." Carston was opening the door to get out.

"You need to just leave, we'll worry about that van," she said pointedly.

Carston paused.

"I'm not kidding," Barbie warned. "Don't go walking around my crime scene."

"You're the boss." Carston shrugged his shoulders, got out of the patrol car and slammed the door closed a little harder than he needed to. He hesitated for a moment, but Barbie was watching him. He went back to where his vehicle was parked and got in. He wasn't ready to leave, though. Just for the principle of it he sat surveying the parking lot from inside the Escalade.

He reached between the seats and felt around for the pair of binoculars in a case on the floorboard behind the passenger seat. He pulled them out and focused them on the van. It was just a late model Ford cargo van, pretty nondescript. You saw them every day delivering locally. It could belong to a hospital or some institution, it just had that look. I could belong to Harmon and Mott, except one thing, it had federal government plates on it. Carston thought about it for a few minutes. It wasn't unusual to see a white Ford cargo van in Council Bluffs bearing federal plates, what with all the regional federal office buildings in Omaha and the Offutt Air Force Base just down the road. Really, the only reason the van stood out was because it was sitting idling at a murder scene. Carston trained the binoculars on the cab. It was dark. The side windows were tinted. No sign of occupants. Carston was sure that Barbie knew exactly what it was doing there. But like Carston drawing the line at telling her who hired him, she drew the line on telling him what a government van was doing at her murder scene. Fair enough.

Carston put his vehicle in gear and pulled away from the curb, made a U-turn at the first intersection and drove back by. He could see Barbie working in her car. The other patrol car was dark. So was the Sherriff's patrol car. They both sat idling unattended, the same as the van. That struck him as even more odd. He wondered where the officers were. It had not registered when he was sitting in Barbie's patrol car with the dome light on. He could hardly see out then. But it was quite evident driving away that there were three apparently empty official vehicles in the parking lot idling and plenty of room in the back of the van. Something was going on.

Carston pulled into the parking lot of the convenience store down the street and parked in front of the doors. The lot and the store were almost empty. He could see the employee standing behind the counter reading a magazine. A red Dodge Ram pickup truck was pulling out as he pulled in. Carston got out of his vehicle and left it running. He knew that he wasn't going to sleep for a while anyway; he needed a cup of coffee. He walked into the store.

"Evening," the man behind the counter said without looking up.

"Evening," Carston replied. He spotted the coffee pots sitting on hot pads on the back wall. He filled a large cup and put a plastic lid on it.

"Donuts and sweet rolls half price after ten," the man behind the counter called to him.

Carston looked at his watch. It was eleven o'clock. He walked to the glass cabinet that contained trays of donuts, sweet rolls and muffins.

"How about muffins?" Carston asked.

"Half price," the man called back.

Carston lifted a blueberry muffin from the case and took it to the counter. He noticed that the man was wearing a pin on his shirt that identified him as Gary. Carston placed a napkin on the counter, placed the muffin on top of it and placed the cup of coffee next to that.

"They close the kitchen at ten, load up case and it's all half price for the night owls," Gary explained. "That it?"

"That's it," Carston replied, holding his billfold open.

"Four-twelve," Gary said.

Carston took a twenty from his billfold and passed it across the counter. "A little excitement over there," Carston nodded toward the funeral home.

"Crazy," Gary remarked. "So I'm working here, not real busy, maybe two or three customers, a couple cars at the pumps, and I hear two pops, I thought, fireworks. Didn't give it much thought, except they were loud. I looked out and didn't see anything. Then just a minute later this truck goes tearing out of here squealing the tires. I looked up and all I saw was taillights."

"You tell the cops this?" Carston asked, taking his change.

"They ain't been over here yet," Gary replied.

Carston looked out the window in thought.

"You got a tape of it?" he asked.

"I bet I do," Gary replied, "I hadn't thought about that."

"Can I see it?" Carston asked.

Gary was already at a computer terminal behind the counter punching a keyboard. "Here, lean over."

Carston leaned over the counter where he could see the screen. Gary had pulled up the video and was watching it. He went back for Carston. "Watch right here," he said.

All the video showed was a Dodge Ram pickup truck coming across the field of view, fishtailing and squealing the tires. The feed was in black and white. There was no way to even tell the color and there was no shot of the license plate.

"You got a video where it was parked? Something where we can get a better look at it?" Carston asked.

"Not really," Gary said.

"You don't have surveillance on the whole lot?" Carston asked.

"Only the pumps and the front of the store," Gary replied. "Pretty much they're only worried about gas drive offs, shoplifters and possible robberies. That's all I got."

Carston leaned back off the counter. "Nothing."

"Nope," Gary agreed.

Carston looked out the window toward Harmon and Mott. It was hard to see beyond the pumps in the dark from where he was standing. He could understand why Gary hadn't seen anything. For just a moment he had hoped that the video would show something more than a Dodge Ram pickup truck tearing out of the parking lot, but it didn't.

"Gary," Carston turned toward the counter. "Listen, I'm a private detective." Carston took a business card from his billfold and handed it to Gary. "I'm doing an investigation and I kind of want to keep the cops out of it, if you know what I mean." Carston held the card as Gary tried to pull it away to get his full attention, then let it go. "Do me a favor, if the cops come and look at the videos, I would appreciate it if you didn't mention that I already saw them."

The Hearse

Gary looked at the card. "I think that I can do that." He looked at the change still on the counter, then looked back up and smiled.

"Also, Gary," Carston said. "If you hear anything, see anything, think of anything, give me a call, would you?"

"Sure," Gary had found a new buddy.

Carston left the change on the counter. Gary had his eye on it. Carston picked up his coffee and muffin. "Keep the change," he smiled and nodded as he left.

Gary grabbed the change and thanked Carston on his way out the door. Carston unlocked the door of his idling vehicle with the fob, then drove to Marzoe's parking lot and went in. The crowd had changed since he had been in there earlier. It was a seedier and rougher crowd.

"Augie's gone," Martin said as Carston approached the bar. Martin was still polishing a glass. "You sure have a hard time catching up to people. What kind of detective are you, anyway?"

Carston let the snide remark pass. He didn't want to alienate Martin. If he was going to catch anyone, Martin might be his best bet for doing so.

"Want a beer?" Martin asked.

"Do I have to?" Carston replied.

"Nah, I guess not," Martin said. "Did you go over to Harmon and Mott?"

"I did," Carston replied. "Talked to Barbie. Dead guy was a Hell Fighter. I'm guessing one of those that was in here asking about Barker and Harper."

"Things are getting serious. You know what you've gotten yourself into?" Martin asked.

118

"More than I'm charging them for," Carston agreed.

Martin was scanning the crowded bar.

"Busy?" Carston commented.

"Every night but Sunday," Martin remarked.

"You know that bar I asked you about over in Omaha?" Carston asked.

"Which one?" Martin replied.

"Flingnasties," Carston answered.

"Is that who you're working for?" Martin asked pointedly in a voice that didn't sound like he thought that was a good thing.

Carston hesitated for a moment, not sure that he wanted to reveal his client to Martin.

"If you're working for Glenda Thompson, a lot of things are making a lot more sense," Martin remarked.

"I didn't say I was working for anyone, I just asked if you know anything about a bar called Flingnasties," Carston backpedaled.

"I can see it in your eyes," Martin noted.

Carston didn't say anything in response.

"Glenda's uncle on her mother's side of the family is Thomas Gunn, known far and wide as Tommy Gunn. Her late husband, Jerry Thompson, was Tommy's right-hand man. He met Glenda through Tommy and they got hitched, a matter of convenience, some say. Tommy got indicted on federal charges and took off to Canada. He put Glenda officially in charge of the show to keep it in the family so to speak, but everyone knew that Jerry was running things for Tommy after Tommy split. A few years ago, Jerry up and disappeared. He's officially presumed dead. Probably down near St. Louis, stuck in a log jam on the river somewhere I reckon. Point is, Glenda never seemed to be very concerned about his disappearance and the cops weren't too concerned, either. It didn't take long to declare him dead and Glenda took over Tommy's business interests in Omaha."

Carston mulled this information over in his head. He knew who Tommy Gunn was. The leader of a crime syndicate that ruled Omaha twenty-five, maybe thirty years ago. He was under indictment for murder, drug trafficking, prostitution, illegal gambling and racketeering when he absconded to Montreal. It was headline news for a while. For years the state of Nebraska and the federal government tried to get him back, but Tommy had too many judges, local law enforcement officials and politicians on his payroll. After a while they gave up. The thing that Carston didn't know was if his criminal influence still reached as far as Omaha. He hadn't heard anything about Tommy Gunn's organization for years.

"Just saying," Martin interrupted his thoughts.

"Uncle Thomas," exclaimed Carston out loud.

"What?" Martin asked.

"Nothing, I'm talking to myself," Carston replied, standing up. "I'm going to head out."

"See you tomorrow," Martin said.

Carston gave him a questioning eye.

"Figure you'll be back tomorrow," Martin replied, shrugging his shoulders.

Gavin checks into the LeVant

Gavin left his office at eight o'clock in the evening. He told himself that he would stay put until the detective called him back, but everyone had gone home a long time ago and the whole floor was empty, which pretty much defeated the purpose of being in the office to have people around him in case someone came after him. Now he was alone and, when he thought about it, trapped in his office.

He stood up from his desk and turned off his computer. It was a habit, good security. A lot of people got themselves in trouble leaving their computers on where anyone could walk in and check them out. Gavin was careful never to let his guard down. He had been thinking the last hour what his next move would be. He realized that he was holed up as it stood at the moment. They had driven him to ground. He should have left earlier, with the rest of the office staff, but he had waited for the detective to call. He didn't know if whoever it was after him was out on the street waiting, or more likely, if they were sitting on his car in the parking ramp ready to ambush him. Maybe both. Gavin decided to make a break for it and take his chances outside, leave the BMW in the ramp overnight. He didn't want to get caught in the parking garage. His chances on the street were better. There was a hotel just a fifteen-minute walk from his office building, the LeVant. It was a flophouse. Rooms to rent by the week, by the night, or by the hour. It was unlikely that anyone would expect him to go to the LeVant and check in for the night. If no one was waiting in the hall, he could make it to the service elevator and out the back entrance into the alley.

He started questioning his thinking. Maybe getting caught in the alley wasn't any better than the car ramp. Maybe they anticipated that he would make that move and had someone waiting for him there as well. What if they had all the possible escape routes covered? He wondered how many people they had watching him.

He mulled over his options while he put on his coat, shoved the pistol in his waistband and got ready to lock up his office. He had to get out, he couldn't stay there all night. His choices were to walk right out the front door or sneak out the back. If he went out the front door they would follow him until they could get him alone. It was more likely someone was watching the front. He would take his chances of making his getaway unseen in the alley.

Fifteen minutes later he walked in the front door of the Hotel LeVant and made his way directly to the front desk. A young lady and a young man were standing behind it as he came up. Both were wearing blazers with the Hotel LeVant logo embroidered on the pocket. The young man had a nametag that identified him as Tip; the woman's identified her as Mona.

"Can I help you?" Tip smiled knowingly. Gavin realized he was checking in with no luggage, no briefcase, nothing to indicate that he was a traveler looking for a place to stay for the night close to the Old Market district.

"I need a room for the night," Gavin replied quickly and with a conviction that he hoped dispelled the young man's unspoken allegations that he might be there for more recreational activities.

"Yes, sir," Tip smirked. "We can put you up for the night." He consulted his computer screen. "Is there a particular floor that you would like? Second floor, close to the lobby and the bar, a bit more noisy during the evening, people coming and going, but quite accessible."

He looked up at Gavin, who didn't reply.

"Fourth floor is usually quiet, fifth floor are suites," the young man said.

"Fourth is good," Gavin replied. "You have something with a window facing the street?"

Mona was looking at her screen while the young man typed something on his. She took a key card and put it in a machine behind the counter. Gavin pulled his credit card from his billfold and put it down on the desk. The young man took it.

"I'll need an ID, please," he said.

Gavin took out his driver's license and gave it to the young man.

"Do you have a car in the lot?" he asked.

"No, I came by taxi from the airport" Gavin replied. "Just flew into town," he added.

"Business?" the young man asked, smiling.

"Yes," Gavin said. "I have a meeting at some law offices close by here tomorrow morning. They gave this hotel a high recommendation."

"487256 Highway 183, Crescent, Iowa," Tip read off his license. "Is that right, Mr. Barker?" he looked up and smiled. The young lady snickered and then cut herself off.

"Yes, it is," Gavin replied, realizing that the young man and young woman knew quite well that the address on Gavin's driver's license was across the bridge then a skip and a jump up the road from where he stood. To all appearances, Gavin was a local from the wrong side of the tracks, or in the case of Omaha, the wrong side of the river.

"Yeh, well," Gavin uttered.

"No problem, Mr. Barker, room 452." Mona handed him the key card, his license, and his credit card.

"Have a nice evening," Tip said with a smile. "Lots of good restaurants over in the Old Market if you are hungry, just a few blocks to your left when you go out the door."

"Do you have room service?" Gavin asked, taking the key card.

"Just a bar, no food," Tip replied. "But you can order a pizza delivered if you like, or something else delivered. There is a list in the room of local eating establishments that we recommend. You can have it delivered here to the front desk and we will call you to come down to get it if you don't wish to be disturbed in your room." Tip punctuated everything he said with a smile. "Or they can bring it up. Whatever works. If you don't see what you are looking for on the list, give me a call, I'm sure we can help you get whatever it is you want."

"Great," said Gavin.

"They have chips and nuts in the bar," Tip added. "If you aren't that hungry."

Gavin left the desk, went to elevator. He rode it to the fourth floor and found his room. Everything was actually nicer than he expected, considering the reputation of the LeVant. The whole hotel had a slightly worn-out look to it, but a glimmer of the one time grandeur still dimly showed through. Gavin could imagine himself staying there in the 50s. Perhaps a big-time cattle buyer, or maybe a rancher from western Nebraska, selling his livestock, taking in the big city sights. Or a big-time railroad man. Gavin took off his coat and sat on the bed. It wasn't as bad as people had told him. There was a dusty smell of nostalgia all around him.

Gavin took in the room for a few minutes, then decided to check out the bar. He wasn't very hungry, and he thought that chips and nuts would suffice. He got up from the bed and went to the window, pulling back the shade just enough to peer out at the street four stories below. It was quiet and well lit. He couldn't spot anyone lurking in the cold. A town car pulled up to the curb. A man in a business suit and a tweed overcoat got out of the back seat, held the door for an attractive woman a bit past her prime and wearing a slutty-looking red dress with a plunging neckline. She stepped out and took the man's arm. He smiled and said something. They entered the hotel. The four-way flashers on the car came on and the headlights went off.

Gavin decided to leave the pistol in his room. It was a big gun and he was not dressed to conceal it well enough to pass scrutiny. He doubted anyone looking for him would imagine him there in the LeVant. Besides, he would be right there off

125

the lobby with people all around him. He went to the elevator and took it down to the first floor. Mona was at the desk alone. She smiled at Gavin and he waved. He was struck that she and Tip seemed to find everything and everyone amusing and that unnerved him a little. The lounge was empty. Gavin took a stool at the bar.

The bartender came up. "What'll you have?" he asked pleasantly.

"Can you do a margarita?" Gavin asked.

"Blended or on the rocks?" the bartender asked.

"Rocks," replied Gavin.

The bartender returned a few minutes later and placed the drink in front of him.

"Do you want to start a tab?" he asked.

"Can I put it on my room?" Gavin asked.

"What floor?" the bartender asked.

"Fourth," Gavin answered.

"Sure," the bartender replied. "What's the room number?"

Gavin gave the bartender his room number. He went to the register and punched some keys, then busied himself at the other end of the bar. Gavin turned on his stool, leaned back against the bar and watched the comings and goings of the Hotel LeVant. A man came strolling in and Gavin noticed that, like himself, the man had no luggage. He was tall and husky, wearing a pair of cowboy boots and a Stetson cowboy hat. He came in with authority, nodded toward Mona and went to the elevator. Gavin watched the lights above the door and noticed that it went to the fifth floor before it stopped, the floor with the suites. He was still imagining himself there in the hotel's heyday.

126

Maybe that fellow coming in was a big-time cattle buyer who came to the hotel to pick up a big-time rancher from western Nebraska and buy him dinner at a fancy steak house. Gavin sat watching and daydreaming, nursing his drink.

Forty-five minutes later Gavin was on his second margarita when the businessman with the tweed overcoat walked across the lobby and out the door. Five minutes after that, the lady in the slutty red dress came into the lobby and walked up to the desk. Tip was back and Mona was gone. The lady appeared to be having a friendly chat with Tip, as if they were familiar with each other. After a short conversation she came into the bar and took up the stool next to Gavin.

"It's warming up," she said to him.

"I heard it is supposed to," Gavin replied with a smile. "It's supposed to be downright balmy tomorrow."

The bartender came up with a drink and put it on the bar in front of her. Gavin didn't remark, but the fact that she had not ordered anything was not lost on him.

"Here on business?" she asked, taking a sip of the drink.

"I have a meeting at a law office down here early in the morning," Gavin replied.

"Oh? Which law office?" she asked.

"Barton," Gavin said without hesitation.

"Barton?" She raised her eyebrows. "I'm kind of a regular around here. I've run into a few fellows who had business with Barton Law Offices. Are you thinking of starting on a new path in life?" She put her hand on his. "Out with the old, in with the new?"

127

"No, nothing like that," Gavin replied. "I work for them. I'm a lawyer."

The woman gave him a questioning look.

"No, I work in one of their branch offices. They have them all over. I just had to come here for a meeting, really."

The lady looked at him dubiously and removed her hand.

"I need to introduce myself," Gavin said hurriedly. "Vince Barker. What's your name?" Gavin had no idea what possessed him to use his father's name. He wished he had come up with something more creative. Perhaps she knew his dad. It was possible. Vince certainly liked the Omaha Old Market district. He would not put it past his father to know someone like her.

"Sylvia," she put her hand on his again, reassuringly.

"It is nice to meet you," Gavin said. "You here on business or pleasure?"

"My business is your pleasure," Sylvia smiled.

"Um, uh-huh." She caught Gavin by surprise. He had suspected Sylvia's occupation, but he had not expected her to be so forward about it.

"Uh-huh what?" She squeezed his hand.

"I don't know," Gavin mumbled. "I have a girlfriend."

"I've got a boyfriend," Sylvia replied.

Gavin called for another margarita. "You need another drink?" he asked.

Sylvia nodded toward the bartender. A few minutes later he brought two drinks and placed them on the bar. A few people had wandered in and taken up seats at one of the tables. The

128

bartender made no move to come out from behind the bar to wait on them. After a few minutes of looking expectantly back at the bar, someone from the table came up and ordered drinks. Other than the table, Sylvia and Gavin had the bar to themselves.

"How much?" Gavin asked pointedly.

"Two fifty," Sylvia replied.

"For how long?" Gavin asked as casually as he could muster.

The cowboy came in, sans hat and jacket, and took a stool at the end of the bar. He caught Gavin's eye and nodded. Gavin nodded and went back to his conversation with Sylvia.

"As long as it takes." Sylvia squeezed his hand again.

Gavin looked into her eyes. She was older than he had thought when he first saw her. She hid it well, but the light gave her away.

"And then some," Sylvia said. "I'm never in a hurry to leave. I'm good company, if you know what I mean. I'm a good listener, if that's something you are looking for. Value added," she laughed and moved her hand up his arm.

"I don't have cash," Gavin said. "I mean, I wasn't planning…" he trailed off, looking toward the lobby. "I could try the desk."

"Cash or credit card," Sylvia said with soft patience in her voice. "I can run a card though my phone. No problem."

Gavin was thinking. He wasn't sure if it was wise to run his credit card through Sylvia's phone.

"It's safe." It was almost as if Sylvia could read his mind.

"Can we finish our drinks?" Gavin asked, stalling for no reason.

"Sure," Sylvia replied. "Take your time."

The cowboy was looking their direction. Sylvia smiled at him and waved casually. The cowboy waved back. Gavin waved and the cowboy turned away. The cowboy was making Gavin nervous and suspicious.

"Do you know him? The cowboy, I mean," Gavin asked. "Is he your pimp?"

"I don't have a pimp," Sylvia retorted.

"Sorry," Gavin backpedaled. "I didn't mean it in a derogatory way. I've just had some run-ins lately with some not so nice guys, I'm a little nervous about strangers watching me. Especially," Gavin paused. "Especially when I'm doing personal business, if you know what I mean."

Sylvia touched his arm. She was starting to wonder about Carston, herself. She would normally take him for granted in the lounge, but he seemed to be particularly interested in her client. More so than she was comfortable with. But long ago Sylvia had learned that if she let herself get paranoid she would never turn a trick.

"Is he a cop?" Gavin asked.

"No, he's not a cop," Sylvia reassured him with a squeeze. She didn't want to tell Gavin that he was a private detective. That was as sure to spook him as a cop would.

"I know him. He lives here, he works down here in the Old Market. He's nobody to be concerned about. He watches people, that's what he does. We both work down here. That's all."

Gavin glanced over at the cowboy, who was talking to the bartender.

130

"Is he a male prostitute?" Gavin asked.

Sylvia stifled a laugh. "No, he is not a male prostitute."

She stood up. "Let's just go up to your room, take our drinks with us," Sylvia suggested. She wanted to get Gavin away from the bar. He was her last trick for the night and she wanted to get it done. She was a patient woman, she took her time and never hurried a client, but she didn't relish the idea of going out in the cold looking for someone else. They were right there, just a few floors from two hundred fifty dollars. She needed to make the move before Gavin shook off the hook.

"Come on," she coaxed him, tugging at his arm.

Gavin got up and went with her, watching the cowboy, assuring himself that he took no notice of them leaving.

Pillow talk

Carston arrived back at the Hotel LeVant, went to his room to deposit his coat, his hat and the Jackass rig on the chair by the door then went right back down to the lounge, as he had done almost every day since he checked in. The thought of losing Megan was too depressing for him to face alone in his room. So he spent his evenings in the bar watching the comings and the goings of the Hotel LeVant, most nights until midnight when the lounge closed.

Carston found his way to the bar and took the end stool, which had become his usual seat. He could see the whole bar and watch people coming in and going out of the lounge and the lobby from his vantage point. Carston had worked ten years with his office on the edge of the Old Market and just a half dozen short blocks from the Hotel LeVant. It was home territory for him. He had spent much of his childhood hanging out at the Hancock building. This was his neighborhood. So it afforded him hours and hours of distraction from his problems to sit in the bar watching people, some of whom he had known since he was a kid, walk in and out of the hotel.

Carston noticed a man at the other end of the bar talking to Sylvia, a high-dollar hooker who had been plying her trade for almost two decades in the Old Market district. The man she was talking to had looked his direction when Carston came in, nodded as if he were a drowning rat about to go under for the third time, then turned back to his fate. Carston watched Sylvia, studied her. There was so much to learn watching her work. She had been at her trade a long time and she was good. Some might say at first sight that she was past her prime, showing wear, but that observation would be incorrect. Sylvia could turn tricks faster than any of the young streetwalkers in the Old Market. She was who they all strived to be. There was an air about her that breathed a timeless, confident sensuality. She was talking, putting her hand on the man's arm, stroking it. She looked past him at Carston who was watching them like some voyeur. She smiled at him. Carston didn't turn away. He smiled back in the realization that she was working both men, keeping Carston's attention on her purely for the sport of it.

The bartender came up to the end of the bar and leaned on it, looking at a table of four across the bar.

"I let them run a tab," the bartender said absently.

"You get any collateral?" Carston asked, not looking around.

"I'm holding a fake driver's license," he responded.

"You think they're going to stiff you?" Carston asked.

"Maybe," the bartender replied.

"Is it worth it, I mean losing their fake ID?"

"I wouldn't think so, but you never know down here." The bartender wiped the ring of water under Carston's drink out of habit when he lifted it off the counter to take a sip.

"The silver streak strikes again," the bartender nodded toward the other end of the bar.

"Sylvia?" Carston asked, not looking over and quite aware of who he was talking about.

"Yep," the bartender watched Sylvia lead the man to the elevator.

"He stiff you?" Carston asked. "Didn't see him pay the tab."

"He had other things on his mind," the bartender laughed. "I got his room number. I'll put it on his bill."

"He's not a short-term tenant?" Carston asked, turning to look, but Sylvia and her newfound friend were already well on their way to his room.

"I guess he's here on business," the bartender said.

"And he's staying at the Hotel LeVant picking up a call girl?"

"Guess so," the bartender shrugged his shoulders. "He gave me a room number and I called the desk. He checked in for the night, said he has business in the morning."

"Okay," Carston shrugged his own shoulders in response.

"So, what were you up to today?" the bartender asked.

"I have a case," Carston replied. "I'm trying to find a hearse that got stolen out from in front of Spaghetti Works yesterday at noontime."

"No shit," the bartender said. "Was there a body in it?"

"Yes, there was," Carston replied.

"Oh man, that sucks," the bartender exclaimed and laughed out loud.

"So are the cops out looking for it, too?" the bartender asked. "I mean what's the deal, why hire you to look for it?"

"My clients want it found before the cops find it," Carston explained, raising his eyebrows.

"Why?" the bartender asked.

"Don't know," Carston replied. "I'm trying to figure that out too."

The bartender didn't respond. He was watching the table. Everyone sitting there had finished their drinks and they were talking. It didn't look like they were interested in more drinks. He was trying to decide if it was worth the effort to leave the bar and see if they needed anything else.

Carston finished his drink and got up.

"Making it an early night?" the bartender asked.

"Gotta make a phone call before it gets too late," Carston answered. "Put it on the room," he nodded toward the empty tumbler.

The bartender grunted. Carston left the lounge and made his way to his room. He kicked off his boots and fell on the bed fully clothed. He pulled a pillow up against the headboard and laid back against it. He took his phone out of his pocket and stared at it for a minute. He had no new emails and no messages. He swiped his contacts and found Megan's name. He waited for a minute, just looking at it, then touched the call button. The phone rang four times.

"Hello, Carston," an unemotional voice on the other end answered.

"Hey, what are you up to?" he asked.

"I'm watching Netflix," Megan replied. "It's late."

"Something good?" Carston pretended that he didn't hear the last part of her reply.

"Just a movie." Megan responded.

"Something we would watch together?" Carston was like a puppy trying to get her attention.

"Carston, did you call me for a reason?" Megan asked.

"I just wanted to hear your voice. I just wanted to talk to you," he replied honestly. "I'm lonely without you. I wish we could patch things up."

There was silence on the other end.

"Megan, I'm so sorry. I'm so, so sorry. There has to be some way I can make you love me again," Carston pleaded. "Please, just talk to me. Tell me what I have to do. I'll do it," Carston trailed off.

Megan didn't respond.

"Your lawyer called. I wasn't able to get back to him. He was out of the office when I called," Carston said. "Do you really need a lawyer? Because I think there is still something between us. I think we can rebuild. It will take time, I understand that. I'm willing to give it as much time as you need. But there has to be something buried deep that we can find and work on. Please, let's try."

"I don't have a lawyer," Megan said after a moment of silence.

"Steph said your lawyer called and needed to talk to me." Carston was confused.

"Well Steph was wrong." Megan spat out Steph's name.

"She said that he called and left a number for me to call him back," Carston said.

"Steph was wrong, it wasn't my lawyer. I don't have a lawyer," Megan reiterated harshly.

Carston didn't respond.

"Listen, I don't give a flying fuck what Steph is telling you. I haven't talked to a lawyer yet. You can believe me or not believe me, I don't really care. So whatever games she's trying to play, that's between you and her. So if that's what you called about, there isn't anything more to say." The phone went dead.

Carston let his head fall back on the pillow, the phone in his hand. He was confused. He didn't know what was going on. A call that he had made to somehow persuade Megan not to go forward with divorce and to resolve things between them had gone totally awry. He had not expected the call to end in such a manner and so abruptly. He closed his eyes. Exhaustion overwhelmed him and he dozed off to sleep fully clothed and laying on his bed. Just before he went to sleep he let the phone drop to the floor in a gesture of finality. Without Megan all was lost.

Gavin awoke to the sound of Sylvia flushing the toilet. She came out of the bathroom naked and walked to the chair where her clothes were draped. Gavin had a moment of panic. He looked frantically around the room. Things had not gone well. He saw that it was just past midnight on the alarm clock next to the bed.

"One last shot, a quickie? It's late but I got the time if you want to try again." Sylvia glanced over at him on the bed.

"I don't think so," Gavin replied.

"I'm charging you two-fifty, regardless," Sylvia told him, poised with her panties in her hand. She had a mature sensuality standing there stark naked, hiding nothing.

"No problem," Gavin replied.

Sylvia turned and started putting on her clothes. Everything had been fine on the way to the room. Sylvia had unzipped his pants and put her hand in them, fondling him as they rode the elevator to the room. Inside she disrobed him and pushed him onto the bed, then went to the chair and began to disrobe herself. That was when things went south for Gavin. He started to think about the cowboy that she had nodded to in the bar. He thought about him watching them. Sylvia had smiled at him. She seemed to be sending signals and he seemed to send them back. Gavin's paranoia took over. He imagined the cowboy working for Glenn, Sylvia a femme fatale, a plant to lure him to his room where she could let the cowboy in. Who knew what kind of nefarious deeds happened in the rooms at the Hotel LeVant? He probably wouldn't be the first body found by the cleaning lady when she came in to clean the room in the morning. When Sylvia climbed into bed next to him, he couldn't get the fear from his mind that at any moment the cowboy would come through the door with a couple other of Glenda's thugs. Maybe even Harvey. He kept looking at the door, the chain unfastened and dangling. He wondered if she had left it that way on purpose, left it unlocked somehow, left it ajar. He failed to perform. He strained to see past her. Sylvia gave it everything she had without success. Finally, she

138

rolled over on her back and lay there. It had been a long day for Sylvia and an even longer day for Gavin, starting with his early morning run for it. His mental and physical exhaustion overcame his fears. Sylvia's rhythmic breathing lulled him to sleep.

"I'm sorry, I just have a lot going on right now. I was hoping that a little time with you would get it off my mind, but it didn't. I'm really sorry," Gavin sat up on the bed and pulled the sheets over himself.

Sylvia was dressed. She took her phone out of her purse and inserted a white attachment into it that allowed her to swipe a credit card. She looked up at Gavin.

"Right, sure," Gavin got up, pulling the sheet with him. He grabbed his pants off the floor and took out his billfold. He had been sleeping while Sylvia was up and he had a moment where he wanted to check to see if his cash was still in the billfold and count his credit cards, but he stopped himself. Sylvia was watching. He took his American Express from one of the slots and handed it to her, closed the billfold and sat on the end of the bed with his hands in his lap, glancing down at the billfold. She swiped the card through the attachment on her phone and waited. After what seemed like forever, she held the phone out to Gavin.

"Just sign with your finger," she instructed him.

Gavin did so and Sylvia pulled the phone back. "You need a receipt?" she asked. "I can have it sent to your email."

"No thanks, it's okay," he replied.

Sylvia took the attachment off her phone and deposited both into her purse.

"Your cash and cards are all there," she commented.

"I didn't—" Gavin said, not finishing the sentence.

"Sure you did." Sylvia put her hand under his chin, pulled his head up and gave him a kiss. "Everyone wakes up wondering if I went through their wallet while they dozed. It's okay. Part of the job."

"You are very nice," Gavin said as she stood up straight.

"Don't fall in love, it isn't going anywhere," she smiled.

"I wasn't," Gavin said sheepishly.

Sylvia was dressed, her coat thrown over the same arm that held her purse. She stopped as she was turning toward the door.

"You know something? You're nice too," she said. "You want to try it again sometime, fifty percent discount. I like to leave my customers satisfied, good for business."

"Thanks, I'll take you up on it," Gavin said.

"I'm usually in the lounge at some time during the evening. Ask there or ask whoever is working the desk, they can get ahold of me."

Gavin nodded. "You can give me your number and I can just call you," he suggested, looking around the room for some stationery and a pen.

"That's not how it works, honey," Sylvia smiled. "You gotta go through channels."

Sylvia turned toward the door again.

"Hey," Gavin was opening his billfold and digging. "I'm going to give you my card. I'm a lawyer. If you ever need an attorney, for anything, I'll take care of you." He held a business card toward her and she took the few steps to retrieve it.

Sylvia read the card while she walked to the door. She turned the lock, opened it and went out. She gave a glance and a smile back at Gavin before the door closed behind her and she was gone. Gavin lay back in the bed. He was a wreck.

Carston woke up and looked at his clock. It was just after midnight. He got up from his bed and went to the bathroom to relieve himself. Then he took off his clothes, brushed his teeth and went back to his bed. He kicked his phone under the bed and had to get down on his knees to retrieve it. It had been a long day and he was no closer to finding the hearse than he had been when he took the case. The murdered biker, the phone call from some phantom lawyer, Steph, Megan, his whole world made no sense. He prayed that the morning would bring some kind of order to it all, but he wasn't going to count on it.

As Sylvia was walking out the front door of the Hotel LeVant on her way home after a long day and four tricks, Carston and Gavin each fell into a fitful sleep.

The call

It was just after midnight. Xavier had been driving around Omaha aimlessly for hours. He had stopped in at two bars, downed a beer and left to continue his driving. Xavier thought best when he was moving. He had just that evening watched Gimp get gunned down and he himself had narrowly escaped the same fate. His adrenaline level was through the roof. He looked over at Gimp's phone in the passenger seat Gimp had once occupied. The business card sat next to it. He had read the business card three times, "Carston Hancock III, Private Investigations." He had driven past the address three times as well. The Hancock building was like most of the buildings in the Old Market district, dated but still somewhat elegant. Xavier wondered what kind of detective agency had a five story building in the Old Market district named for them. Who the hell was this Carston Hancock the Third, and why was he looking for the hearse that he and Gimp hadn't jacked? And if they hadn't jacked it, where was it? And Gimp never did explain what he thought was going on at that place north of Crescent. It was clear that Gimp was looking for the hearse, but Xavier had no idea why Gimp would think it was there. And maybe Gimp didn't know. Xavier had been taking orders from Gimp, and Gimp was taking orders and getting information from someone on his phone. The whole thing made absolutely no sense to Xavier.

Then Gimp's phone rang. It startled Xavier. He looked at it long enough that he started to swerve off the road and kissed the curb with his front tire. He regained control of his vehicle and peered through the rearview mirrors for cops. It would not bode well to get stopped at midnight driving around with a murdered man's phone on the passenger seat. The phone stopped ringing. Xavier pulled off into the parking lot at the Crossroads Mall and parked. He picked up the phone. He was surprised that the screen wasn't locked. He brought up the call history. The last number showed seven times. There was a voicemail message. Xavier tried to access it, but he didn't have the pin. He hesitated, then hit the callback button. The phone rang twice before a voice answered.

"Gimp?"

"X," Xavier answered.

There was a pause. "Where's Gimp?" the voice asked.

Xavier thought for a moment how to answer. He decided to be straight. It was no time to try to be clever. "He's dead I think," he answered.

There was another pause. "How?"

Xavier used the moment of silence to collect his thoughts.

"Start to finish," the voice on the other end prompted.

"I picked up Gimp at the airport yesterday and we were going to jack a hearse, but we missed it. You probably know that," he said.

"Don't worry about what I know," the voice responded. "Keep talking."

143

"We missed the hearse, so then we spent the whole day looking for it. We drove all around Council Bluffs and Omaha. We went everywhere until it was so late that we couldn't look anymore. Then this morning first thing, early, we went to some place across the river in the bluffs up north of Crescent and checked that out. Whoever lives there did a rabbit on us. We chased after him but lost him. We spent the day looking for him, and then we went looking for the two guys that were driving the hearse that picked up the body. It got dark and Gimp wanted to go to the funeral home, so we did. We were going to break in and see if the hearse was there." Xavier stopped and took a breath.

"And then what?" the voice asked.

"Gimp had me bring a tire iron from the truck and he was shaking doors and looking through windows. Then he shook this one door out of sight from the street, stepped back and told me to pry it open. As soon as I stepped up to the door. I heard two shots." Xavier paused. "Actually, I heard the bullets smack into Gimp and then heard the shots. He hit the ground and I took off."

"How do you know he's dead?"

"I went back an hour or so later, found a place far enough away to watch without drawing attention to myself. The cops were still there and Gimp was still lying on the ground, a tarp pulled over him. Two cop cars were there and a detective showed up. That's it." Xavier took another breath and waited.

"You got his phone?" the voice asked.

"He left it in my truck when we went to break into the funeral home," Xavier answered.

144

There was silence. "That's good," the voice said after at least a minute. "What do you know?"

"Just that he's dead," Xavier answered.

"What do you know about what he was doing there?"

"I know that a body came in on the same flight as Gimp from Montreal. I know that a funeral home, Harmon and Mott, was supposed to pick it up. I know that there is contraband hidden in the coffin and Gimp planned to jack the hearse on the bridge over the river, get the contraband, whatever it is, and take it back to Montreal. I know that we missed the coffin somehow and that we've been looking for it for two days. I know that the contraband has to be pretty serious, because I know that someone killed Gimp over it. That's what I know." Xavier stopped talking. There was no response. "I know that Gimp was taking calls and getting his orders from you since he got here," he added.

"That it?" the voice asked.

Xavier thought for a moment. "That is what I know," he said. "I also know that even though Gimp is dead, I'm still here. I'm still looking for the hearse."

"Is it at the funeral home?" the voice asked.

"I think that was a long shot," Xavier replied. "I got the feeling we were still looking. It seemed to me that we were grasping for straws. We were just checking the funeral home on an off chance because Gimp was out of ideas."

"What happened?" the voice asked. "Gimp didn't jack the hearse, so what made him think that it didn't make it back to the funeral home? Where else would it be?"

"I assumed that you had some idea on that," Xavier said. "He was talking to you and I guess I thought you were giving him leads and telling him where to go."

"Look at the call history," the voice told him.

Xavier put the phone on speaker and pulled up the history. "Okay," he said.

"Is there a number other than this one there?"

Xavier could see another number that showed several times. "I see one."

"Give me the number," the voice instructed.

Xavier read it off.

"That's where Gimp was getting his leads," the voice explained. "Someone local that he got connected up with. Those calls to me were him reporting back to me. Whoever was giving him those leads was setting him up." The voice let this information sink in. "Here's what you're going to do," the voice instructed. "You're going to go home, get some sleep. Wide awake tomorrow, you're going to call that number and tell whoever answers what happened to Gimp. You are going to tell them that you've been told to keep looking for the hearse and that when you find it, you're going to jack it. Nothing has changed. But this time around, whenever they give you a lead, you're going to call me before you chase it. You are taking Gimp's place, but you are not going to follow the leads they give you without going over it with me. You are going to report in before you do anything." The voice paused. "You got it?"

"I got it," Xavier said.

"Another thing," the voice said. "You say absolutely nothing about me. Whoever it is, as far as they are concerned, it is just you and them."

"Got it," Xavier replied

"Any questions?" the voice asked.

"Listen, I got this gig because our chapter president told me that if I could demonstrate that I was up to the task, there was a good chance I can move up in the organization. I'm just saying, I want to do good for you. I want to move up. You can count on me," Xavier explained.

"You find the hearse, you get that coffin and body, you report back to me that you have it, and you are going to get catapulted up the ladder," the voice told him. "You understand, this is international shit. You pull this off, you move up internationally."

"I'm your man," Xavier replied enthusiastically.

"You bet you are," the voice said. "And if you don't find that hearse, you fuck this up, you can kiss your ass goodbye."

Xavier caught his breath. "I understand," he said.

"What did you say they call you?" the voice asked.

"I'm X," he replied.

"You call me Zee," the voice said.

"Right," Xavier replied. "Anything else I need to do?"

"You have a gun?"

"I got a forty-five. It's a nineteen-eleven. Not a Colt 1911, a Springfield Armory," Xavier answered.

"I don't care what it is, just don't leave home without it. You might need it before this is over."

"Considering what happened last night to Gimp, probably good advice," Xavier agreed.

"That's it," the voice replied.

The call ended and Xavier was startled by a knock on the window. He looked out quickly but couldn't see. His eyes were dilated by the glow from the screen. He thought that he saw a police officer standing outside. He panicked, threw the phone on the floor, kicked it under the seat and rolled down the window.

"Everything okay?" the uniformed officer asked.

"Yes officer, I just pulled over to make a call. I didn't want to be talking and driving at the same time." Xavier left his hands in sight on the steering wheel.

"I'm not an officer," the man replied. "I'm mall security. And if you are done with your call, I'm going to have to ask you to move on."

"Yes sir," Xavier replied.

The security officer flashed his light around the interior of the Ram. He stepped quickly back away from the door and lowered the light.

"No problem," Xavier called to him, recognizing the security officer had just realized that he had a bigger-than-life Hell Fighter motorcycle gang member in the vehicle. Normally Xavier might have taken the opportunity to have some fun with the security guard, but under the present circumstances he couldn't take a chance that he would draw unwanted attention in the process. Xavier put the Ram into drive.

"Thanks, have a good evening." Xavier pulled away.

Xavier drove home. Xavier's father had passed away just a few years earlier. After his dad died he sold his house, which he was about to lose

148

anyway, and moved back home, telling himself that he was moving in to take care of his mother. In reality, his mother took care of him. In a feeble attempt to disguise the image that he was a twenty-eight-year-old Hell Fighter motorcycle gang member who still lived with his mother, with the help of a Hell Fighter who had some building experience Xavier turned the two car unattached garage next to his mother's house into an apartment by installing a toilet and a shower in one corner and a kitchenette in the other. And that was home for Xavier and his Harley.

Most of the younger Hell Fighters were in the same circumstances, still living with a parent. Young Hell Fighters didn't have a lot of income. If they did have a job it was a low paying one. And there was a monetary cost to being a Hell fighter. There were monthly dues, and at every meeting it seemed like there was always someone in the club who had it worse off and everyone was expected to pitch in to help out. Xavier couldn't count how many hard-earned Hell Fighter bucks were collected to post bail for a luckless member who found themselves in trouble with the law. And if there wasn't anyone to free at the moment, they passed the hat anyway and started a fund for the next one. A lot of the Hell Fighters worked construction, and in the winter they were laid off. It was a Hell Fighter's life, having nothing but time on their hands during the cold months when they couldn't ride their motorcycles and busting their ass on construction sites in the warm months when they could be. The only way to break out of the rut was to move up in the organization. The higher up in the club one climbed, the more money they skimmed from the sundry and assorted criminal activities sponsored by the club. Xavier had just been handed an opportunity to move out of his mother's garage. He intended to take advantage of it.

Xavier jumped out of the Ram and went into the garage. For such spartan accommodations, it was warm and inviting. Xavier stripped down and climbed into bed. It took him a long time to fall asleep. He was wound up. He stared at the ceiling that was softly illuminated through the windows by the street lights. Xavier wasn't stupid. He could put things together. Whoever Zee was, he was high up. Gimp was reporting to Zee and nomads didn't report to the lower echelon. They were not bound by a chapter affiliation, they didn't take orders and even chapter presidents bent over backwards to accommodate a nomad when they came in. So Zee was running the show in Omaha, not the local club. That was clear enough. It was also clear that someone set Gimp up. Someone knew that he was going to show up at Harmon and Mott Funeral Home at the time appointed. So now it was going to be a game of cat and mouse, and Xavier needed to be the cat. He was going to have to turn the tables on whoever set up Gimp, and to do that he was going to have to convince them that he was just as capable, just as dangerous as Gimp. He was going to use himself as bait. Simple as that. But he knew the score and that gave him an advantage over Gimp. Xavier rolled it all around in his head. Then there was the detective, Hancock. He began to wonder how Hancock fit into everything. A distraction perhaps? He would have to figure that out as well. If he was going to pull this off, he would have to figure out who the hell the detective was and what exactly he was investigating. Xavier fell asleep and dreamed of himself with a nomad patch on his colors and his own garage, attached to his own house and filled with Harleys.

Epiphany

Carston woke much earlier than usual. He closed his eyes to go back to sleep but he couldn't. First off his mind was racing, going over the events of the day before, and secondly he had to pee. He rolled out of bed and went to the bathroom. A half hour later he was showered, dressed and going out the door. The lobby of the LeVant was empty except for the middle-aged man in a sports coat who sat at the desk. Carston glanced toward the deserted lounge. He wondered briefly how it went with the fellow Sylvia had been working last night. The clock over the bar showed five after seven. It was an ungodly hour to be up, he thought. There was no use going to the office, Steph never got there before eight. Carston walked to the parking lot. It was always ten degrees colder in the lot than it was anywhere else. The temperature was supposed to get above freezing before the day was out. It would be a welcome respite from the polar express that had been sweeping the Midwest for the last two weeks. Carston got into his Escalade and started it up. The leather seats were cold. It would take them a minute or two to warm up.

Carston drove out of the lot toward Dodge Street and toward the Aksarben bridge. He decided to head over to Council Bluffs to Kenny Smart's garage first thing. He knew that Kenny opened at seven. It would be a good place to hang out for a half hour or so, see if Kenny had come up with anything, then he could run up to Harmon and Mott and try to catch Vince and Bill coming in to work, before they disappeared for the day. He also wanted to get a look in the daylight at the parking lot where the biker had been shot.

Traffic was light and he made it to Kenny's right at seven-thirty. The day was already warming up. He was tempted to just leave his vehicle running, but the thermometer on the dash said it was already thirty degrees. He turned off the ignition, grabbed his cup from the cup holder and went into the garage. He made his way straight to the office. He could hear someone, probably David, back in the corner banging a wrench on something. He was surprised that Kenny wasn't sitting at his desk. The coffee pot was cold, half full of coffee from the day before. Carston put it back on the cold burner and went out into the garage toward the clanging wrench.

"Hey, where's Kenny?" Carston called to David as he came into view.

David looked up. He was working on the same Ford pickup that he had been working on the day before.

"Had to go to the doctor," David replied. "Getting himself a finger wave."

"His colon acting up, is it?" Carston asked, sitting on a stool by the workbench where David was working.

"Yeah," David said, putting down the huge wrench that he had been using more as a hammer than a wrench.

"Don't you have tools specially made for beating on things?" Carston asked.

"It was handy," David replied, setting the wrench down and reaching into his toolbox for a hammer. "Kenny's been having trouble pissing again. His wife got him an appointment this morning. He'll be in later. He can't stay away from this shit hole. I wish he would just stay home and take care of himself."

Carston shrugged his shoulders. "Maybe coming in is better than sitting at home," he suggested. "A lot of old people go to work just to get away."

"I suppose," David replied. "Did you find your hearse yet?"

"Nope, I was actually hoping against hope that Kenny might have heard something. I got nothing," Carston said.

"He didn't say anything to me yesterday before he left," David replied.

Carston was looking around. David's description of the garage as a shit hole was pretty accurate. There were a half-dozen cars in various stages of disrepair in stalls on both sides of the huge bay. It was a big place for just David and Kenny, especially since Kenny had slowed down considerably over the past couple of years, leaving most of the work to David. It looked to Carston like he was running behind.

"You look into Vince's son, Gavin?" David asked thoughtfully. "I been thinking about it since yesterday when you were in. It just sounds like something he would do."

Carston looked up at him.

"He never was any good," David continued. "He was always in and out of trouble when we were kids. I think he got picked up for joyriding a

154

couple times when we was younger. Who knows what he's graduated into now."

"I remember you mentioning him yesterday," Carston replied. "Why would Gavin steal his dad's hearse though? It seems like one hell of a leap if you ask me."

David shrugged his shoulders. "You got anything else that's not such a leap?" he asked. "Just trying to help you. I know these people."

"I got nothing," Carston admitted.

"I'd put money on it that if Gavin didn't do it, he knows who did," David said.

Carston thought it over. "I'll run him down, check him out."

David smiled and nodded.

"Okay," Carston said as he stood up from the stool. "I better get going. I want to check out the parking lot at the funeral home. Some biker got shot there last night."

David perked up. "No shit? Shot like shot dead?"

"Yep," Carston replied.

"Holy crap," David exclaimed. "What's up with that? Does it have something to do with the hearse that got stolen?"

"I don't know," Carston replied, purposely not mentioning that the dead biker had been in the same bar that Carston had been in the day before, asking the same questions that Carston had been asking.

"That's fucked," David exclaimed.

"Yes, it is," Carston agreed.

"Okay, I'm out of here," Carston said. "Tell Kenny to call me later if he comes in. I just want to touch base with him. If he hasn't heard something maybe he thought of something."

"Will do," David replied and went back to the Ford.

Carston went out of the garage and got in his car. Traffic was picking up and he had to fight it to get onto Broadway so that he could get over the tracks then north to the Harmon and Mott Funeral Home. When he got there, he found the entrance to the parking lot still blocked with crime scene tape. A pool of frozen blood in the far corner of the lot was barely visible from the street. Carston parked his car at the curb and got out. He took the drive and ducked under the yellow ribbon of tape rather than crunch his way through the snow to the front door. There was a piece of typing paper taped to the door.

"Due to unforeseen circumstances, Harmon and Mott Funeral Home and Crematorium is closed today. Sorry for any inconvenience." There was a phone number to call in case of emergencies. Carston took out his phone and called the number. It rang six times then went to a phone message. "Due to unforeseen circumstances Harmon and Mott Funeral Home and Crematorium is closed for today. Sorry for any inconvenience." Carston ended the call and put his phone back in his coat pocket. He walked to the corner of the building where he had a better view of the frozen pool of blood. From its position, it appeared that the biker had been doing something at the back door when he was shot. Carston surveyed the lot. The door was hidden from the street. The biker might have been trying to break in through it.

Out of the corner of his eye, Carston saw one of the blinds in the window move. It could have just been near a heater vent and the furnace had just come on. He turned and watched the window. The blinds were still. He waited a moment. A bony finger pulled one of the blinds down again and an eye peered out at him. Carston waved. The finger disappeared and the blind snapped back into place. Carston stepped into the crusty snow piled between the lot and the window and tapped on it. There was no movement. Carston tapped again and the bony finger came back in sight and pulled down the slat.

"I want to talk to you," Carston yelled at the eye looking out at him. The slat snapped shut again. Carston stood waiting. A minute later he heard the front door open and saw Henry Mott stick his bald head out of it. Carston took two leaping steps over the snow and back onto the pavement and made his way to the door. Henry held it open for him, then closed and locked it behind him.

"Henry," Carston greeted him. "Sounds like you had a little action here last night."

"I guess we did," Henry agreed.

"Did they get you down here last night, or did you just show up this morning to the crime scene tape and blood in your lot?" Carston asked.

"They called me out," Henry replied. "I've been here all night. I slept here in my office."

"How about Bill or Vince, are they coming in today?" Carston asked.

"We're closed for the day, but they might come in later. I don't know," Henry said.

157

"Man," Carston exclaimed. "I just want ten minutes to talk to those guys. How can two guys like that who work for a funeral home be so hard to catch up to?" His voice was a little exasperated and it took Henry aback.

"I'm really sorry," Henry replied. "I really am. I've told them several times to call you."

"But I'm not going to get to talk to Bill or Vince, am I?" Carston retorted sarcastically.

Henry shrugged his shoulders.

"What's the deal with the biker?" Carston asked. "Do you have him here? I mean, how much more convenient can it be, get shot in the parking lot of a funeral home? Handy for you."

"They took him to the morgue," Henry explained in a calm and informative funeral director tone, unaffected by Carston's earlier outburst. "We may or may not get him once they finish with the autopsy and identify the body."

"What was he doing in your parking lot?" Carston asked.

Henry shook his head. "Maybe he was passing through on his way somewhere?"

"Could be," Carston replied. "Or it could be he was trying to break in through that back door there."

"Why would he be doing that?" Henry asked.

"You tell me. Maybe looking for a stolen hearse?" Carston suggested.

Henry wrinkled his brows. "Detective Hancock, why would a motorcycle gang member be looking for our stolen hearse? And if he was looking for it, why would he want to break in here during the middle of the night and search for it? If someone stole it, is it likely they hid it here?" Henry shrugged his shoulders.

Carston could see where it would make no sense to Henry, knowing what he knew. "Because that biker that got killed was over at Marzoe's last evening asking Martin the bartender if he might know the whereabouts of Bill and Vince. They were asking Martin the same questions that I asked him earlier when I was in there looking for Bill and Vince."

Henry rolled this information around a moment. "That is interesting, isn't it?" he finally replied.

"So what do you think?" Carston asked.

"I don't know," Henry said. "This is just all beyond my comprehension. I do not know what to make of it. And that is as honest as I can be."

"What do you know about Gavin Barker?" Carston asked.

"Gavin Barker, Vince's son?" Henry clarified.

"Yes, that Gavin Barker," Carston replied.

"He's our lawyer," Henry answered.

It was Carston's turn to have a look of confusion on his face. "Gavin Barker, Vince's son, is your lawyer?"

"Yes, he is," Henry reiterated. "Why do you ask?"

"Okay," Carston said. "I was told that Vince's son Gavin was a bit of a juvenile delinquent when he was a kid and might have had something to do with your stolen hearse."

Henry laughed out loud. It was the first time Carston had seen him crack a smile.

"Gavin was a handful as a teenager, that's for sure" Henry began. "But he got his act together his senior year. He was a very good baseball player, which earned him a scholarship to Creighton. He played four years and graduated with a degree in political science. He was talking about going pro, but then he decided to continue with school. He finished law school, took the bar, and now he is a junior partner in Barton Law Offices in Omaha. I sincerely doubt that he had anything to do with our hearse getting stolen off the street."

Carston was taken aback by the mention of Gavin's affiliation with Barton Law Offices. "Is he not a divorce lawyer, then? I thought Barton Law Offices was divorce attorneys," Carston said.

"Barton Law Offices is a lot of things," Henry explained. "Gavin doesn't specialize in divorce. But he is our attorney here. He handles all of our legal concerns. I believe he also represents other businesses around the Council Bluffs and Omaha metro area. That's what got him junior partner."

Carston stood mulling it all over for a moment. "Why would someone want to point me in the direction of Gavin Barker?"

"No reason that I can think of. How did this person you talked to know Gavin?" Henry asked.

"They went to high school together," Carston replied. "They played baseball together."

"And did this person talking to you get a baseball scholarship to Creighton?" Henry asked. "Maybe Gavin took a girl that he had a crush on to the prom? Any number of reasons that someone might want to make trouble for Gavin. High school is like that, petty you know. Perhaps this person hasn't gotten past it."

"You make some very good points," Carston admitted.

"There you are," Henry observed. "Someone is still a little jealous, maybe."

"You could be right," Carston replied shaking his head. "That makes sense, but at the same time it doesn't."

"How's that?" Henry asked.

"Because someone from Barton Law Offices was trying to get ahold of me yesterday and I've been dodging him. I thought it was a divorce lawyer that my wife hired. But when I called her last night to plead my own case without getting the lawyers involved, she told me that she didn't hire a divorce lawyer. Now I wonder why someone from Gavin Barker's law firm is trying to talk to me. Make sense of that."

Henry looked at Gavin. "That is quite coincidental," he remarked.

"I gotta get to the bottom of this." Carston held out his hand and Henry shook it. "You know something? You're a smart guy."

"Well, thank you," Henry smiled for the second time.

"Let me know if you think of anything. I'm heading to the office. I need to contact whoever it is who called me from Barton Law Offices."

"Do you think it is Gavin?" Henry asked.

"I don't know," Carston replied. "But I need to find out who it is and why they called."

How it was

Gavin was lying in his hotel room trying to decide what his next move should be. He had until eleven to decide, that was checkout time. At the moment he was revisiting the circumstances that landed him where he was. As he lay on his back on the bed staring at the ceiling and thinking, Good Morning America was on the TV in the background. He thought back over his entire life, trying to make sense of it.

Gavin's earliest clear memories began with his mother's departure when he was seven years old. As far as he knew, she just left. He had not been hurt over it, particularly. He might have missed her at first, but he didn't remember it if he did. Kids that age are resilient. But she moved to California with a fellow she met at work, and he didn't see her again until he graduated from high school. She came to his graduation. She sat with his dad in the big auditorium and they smiled and waved at him as the class entered the auditorium and took their seats. His dad introduced her to the other parents as Gavin's mom. When he crossed the stage to receive his diploma his father whistled the shrill, piercing whistle he was so good at and he heard his mom cheer and call out his name. For that one day his life went back to the way it was when Gavin was seven. The next day she left and went back to her husband in California. He had not seen her since. She did start sending him Christmas cards and birthday cards after that. She sent him a graduation card with a hundred-dollar check in it and a letter telling him how proud she was when he graduated from law school. The check had the names of two people that Gavin did not recognize. It struck him as strange that he did not know his mother and her husband.

When she left it devastated his father. Gavin's earliest memory of the relationship between his father and his mother was his father's feeling of betrayal, which he did not hide from Gavin. Looking back at it, and Gavin revisited it periodically, Vince never expressed to his son any feeling of lost love for his mother, it was the betrayal that devastated him. A sense of betrayal so profound that by extension and with few exceptions, to his father from then on all women were bitches, sluts and whores. His father never trusted his affections to another woman again.

Vince had worked at Harmon and Mott Funeral Home and Crematorium for as long as Gavin could remember. The job was fitting for Vince. Vince was neat in appearance. He was a quiet man, composed. He stifled all emotion well. Vince drove the hearse, picked up bodies and delivered them back to the funeral home. He did odd jobs, he did maintenance on the hearses, and he kept busy. During the funerals he handed out programs and greeted mourners at the door. Then when the family gathered in the chapel before the ceremony, Vince stood with them and mourned as well, guiding them though their grief. He was an expert at grief and sadness. His decorum was impeccable. It was the perfect job for a man with no ambition, and it paid surprisingly well. Vince loved his job with Harmon and Mott. He could depend on it to be there every day and never change.

Except for his mother leaving, Gavin's childhood was generally uneventful. He was your average kid. He did well enough in school, he never wanted for anything, he had friends, his teachers liked him and he took piano lessons at his dad's insistence from fourth grade until he graduated from high school. Looking back, Gavin wondered if his father didn't harbor some idea that someday Gavin would work for Harmon and Mott Funeral Home himself, and the ability to play the piano might come in handy. Gavin did not have a passion for the piano or the desire to work at the funeral home. If there was one talent that Gavin possessed growing up, it wasn't playing the piano, it was hitting an object coming at him through the air at a high rate of speed with a stick. He had extremely well-defined spatial awareness, something that made him a natural born baseball player and a pretty good juggler. While his father and his coaches considered the former to be a talent and the latter to be a stunt, Gavin considered them much the same, and he was equally proficient at both.

Gavin grew up in Council Bluffs and went to Lincoln High School. He and his father lived in a three-bedroom ranch on Kimberly Drive. He had two best friends growing up: Harvey Grant and David Long. David played baseball with Gavin on the Lincoln High team. David had been a third-string third base player while Gavin was first-string all-star left fielder. David had taught Gavin how to juggle. All the third and second stringers in the dugout learned to juggle. David was also prone to getting himself into trouble. That was why he played baseball. David would have liked to spend his summers looking for mischief and excitement instead of learning how to juggle in the dugout, but his parents thought otherwise. Harvey was never a baseball player. Harvey was a football player, and he was big, strong and mean. He liked to hurt people. When the three graduated from Lincoln High, both Harvey and Gavin got sports scholarships to Creighton in Omaha. David went to auto mechanics school at Iowa Western Community College in Council Bluffs. Harvey and Gavin lost touch with him. They heard that he had a few run-ins with the law right out of high school, but nothing specific. Two years after graduation David married the girl that Harvey had dated in high school and Gavin was asked to be the best man. Harvey didn't get an invitation. Since the wedding Gavin hadn't talked to David to any extent. Their paths crossed occasionally. He saw him around once in a great while, they exchanged nods and salutations, but it was a friendship past.

Harvey lost his eligibility and flunked out of Creighton his junior year. It would have been earlier if it not for the coach's interventions. Gavin tried to keep the friendship between him and Harvey going, but it wasn't to be. Gavin was doing well in school, well in baseball, and he had too much going for him. He had to make a choice to hang out with Harvey or buckle down and keep his grades up. The two drifted apart and the friendship fizzled, much like his friendship with David.

Gavin's senior year at Creighton he was wined and dined by the Iowa Cubs minor league baseball team. Gavin would have rather been wined and dined by the Chicago Cubs major league team, but none of the major league teams seemed interested in him. Gavin came to the realization that he was a very good college baseball player. He was not major league. He had a choice to make. He could go to the Iowa Cubs and hope that he got to a major league level there, or he could go to law school. Much to his father's unspoken and well stifled disappointment, he went to law school. It was a decision that he did not regret.

By the time he graduated from law school and passed the Nebraska bar, Gavin's celebrity on the Creighton ball diamond was still enough in some circles to land him a job with Barton Law Offices, a well-known agency in downtown Omaha. The job suited Gavin well. He fit right into the Barton Law team. His years of organized baseball had taught him many life lessons that would serve him well there: keep your eye on the ball, follow the coach's signals, if you get a hit, hold up on base and don't run unless they tell you to, and always remember to be a team player. Sometimes you had to make sacrifices for the team, it is just part of the game. Gavin knew how it worked. It was all about scoring more points than the opposing team. Nothing else counted. Gavin knew how to win cases and score points.

Everything was going fine. Gavin prospered. He started out working divorce cases, the bread and butter of Barton Law Offices. Every time he got up to bat Gavin knocked it out of the park, one after another, inning after inning, month after month, year after year. Then one day Walt Barton himself came into Gavin's office and introduced Glenda

Thompson. He left her there without any further discussion, closing the office door on the way out. That's when the mess that Gavin found himself in at the moment started.

Glenda explained that her beloved husband Jerry had disappeared under suspicious circumstances four years previously. Authorities had exhausted all avenues of investigation into his disappearance. The circumstances under which he disappeared, however, were termed suspicious by investigators, primarily because they kept changing. When she first reported his disappearance, Glenda told authorities that her husband had left on a business trip somewhere and just didn't come home. But then under scrutiny the story became that Jerry went out fishing on lake Manawa one evening by himself and didn't come home. Then it was that he went fishing out on the Missouri River and didn't come home. While the authorities could find no evidence of foul play that they could pin on anyone in Jerry's disappearance, the fact that the story changed three times and no empty boat was ever found floating on either Lake Manawa or anywhere on the Missouri River, and considering that Jerry didn't own a boat at the time of his disappearance, they kept the case open. Glenda wanted Gavin to start the legal proceedings to officially pronounce Jerry dead and transfer all of his assets and holdings to her. Considering the fact that Walt himself had walked her into his office, Gavin was sure that there would be a promotion at the successful culmination of the proceedings, even though Walt had essentially washed his hands of the whole affair when he walked out the door and closed it behind him.

167

Gavin dove into the case, kept his eye on the ball, watched for signals from Walt, didn't take any chances unless he was told to by the coaches or run to the next base unless it was safe, and brought the case in to home plate two years later for a score. That moved him to Junior Partner and landed him Glenda's account and her as a permanent client. He got out of being a run-of-the-mill divorce lawyer and took on representing all of Glenda's newly acquired business ventures, and there were several. Enough of them to keep him busy almost full time.

Along the way there were plenty of rumors, insinuations and inuendo floating around the agency about Glenda. The first one that he heard about at the water fountain was that Glenda's husband Jerry was connected to Tommy Gunn, the crime boss who had absconded during a murder investigation and escaped to Canada. Or Mexico, or Brazil, depending on who was telling the story. The story was that old cliché that Jerry grew up in the poor part of town and started out running errands, working his way up in the organization to be Tommy's right-hand man. But behind every successful man there was a woman, and most agreed that although Jerry appeared to be running the business in Omaha for Tommy, his wife Glenda was really running the show. The speculation was that Tommy trusted Glenda to run things more than he trusted Jerry, and Jerry pushed back on both of them a little too hard, so Tommy made Jerry disappear. There was also talk that Walt himself was Tommy's lawyer and that Walt had been fighting Tommy's extradition for years. It was even suggested that Barton Law Offices was built with Tommy Gunn's money. Gavin let all the whispering go past him like an errant pitch. All the speculations sounded more like a movie script than reality to Gavin. He kept his eye on the ball and all of that other was just buzz from the bleachers. Gavin had a game to win.

While all of the talk about the connection between Walter Barton and Tommy Gun was purely conjecture and ignored by Gavin, over the two years that he represented Glenda and her business interests he began to have his own suspicions about her connections to Tommy Gunn. He spent a lot of time in civil court, pushing for injunctions on rulings while they were being appealed, requesting zoning waivers for projects that were already in noncompliance, seeking tax exemptions and tax extensions. She applied for every grant and no-interest business loan that she could get, with no intentions of meeting the requirements and every intention of defaulting. She owned rental properties so full of violations that it was cheaper for her to keep them in perpetual court proceedings than it would be to bring them up to code. She pushed the limits of the law in every way, always right to the edge of criminal conduct. Several times he had warned her that she was crossing a line. But he always reminded himself that the law was the law, and playing it close to the line was not criminal. He made every effort to keep Glenda on the right side, and even if he wasn't always successful in that, he was doing his job.

During this time Glenda got to know Gavin well. She was a very good listener. Gavin told her his life story many times. He confided in her. She

was a mother figure to him. A year ago Harvey
Grant had gone to work for Glenda. Even though
he hadn't seen Harvey for years, Glenda said that
Harvey used Gavin as a reference. Gavin always
wondered how Harvey would even be aware that
he was representing Glenda, and when he thought
about it, the reference was more that he was
vouching for Harvey than anything. Glenda hired
him on Gavin's word. But even though Harvey
was on the payroll, Gavin hardly ever talked to
him and if he did it was just a hi or see-ya. Gavin
got the impression that Harvey was Glenda's
personal bodyguard. While he didn't want to think
about it too much, it probably wasn't a bad idea for
her to have one. She certainly ruffled feathers
around town.

That brought Gavin's thinking to three weeks
ago when Glenda insisted that Gavin meet her at a
boutique restaurant in the Old Market that was
above even Gavin's pay grade. When he got there
he found Glenda and Harvey both waiting for him.
The restaurant was empty other than the three of
them and a waiter who discreetly stayed out of
hearing but not out of sight. First Glenda reminded
him of all the times he himself had pushed past the
line, turned a blind eye to what she was doing. All
the times he had twisted and turned the law to
favor some sketchy deal that she had found herself
involved in. Gavin had to admit that she made
some valid points, he had dipped his toe into the
waters on the wrong side a few times for her, and
he realized right away that she was about to use it
to her advantage.

The job would be simple, she explained. He
had told Glenda a number of times that he also

represented Harmon and Mott, that his father had
worked there for decades, how when he was a
teenager he used to hang out at the funeral home
waiting for his dad to get off work. He told her
about going over to Eppley with his dad to pick up
bodies coming in on planes, just for the ride, and
how his dad always figured out how to time it so
that they could go to Spaghetti Works while they
were over there. He might have even bragged a
time or two about snitching his dad's keys and
taking his friends for a little after-hours ride
around the block in one of the hearses. Now all
Glenda wanted him to do was get a set of keys for
both of the Harmon and Mott hearses. That was all.
Deliver them to Harvey and Harvey would take
care of the rest. It wouldn't be hard. Glenda knew
he had access. Just the keys, she told him, and don't
ask questions. It would just be another one of those
things he knew nothing about.

The whole time Gavin listened to Glenda he
watched Harvey and Harvey stared back at him,
not uttering a word. Gavin recognized the look on
Harvey's face; he had seen it many times before.
There was no doubt that Harvey wanted to hurt
someone, and Gavin couldn't help but feel like he
was a prime candidate sitting there.

The following evening Gavin showed up at
Harmon and Mott Funeral Home under the pretext
that he needed to review some files, right as Henry
was about to lock up and leave. Henry had
informed him that he had just missed his dad.
Gavin told Henry to go ahead and take off, he
didn't know how long it would take and he had
keys to the front door. There was no reason for him
to have to stay. Henry was happy to leave him to

his work. As soon as Henry left, Gavin went to the garage, took the keys from both hearses, then ran to the True Value hardware store down the street to get copies made. He returned the originals and locked up. He called Harvey on his way out the door to arrange a meet-up. Harvey didn't answer his phone, so Gavin just went home with the keys and didn't give it a thought. He would get them to Harvey the following day. No problem.

But that's actually when the problems started. Because Gavin didn't get the keys to Harvey the next day, or the day after that. He never did get them to Harvey. Harvey kept putting him off, telling him to hang on to them for a while, using one excuse after another. Then three days ago Glenda called him to meet her at the same restaurant. This time when Gavin got there it was only Glenda, and Glenda told him she had something she needed him to do for her. She explained that she had planned to have Harvey do it, but he was busy taking care of something else. She wanted Gavin to go to Spaghetti Works at noon and steal the Harmon and Mott hearse. She said that Harmon and Mott was going to pick up a body at the airport and that Vince would be driving. She said that he had told her many times that his dad always worked in a stop at the Spaghetti Works when he had business in Omaha. While Vince was in Spaghetti Works, she wanted Gavin to steal the hearse and run it down to a rental garage on the southeast side of Council Bluffs. Someone would meet him there to bring him back to Omaha. Nothing more, no big deal.

Gavin tried to protest, but Glenda cowed him. Gavin was a team player; he knew he had to make sacrifices for the good of the team. He tried to ask Glenda why in the world she would want him to steal his father's hearse with a body in it, but she assured him that the less he knew the better off he would be. He grudgingly agreed to do it. He had no choice. So a half hour before noon he stationed himself in the little store across the street from Spaghetti Works in the Old Market and waited, hoping that something would come up and his dad wouldn't show. But that wasn't to be. True to form, his dad and Bill were creatures of habit. They were predictable. They came by and parked the hearse a block down the street and went into the restaurant.

Even though his heart was beating so hard that he thought he was having a heart attack, Gavin walked casually to the hearse, unlocked the door and backed it out of the parking place. He had the presence of mind to drive the other direction so that he wouldn't pass in front of the restaurant and be seen by his dad and Bill while they ate. He headed toward the bridge as if he was taking the hearse to Harmon and Mott Funeral Home, hoping that the charade would make him less noticeable. On the bridge he got the call from Harvey. The gruff voice was brief and to the point: Do you have the hearse? Be careful, watch your ass. Don't trust anyone. Gavin was already scared shitless. Harvey's stark warning pushed him over the edge. When he got across the bridge, instead of turning south to the rental garage as Glenda instructed him, he turned north and didn't stop driving until he was out of town.

Gavin took a deep breath. He was not as cool in a clutch as he seemed when he stood at third base getting set to steal home plate. Gavin was in fact just the opposite. As he sat on the bed in his room at the Hotel LeVant, Good Morning America was going to the local news and the picture on the TV screen caught his attention. It was cop cars sitting in the parking lot of Harmon and Mott Funeral Home. He grabbed the remote and turned up the sound.

"Council Bluffs Police are investigating a homicide that took place at the Harmon and Mott Funeral Home and Crematorium last night. It was reported around ten thirty. When police arrived they found the victim laying in the parking lot. He was pronounced dead at the scene and it was determined that the cause of death was two gunshot wounds to the back. At this time the Council Bluffs Police have not identified the body, but they believe the incident to be gang related. The victim was wearing clothing that identified him as a member of the Hell Fighters motorcycle club. Calls to Harmon and Mott Funeral Home have not been returned. We will update when more information becomes available."

Gavin felt sick to his stomach.

Xavier takes over

Xavier woke up late. It was after eight o'clock. He turned his head and looked at Gimp's phone charging on his nightstand. He rolled over, unplugged the charger from the phone and switched the charger to his own phone. He sat up in his bed, settled back against the headboard, hit the button on the side of the phone and the screen came alive. He was still in disbelief that Gimp's phone wasn't protected by a pin. He opened up the call history and studied the numbers. The calls with Zee were all incoming, same as the call last night. One number that Gimp called last night was repeated several times in the list. Gimp had called three other numbers the day before, and one of the numbers had a seven-one-two area code, a Council Bluffs number. Whoever Gimp had been getting his leads from, he was a local.

Xavier touched the number tentatively and it startled him when it went straight to call and started ringing. He had expected a step or two to work himself up to it. The phone rang six times, then a voice came on saying to leave a voicemail. Xavier ended the call before it went to the tone. He stared at the phone for a full minute. He pushed the number again and this time he got an answer on the second ring.

"Who is this?" a voice on the other end asked.

"This is X. Who are you?" he asked with authority.

175

"I think you dialed a wrong number," the voice replied.

"Who am I talking to?" Xavier asked with authority again before the person at the other end could end the call. He didn't want whoever it was to blow him off or take him as a pushover. He had to make it sound like he was just as capable as Gimp, taking no bullshit, for the plan to work.

"What do you want?" the voice asked.

"Gimp met with an accident last night and I'm taking over." Xavier took on the persona of a man of few words.

"I don't know any Gimp," the voice replied.

"Okay, fuck you," Xavier ended the call. As soon as he did, he wondered if he had pushed too hard. He stared at the screen, trying to decide if he should call the number back. His instincts told him to wait.

The phone rang. "Who am I talking to?" Xavier answered it curtly.

"That's not important," the voice on the other end replied.

"It is to me," Xavier said calmly but assuredly. "I need to know who I'm working with if I'm putting myself on the line. Who are you?"

The voice was quiet for a moment. "You said Gimp had an accident. How do I know you aren't the cops calling numbers on his phone, seeing who answers?"

"Fuck you," Xavier ended the call.

The phone rang again and Xavier answered it. "Who am I talking to?"

"Tell me what you know," the voice asked.

"Tell me who I'm talking to," Xavier demanded.

"Christ, Bronco Billy, whatever. I don't know what you are trying to prove, I can tell you my name is George, you won't know the difference. What the fuck?" The voice was exasperated.

"You want to go by George, or Bronco Billy?" Xavier asked. "It makes no difference to me, but I'm talking to someone and that someone better come up with a name if they want to keep talking to me."

"George," the voice on the other end replied. "Call me George."

"Okay George, Gimp's not in the game anymore. I am," Xavier replied. "What bullshit were you feeding him?"

"I wasn't feeding him any bullshit," George replied. "What happened to him, and why are you taking over?"

"He got himself shot last night," Xavier said. "And I'm taking over because I'm next in line and we aren't going to stop just because one of us is stupid enough to walk into some shit. You were talking to him all day yesterday and last night, telling him where to go and what to look for. Maybe you set him up, maybe it is just a coincidence that he walked into a bullet, but I'm taking over and if it was you, and if you try to set me up, I'll hunt you down and you will wish you never answered that fucking phone."

"Calm down, it wasn't me," George assured him. "You tell me what you know. I'll fill in what you don't. Trust me."

"I know that the day before yesterday I picked up Gimp at the airport and he wanted to jack a hearse that was picking up a body that came in on the same plane out of Montreal, Canada. We somehow missed the hearse and we looked for it all day yesterday and the day before. I know that Gimp was talking to you and you were giving him leads." Xavier paused for a moment. "I know that you are local, so I figure you were giving him inside information."

"What makes you think that I'm local?" George asked.

"Because who else would be close enough to be giving him leads, and you got a Council Bluffs area code, dumbshit." Xavier was enjoying his role as a hard case and a tough guy. He was feeling like a nomad. He didn't take orders, he gave them.

"Do you know why Gimp was going to jack that hearse and what he was going to do once he did?" George asked with no hint that he was offended by Xavier's taunt.

"You tell me," Xavier replied. "I think we both know the answer."

"I'm just wondering how you are going to take over for Gimp when you don't even know why he was here or what he was doing," George replied.

"Let's just call it contraband that needs to go back where it came from. Then we can both pretend we don't know what it was he was looking for, if that's the way you want to play it," Xavier said.

"Okay, fine," George said. "You're right, there's some contraband that someone wants back. It is in the coffin with the body. Gimp was going to jack the hearse, retrieve the contraband and take it back in a rental, or whatever he could get his hands on to drive back. You are also right that he missed his chance. That's because the guys driving the

178

hearse decided to stop off in Omaha for lunch instead of going straight back to the funeral home. But someone else got wind what Gimp was up to, so they got the jump on him and stole the hearse before he could. I was Gimp's local contact. I was helping him try to find it before it got to the wrong people."

"Then you know who stole the hearse?" Xavier asked.

"Yes, I do," George answered.

"Someone working on the inside, someone from the funeral home?" Xavier asked.

"No, no one from the funeral home. They were just the patsies. They were just going to collect the body and Gimp was going to take it from them," George replied.

"I think that Gimp assumed they had something to do with it. That's why he went to the funeral home last night. You told him that it might be there," Xavier accused.

"I didn't tell him any such thing," George replied defensively. "He went there on his own."

"Who stole the hearse then?" Xavier asked.

"A guy named Gavin Barker," George replied. "He works for some really bad people who want to get their hands on that contraband. If you're wondering who shot Gimp, they would be my first bet. But this Gavin Barker is playing his own game now. He hid the hearse and no one knows where it is. Everyone is looking for Gavin and he's laying low. He's putting the hearse up to the highest bidder. That's who Gimp was looking for yesterday all day. That's whose house you guys went to yesterday up north of Crescent."

"Okay," Xavier said. "So what are we doing today?"

"The people who Gavin works for hired a private detective to look for Gavin and the hearse. Detective's name is Carston Hancock. Now I'm not telling you what to do, I'm not in charge here, I'm just local. You might say that I'm a consultant. But if it were me, instead of looking for Gavin, I would find that detective and follow him. Because he is probably getting his leads from the people who Gavin was working for before he turned traitor on them. And I'm thinking his leads are better than any I have. Besides, he's going to be easier to find. So that's what I would do."

The business card Gimp had left on the seat of his Ram was on the nightstand. Xavier picked it up thoughtfully. He didn't feel a need to tell George that he was looking at Carston Hancock's card as they spoke.

"I'm just saying, instead of running around in circles, you might as well let him do the work," George said to the silence.

"We'll see about that. I got some other leads I might follow up today," Xavier lied.

"You a Hell Fighter?" George asked quickly.

"Yep," Xavier answered.

"Local?" George asked.

"Nomad," Xavier replied. "You?"

"Well I'm just a local here, so if you need anything at all give me a call. Sorry about the shit to start with, but you can't be too careful," George said. "Let me know if you need something."

"I'll do that," Xavier said and finished the call.

Xavier turned the card in his fingers, looking at it from every angle while he thought. After a few minutes he called the number. The phone rang twice.

"Carston Hancock Investigations," a female voice answered the phone. "This is Stephanie."

"Stephanie, is Detective Hancock around?" Xavier asked.

"He isn't in yet," she replied.

"I need to talk to him. Do you expect him in soon?" Xavier asked.

"I expect him anytime," Stephanie replied.

"Could I maybe make an appointment? The sooner the better, maybe nine or nine thirty?" Xavier asked.

"Nine thirty would work, I think," Stephanie replied. "He's usually in before that."

"Good," Xavier replied. "I will see him then at nine thirty."

"Is this about your call yesterday?" Stephanie asked, surprising Xavier.

"Yes, it is. You told him that I called?" Xavier replied quickly.

"I did," Stephanie replied. "He must not have gotten ahold of you yesterday."

"No, he didn't," Xavier replied. "It's probably better that I talk to him in person, anyway."

"Probably," Stephanie said in a serious voice. "Might as well get it over with. I'll tell him you are coming over. Will it take long?"

"Not long at all," Xavier said. "Talk to you then."

He ended the call. He thought himself quite clever. He would stake out the Hancock building at nine thirty. Then when the detective figured out that he was a no-show, Xavier could pick him up and tail him from there. It was a brilliant plan.

Glenda rolled over in her bed and looked at the alarm clock on the nightstand. It said nine o'clock. She had slept well, all things considered. She glanced at her phone, which she kept on do not disturb until eleven. There were three calls from a number she recognized. Glenda made it a habit to keep certain numbers in her head. She seldom put important ones in her contacts and she routinely cleared her call history. No use making it easy for the authorities if they showed up some day at her doorstep with a warrant for her phone. The last thing she needed was for the authorities to know who she was talking to. She hit the callback.

"Glenn," a man's voice answered.

"Yes," she replied in an annoyed voice.

"I've been trying to get ahold of you."

"I see that," Glenda replied. "I think that I've told you before that I don't answer calls until after eleven."

"Listen, there's another Hell Fighter that took over from that guy from Montreal. A local guy. He called me earlier on Montreal's phone. Spooked the hell out of me."

Glenda didn't say anything for a moment. "Okay, what's the story on this new guy?"

"I think he's the mope that was trailing around with Montreal. It sounds like he wants to make a name for himself. He tried to sound like some hard case on the phone."

"And how did he get your number?" Glenda asked.

"He said that Montreal left his phone in his truck."

"And how do we know it isn't the cops that found Montreal's phone in his pocket and are calling around and acting like a mope who is taking over?" Glenda asked.

"I thought about that. I quizzed him and he knows too much to be the cops. Also, he wasn't fishing."

"Just what does he know?" Glenda asked after a pause to think.

"He knows the what, he doesn't know the why."

Glenda paused again to think. She always thought before she spoke, a habit that she had learned from her late husband. One of many things he had passed on to her before he so conveniently disappeared.

"What's in it for him?" she asked. "Why would he pick up the ball and run with it?"

"Wants to move up I would suspect. It's an opportunity to get noticed. Move him up in the Hell Fighters where maybe he makes a little money."

"That's what you think?" she asked.

"Yes."

"So how did you leave it?" Glenn asked.

"He started out a little suspicious, but I got him licking my hand. I sent him to follow Hancock until we decide how we want to proceed."

"Do you think that's wise?" Glenda asked.

"That way I don't have two people to keep tabs on all day. They're both in the same place. I can watch them both that way, without getting anyone else involved."

"Does this mope have a name?" Glenda asked.

"X."

"X?" Glenda repeated.

"All the Hell Fighters have some name that they use. When he called me, he was all pissy and demanded my name. I told him my name was George."

"George?" Glenn laughed. "Where did you come up with George?"

"I don't know, it just popped into my head to get him out of his goofy game so I could find out what the hell he was up to."

"Are you in contact with him, can you feed him?" Glenda asked.

"Putty in my hands."

"See if you can get his real name," Glenda said. "I want to check him out."

"Will do."

"Keep me informed," Glenda said, getting ready to end the call.

"I've been trying all morning to keep you informed."

"Yeah, well," Glenda paused. "We need to deal with him eventually."

"I know," the voice on the other end replied with a serious tone.

Glenda ended the call. Siccing this X on Carston probably was a good move. It sounded to her like this guy wasn't as big a threat to them as Montreal had been and keeping him close to Carston might eventually play well into the plan. Glenda got up out of bed. There was no going back to sleep now. She turned off the phone's do not disturb and went into the bathroom to start her day.

All I do is sit and wait

Carston walked into the office to find Stephanie at her desk, her shoes off and her feet propped up on the corner of her desk, the computer mouse in one hand surfing the net. She was digging in her hair with the middle finger of the other hand.

"Doing research for me, or just surfing porn?" Carston asked.

"Porn," Stephanie replied.

"Got anything for me?" he asked.

"That lawyer you were supposed to call yesterday made an appointment for nine thirty." Stephanie kicked her feet off the desk and sat up.

"You mean Megan's divorce lawyer who called yesterday?" Carston quizzed her.

"Yeah, he called and made an appointment to see you," Stephanie replied off-handedly.

"Well, that's pretty interesting," Carston replied. "Because I talked to Megan last night and she said that she hasn't hired a lawyer."

Stephanie gave him a confused look.

"This lawyer who called up yesterday, what did he say? Did he tell you he was Megan's lawyer?"

"He left his phone number. I looked it up and it came back to Barton Law Offices. Their website says that they specialize in divorce." She held out her hands palms up and shrugged her shoulders. "Research."

"You didn't ask him his name, ask him what it was about, anything?" Carston asked pointedly.

"He didn't give me his name and he told me it was personal when I asked him what it was about," Stephanie shot back. "So I did a little detective work."

"How many lawyers work out of Barton Law Offices?" Carston asked.

"I don't know," Stephanie replied.

"Do all the lawyers there do divorce cases, or do some of them do something else, like maybe personal injury, or worker's comp, or any of those other slimy cases that big law offices like to use to suck people dry?"

"Why are you attacking me?" Stephanie asked, hurt that he would be so harsh with her for just doing her job.

"That's what I thought," Carston said. "Because Gavin Barker is Vince Barker's son, and he works for Barton Law Offices. Do you think that Gavin Barker, Vince Barker's son, might want to talk to me about a stolen hearse?"

"Who is Vince Barker?" Stephanie asked.

"One of the guys who was driving the hearse when it got stolen," Carston explained, exasperated.

"How was I supposed to know all that?" Stephanie acted like she was offended at Carston's accusations. "It could be a coincidence. Maybe he wants to talk to you about something else altogether," Stephanie replied. "You'll know in a half hour, because he's coming in to see you." She smiled triumphantly and went back to her computer screen.

"Yep," Carston conceded and walked toward the door to his office. "I'm sure it isn't a coincidence."

"Probably lucky that I didn't call Megan yesterday and try to talk her out of divorcing you," Stephanie called after him.

"Very lucky," Carston called back.

Carston hung his coat and hat on the tree behind his desk and sat down. He put his head in his hands. Stephanie was the worst receptionist, office manager, whatever she was, that he could have hired. He needed to get rid of her, something he had contemplated many times over the last months and something that he could not bring himself to do. He was such a coward. Megan wanted her gone. Life would be so much easier if he just fired her and found someone halfway competent. He had come to think of her as his punishment for his transgressions. It was like self-flagellation, he deserved her.

He looked up at the clock on the wall, then back at his desk. He was trying to think of something he could do there at the office while he waited that might help him with his case. He wished that Stephanie would do something that would help him with his case instead of sitting at her desk all day giving him her minimums. Carston wanted to scream. He was getting nowhere. He turned on his computer and watched it slowly boot up. As soon as it was finished clicking and spinning he searched Glenda Thompson on Google. There were pages and pages of results, none of which appeared to concern the Glenda Thompson he was working for. He went to Facebook and typed in her name. Again, he found hundreds of Glenda Thompsons. He went down four pages of Glenda Thompsons with no luck. He typed in Glenda Thompson Omaha. He checked LinkedIn and came up with nothing. What kind of person as high profile as Glenda had absolutely no footprint on the internet? He tried Instagram.

Carston switched gears. He typed in Gavin Barker, attorney at law. The top result was the one he wanted: Gavin Barker, Junior Partner, Barton Law Offices, Omaha, Nebraska.

"Well fucking A, that was easy." Carston said out loud and pulled up Gavin's bio.

"Gavin Barker, Attorney at Law. Gavin Barker is a Junior Partner at Barton Law Offices. Gavin Graduated from Lincoln High School in Council Bluffs, IA. He holds a Bachelor of Arts Degree in English and a Juris Doctorate degree from Creighton University where he received his undergraduate degree on a baseball scholarship. Gavin specializes in business law and represents numerous clients in the Omaha metro area." Carston recognized the photo in the bio.

"Hey," Carston called out to Stephanie. "The number of Barton Law Offices from yesterday. Is this it?" Carston read the number for Gavin Barker off the site.

"That's it," Stephanie yelled back.

"Fuck me," Carston said out loud.

Stephanie came to the door. "You need something?" she smiled.

Carston looked up at the clock, it was nine thirty-five. "You haven't heard anything from Barker?"

"Nope," Stephanie answered. "Maybe he's running late."

"Well that's a given, that he's running late. He was supposed to be here five minutes ago. I was wondering if he called or anything," Carston remarked.

"If he had I would have told you," Stephanie replied.

"I'm not sure of that," Carston remarked under his breath.

"You would have heard the phone ring if he had called," Stephanie observed. "Did you hear the phone ring?"

Carston gave her a stern look.

"Why are you so pissy today?" she asked. "Don't you have somewhere to go or something to do?"

"I'm waiting for my nine thirty," Carston replied incredulously.

Stephanie turned and went back to her desk.

Carston picked up his office land line and punched in the number Gavin had left the day before. The phone rang once.

"Barton Law Offices, my name is Margarite. May I help you?"

"Yes, Margarite, this is Carston Hancock of Carston Hancock Investigations. I'm returning a call from Gavin Barker," Carston replied.

"Mr. Barker has not come in yet today," Margarite replied.

"When do you expect him to come in?" Carston asked.

"I don't know," Margarite replied. "He is usually in his office before nine, but he has not come in yet today. He may be meeting with a client outside the office. He hasn't called in," Margarite explained.

"Does that happen often, Mr. Barker not coming in and not telling anyone?" Carston pressed.

"No, that is not usual," Margarite replied.

"Do you have any idea why he was trying to contact me yesterday?" Carston asked. "By the time I called back I think that the offices were closed. I was just wondering what he needed."

"I do not, Mr. Hancock, sorry. You'll have to talk to Mr. Barker."

"Does he have another number that I can reach him at?" Carston pressed. "A cell phone?"

"I'm sorry Mr. Hancock, I cannot give that number out. I can call him and give him your number if you like and he can call you," she suggested.

"That would be fine," Carston replied and rattled off his cell number.

"I will let him know that you called. Is there anything else?"

"No, thank you. You've been a lot of help," Carston said, even though he was thinking that she hadn't been much help at all. She was just doing her job, he told himself. Better than Steph did hers. He wondered what she looked like.

Carston looked up at the clock. It was a quarter to ten. He was getting tired of waiting. He was getting nowhere fast and marking time in his office was not helping him find the hearse. He reminded himself that Gavin Barker very well could break the case for him and that patience was something that he needed to practice a little more of. He sat back and stared out the door at Stephanie's back. She was surfing the internet. It was all she did, all day every day. He had to admit that at the moment there wasn't much she else she could do. Have patience, he told himself.

Carston watched the second hand go around the clock from nine fifty-nine to ten o'clock. He got up from his desk, took his coat and hat from the tree, and went out into Stephanie's office.

"I'm leaving. I need to follow up some leads," he said. "If Barker, or anyone else for that matter, comes in looking for me, call me and keep them here. I will come straight back. Do not let them leave."

"What kind of leads?" Stephanie asked.

Carston was caught with no answer. He had no leads. "I'm just going over everything from yesterday, see if anything has changed or if there is anything I missed. I'll probably go down to Kenny's and ask Dave why he really thinks Gavin Barker had anything to do with the stolen hearse, then to that bar, Marzoe's, and talk to Martin."

"Okay," Stephanie replied in a tone that made Carston feel like she was giving him her permission to go.

"I'll call you later then, providing Barker doesn't come in," Carston tried to sound authoritative.

"Sure." Stephanie was already staring at her computer screen and moving the mouse across her desk.

Carston put on his coat and hat and went out the door to the elevator. He rode it to the first floor and went out onto the street. The air was noticeably warmer. He went to the Escalade, climbed inside and shut the door. He pulled out his phone and made sure that his ringer was turned up. He felt like Gavin Barker was his best lead to work at the moment. He was not sure exactly why Gavin was trying to get ahold of him, but it must have something to do with the hearse. Henry had told him that Gavin represented the Harmon and Mott Funeral Home. Maybe he was just calling to touch base and see where Carston was on the case. Maybe he was dealing with the insurance claim. Maybe he had been talking to the police and wanted to check in with him. In the course of a few minutes Carston convinced himself that whatever it was that Gavin wanted to talk to him about, it was nothing more than checking in with all the people involved, generating some paid hours, padding the bill and nothing more. Carston felt depressed. It was the only reason that made sense. He did it himself, make lots of calls, talk to lots of people, charge by the hour. He realized that for a brief time he had been counting on Gavin, but that there was likely nothing there. Just a lawyer piling up billable hours. He pulled out on Dodge Street and drove toward the Aksarben Bridge to Council Bluffs.

On the way over the bridge, Carston shifted his thinking to David. He asked himself why David was so sure that Gavin was involved somehow in the theft of the hearse. Surely he knew that Gavin was an attorney, a successful attorney working in a big law office. Lincoln High was not a big school, nothing like Carston's graduating class of sixteen hundred. Carston found it hard to believe that no one that David ran into from their class ever said, hey David, did you hear about Gavin Barker? He's a big shot lawyer over in Omaha now.

Carston had David on his mind when he pulled off of Broadway and decided to swing by

Marzoe's first. His gut told him that running his thoughts past Martin first might help him get his mind organized. He pulled into the lot and parked. It was early and there were only a few cars parked outside. Carston got out of the Escalade and went into the bar. When his eyes accustomed themselves to the dark interior Martin appeared like an apparition, cleaning a glass with his dirty dishrag.

"Early lunch?" Martin asked as Carston took a bar stool. "Kitchen isn't open until eleven."

"You haven't by chance seen Vince or Bill today?" Carston asked.

"Nope. Find out anything more about the dead biker?" he asked

"Nope, nothing more than I knew last night," Carston replied.

Martin thoughtfully quit rubbing the rim of the glass with the dirty dish cloth and looked across the room.

"What are you thinking?" Carston asked.

"Nothing," Martin replied. "Just sort of drifting off."

Carston chuckled, Evidently Martin just went into sleep mode, like his computer sometimes did. He wondered if there was a setting that kept him on track conversationally speaking that could be set for more than thirty seconds.

"Remember the other day I asked about Gavin Barker?" Carston asked.

"Vince's kid," Martin replied.

"Exactly," Carston said.

"Sure, nice kid. Comes in with his dad sometimes. Was a hell of a baseball player when he was a kid. Vince was pretty proud of him."

"When was the last time you saw him?" Carston asked.

Martin had to think for a moment. Carston was wondering if he had gone into sleep mode again when he answered.

"He was in here with some old high school buddies, I don't know, around Christmas."

"Do you happen to know who these high school buddies were?" Carston's curiosity was piqued. He had a hunch that he might already know the answer.

"Ol' Kenny Smart's son-in-law, Davie," Martin replied. "And that other kid, the one that played football for a while. I can't think of his name."

"That's very interesting," Carston nodded his head.

"How's that?" Martin asked.

"Nothing," Carston replied. "I think that I need to get a little clarification about something. Someone might be bullshitting me."

"Who?" Martin asked.

"Just someone," Carston replied.

Martin wrinkled his brow, put the glass down, placed both hands on the bar and leaned toward Carston. "That's not how it works here. I'm not like the juke box that you stick a couple of quarters in and I sing a song for you. This is a two-way conversation we're having, so what's up?"

Carston could see that Martin was quite serious. He had to admit to himself that most of the information he had gotten in the last twenty-four hours that had been worth anything had come from Martin.

"Well, I know Kenny pretty well," Carston opened up. "I've known him for a long time. Whenever I'm trying to run down a stolen car out of Omaha, Kenny knows something about it. He hears a lot. I don't question it, I just appreciate his sharing. So yesterday, as soon as I got this missing hearse case I went over and asked Kenny. And Kenny didn't have any ideas, which is unusual. But ol' David, he was ready to bet the farm that Gavin Barker had something to do with it. He left me thinking that Gavin was some kind of mope that was good for anything, especially his pappy's hearse coming up missing. He never once mentioned that Gavin was a big shot attorney with some big shot law firm in Omaha. I kind of thought Dave had lost track of Gavin, didn't realize he had grown up and become respectable. This new information kind of changes my mental picture of David's prime suspect."

Martin laughed. "I would point the finger at Davie long before I would Gavin, if you're just looking at ne'er-do-wells as suspects."

"You think that David might know more than he's letting on?" Carston raised his eyebrows.

"I'm just saying that of the two, Davie has a lot less going for him," Martin replied. "I'll tell you one thing, all this info that Kenny always has, I'll bet that most of it comes from Davie. He's always been on the shady side."

"So do you think that David might know something about the stolen hearse that he's not sharing?" Carston asked again.

"I ain't saying that," Martin backpedaled a bit.

"What would David's motivation be to point me toward Gavin Barker?" Carston asked.

"Who knows?" Martin replied. "Davie likes to talk."

Carston watched Martin straighten up, pick up the glass and start polishing it again.

"You aren't holding back on me, are you?" Carston asked.

"I don't know why he would point you toward Gavin," Martin answered. "Honestly, they've been friends forever. Davie likes to talk. Gavin is Vince's kid. Davie isn't bright."

"You're probably right," Carston conceded.

"You want something to drink?" Martin asked. "Or you just want to waste my time jawing, because I got stuff to do."

Carston looked around the bar. There were two other customers in the place, a middle aged man and a middle aged woman far back in the corner who looked like they were having a morning rendezvous. They looked to Carston like two people who were married, but not to each other. He felt like he should take a picture on his phone, just out of habit.

"I'll take a Fat Tire, bottle," Carston said. He wanted to stay on Martin's good side. So far everything he had to go on came from Martin.

Bits and pieces come together

Gavin was about to leave his room at the LeVant when his phone rang. He answered it.

"Where are you at?" He recognized Harvey's voice.

"Why?" Gavin asked.

"You know why," Harvey said. "Glenn wants that hearse. You are being totally fucked up about it. We have no idea why you are acting the way you are. Just tell us where it is and we'll go get it."

"You told me to call that detective and tell him," Gavin replied.

"But you didn't," Harvey retorted. "So now it is back to you. Where's the hearse?"

"You know those two bikers from yesterday?" Gavin asked.

"What two bikers?" Harvey replied.

"Those two bikers that were nosing around my place yesterday morning," Gavin answered.

"You didn't say it was two bikers at your place yesterday morning," Harvey replied calmly, trying to keep Gavin from going off the deep end.

"Well, one of them is dead. He got shot last night in the Harmon and Mott Funeral Home parking lot."

"No shit?" Harvey remarked.

'Yes, no shit," Gavin replied. "I suppose you don't know anything about that?"

There was a pause. "Gavin, you need to tell me where that hearse is. You are in way over your head. You need to get yourself out from under this."

"No shit," Gavin replied.

"Where's the hearse, Gavin?"

Gavin heard a tone that told him someone was trying to call him. "Right now, at this moment, while I try to figure out what is going on, that hearse is my insurance policy," Gavin said. "You and Glenn, and your bikers, just back off and give me some room to figure this out. I'll tell you where it is when I'm good and ready."

"Listen, Gavin," Harvey said harshly. "Every minute you are trying to figure it out, you are sinking deeper and deeper into quicksand. I want to help you, but you need to let me. Because what you got yourself into is beyond your wildest dreams. Do you understand me?"

"I think that I understand you just fine, and that's why I'll tell you when I'm good and ready." Gavin ended the call.

He looked at his phone to see who had tried to call him while he was talking to Harvey and saw that his hand was shaking so much that he couldn't read the screen. He laid the phone down on the mattress. It was his receptionist at Barton's. He managed to pick up the phone and push the right button. The phone rang twice and Margarite answered.

"Mr. Barker, are you coming in today? A private detective named Carston Hancock is trying to contact you. He wants you to call him. I have his number here if you want it."

Gavin found the notepad and pen on the nightstand. "Give it to me," he said.

Margarite read off the number and Gavin wrote it down. "Okay, I'll call him," he said.

"Are you coming in today?" Margarite asked.

"I don't know," Gavin answered.

"What should I tell people if they come in to see you or try to call you?"

"Tell them I'll be in later," Gavin replied.

"Then you are coming in eventually?" Margarite asked.

"I don't know," Gavin answered.

There was a pause.

"Anything else?" he asked.

"I guess not," Margarite said. "I just wanted to tell you that detective was trying to get ahold of you. He wanted me to give him your cell number, but I didn't think that you would want me to do that."

"Okay, you did right. You can call me if something comes up. Otherwise, you don't know where I am."

"I don't know where you are," Margarite replied.

"Right." Gavin ended the call and looked at the number he had written down on the paper. Gavin had tried to call the detective the day before, but now he was questioning himself. He didn't trust Glenda, he didn't trust Harvey, who worked for Glenda, so why should he trust a private detective that Glenda had hired? The risk was too high. If he did contact this Hancock guy, then what? Glenda and Harvey find him, torture him, kill him? "What you got yourself into is beyond your wildest dreams," Harvey's own words. Gavin had to think before he talked to Glenda's private investigator. He had no idea which way to turn; he was an attorney for Christ's sake.

It was eleven o'clock, check-out time. He had to decide if he was going to stay at the LeVant another night or stay somewhere else. He was still paranoid about Sylvia and the cowboy. He rationalized that if they were agents of Glenda, why wouldn't they have gotten him while he dozed last night while Sylvia was up there alone with him and the cowboy was down at the bar? They didn't. But what did that mean? Even if they weren't working for Glenda, they were bound to talk, and Glenda had ears all over Omaha, and especially in the Old Market district. Gavin decided that he would drive down to Bellevue and find a hotel to hole up in while he tried to figure something out. The last thing he wanted to do is be predictable. Two things first, though: he needed to get out of the Old Market district and stay out of Council Bluffs. That was clear to him. Beyond that his immediate concern was what he was going to do all day. If he made it out of the hotel and to his car without getting nabbed, he needed to keep moving.

Carston drove into the lot at Smart Auto Body and Repair and parked. Kenny's car was parked right outside the door in his handicapped parking space. Kenny was not handicapped. He stole the sign somewhere and put it up so that no one would take his parking place. Eight parking spots, and Kenny wanted to make sure no one else got the one closest to the door. David's Silverado was parked next to Kenny's car. Carston went into the building and saw that Kenny was in his office. He could hear wrenches clanging in the back. The sights and sounds of Smart Auto Body and Repair never changed. Carston went to the door of the office, knocked on the door frame and when Kenny looked up, he went in and took his seat.

"Find your hearse?" Kenny asked.

"Nope," Carston replied. "You hear anything?"

"No, and I been asking around," Kenny replied.

"How was the finger wave?" Carston asked.

"Fucking swollen prostate," Kenny replied. "The doctor felt around and gave me a prescription for some medication that is supposed the make the swelling go down. Got to get a colonoscopy next month. Earliest they could get me in. Until then I just feel like I gotta piss all the time."

"Pretty stimulating conversation," Carston remarked.

"Well, you are the one that brought it up," Kenny shot back.

"Irritable?" Carston remarked.

"A little," Kenny replied. "You would be irritable too if you just got back from someone sticking their finger up your ass and feeling around. What about the hearse?"

"You know a guy named Gavin Barker?" Carston inquired.

"Vince Barker's kid," Kenny replied. "Sure. He dated my daughter Kathy a couple of times when they were in high school. Him and David and some kid named Harvey something were pals. I think David and Gavin played baseball at Abe Lincoln."

"Harvey something?" Carston repeated.

"Yeah, big kid, mean."

Carston pondered that bit of information for a moment and put it away for later. "Do they still keep in touch?" Carston asked.

"I don't know," Kenny said. "I doubt it. Barker became a lawyer and works over in Omaha. I don't know what happened to the Harvey kid. He got a scholarship to play football somewhere. Why?"

"If I asked David what he knew about Barker, what would he tell me?" Carston asked.

"Why you asking me what David would say?" Kenny inquired. "Go ask him yourself."

"I'm asking you," Carston replied.

"Probably what I just told you," Kenny said. "That they was friends in high school and that Barker went to college and became a lawyer."

Carston thought for a moment. He wasn't sure how much of his hand he wanted to reveal.

"Yesterday and today, two times I've talked to David. Just chatting about the stolen hearse, not about his glory days or anything else. And both times he told me that I needed to take a close look at this Gavin Barker. That he had something to do with my missing hearse. He was sure of it."

Kenny snorted. "Shit, David thinks he knows everything, just ask him. If he don't know something, he'll make something up."

Carston paused to think again.

"Gavin Barker's dad was driving the hearse when it got stolen. Him and another guy parked it and went into Spaghetti Works to eat, and while they were in there eating the hearse got stolen. I mentioned that to David, and he came up with Gavin Barker without even thinking about it."

"There you go," Kenny nodded his head. "First name that comes to mind and he throws it out there to make himself sound like he knows something. He likes to hear himself talk."

"What are you guys talking about?" The two turned abruptly toward the door where David was standing.

"Nothing," Kenny replied quickly. "Talking about some guy we both know."

Carston was nodding his head in agreement.

"I got that F-250 done and it's ready to go out," David addressed Kenny and ignored Carston. "I'm going to start in on that Sentra that we got in yesterday."

"I'll let the owner of the F-250 know," Kenny said.

David leaned against the door frame and didn't move, creating an uncomfortable silence.

"I think I better get going. I'm not finding that hearse sitting here." Carston smiled at David. David did not return it.

Carston got up and squeezed past David, who turned just enough to allow him to pass through the door.

"Talk to you later," Kenny called after him.

Carston sat in his car enjoying the sun coming through the windshield. He was thinking about David and he wanted to agree with Kenny, David just liked to hear himself talk. It made no sense to him that someone like Gavin would plot to steal a hearse that his dad was driving, doing the job he had done Gavin's entire life. Not to mention that the owner of the hearse was also one of Gavin's clients. Why would he do that? What made more sense was that David's friend, who used to date his wife in high school, who went to college on a baseball scholarship and became a successful attorney working for an established law office in Omaha, made David feel like a loser in comparison, and maybe David might want to marginalize him. But then again, Carston thought, that didn't explain why Gavin Barker was trying to get ahold of him. If it wasn't for that, he would write Gavin off as David's bugaboo. And then there was Harvey something. "Glenda's Harvey?" he asked himself out loud. He was about the same age, big and mean. The three of them, Gavin, David, and Harvey something. There was a connection, the first one he had made in two days.

Carston found the number for Harmon and Mott and placed the call.

"Harmon and Mott Funeral Home and Crematorium," Henry's now-familiar voice answered.

"Henry, this is Carston."

Henry sighed. "Yes," he said apologetically.

"They're not around?" Carston asked.

"They went to pick up a body in Atlantic," Henry said. "I don't know when they will be back. I'm sorry."

"What's with those two?" Carston was irritated. "Why are they avoiding me?"

Henry sighed again. "I inherited this business from my father, and when I did, I inherited Vince and Bill. They have been here since I was a kid. They do what they have to do. Otherwise, they do what they want to do, and they don't want to talk to you."

"Why?" Carston asked, more irritated than before.

"Because you want them to," Henry replied. "That is all there is to it. You want to talk to them, so they don't want to talk to you. That's Vince and Bill. That's the way they are. If you didn't want to talk to them, they would be talking your ear off."

"Damn it!" Carston exclaimed.

"There's an Omaha police detective trying to get them to call, too. He isn't having any more luck than you are," Henry said in an attempt to console Carston and let him know that it wasn't anything personal.

"An Omaha police detective?" Carston asked.

"Yes, called about an hour ago, just after they left. I called Vince's cell to tell him and he didn't answer. And his voicemail is full, so I couldn't leave him a message. I don't know what else to do," Henry apologized. "I'll remind them again when they get back."

"I suppose you wouldn't do me a favor and not tell them that a detective from the Omaha PD is also trying to contact them," Carston suggested.

Henry laughed. "They aren't going to call him either, so don't worry about that," he replied. "Why?"

"Just that I get a bonus if I find the hearse before the cops," Carston replied.

"A bonus for finding it first?" Henry asked.

"That's the deal," Carston replied.

"I just want my hearse back with that body," Henry exclaimed. "I don't care who finds it first."

"I understand that," Carston replied. "I want you to get it back too. I just want to be the one who gets it back."

"Well, I'm not going to tell them not to call the Omaha PD detective," Henry replied. "But they aren't going to, so what's the point?"

"Henry, I want you to get your hearse back and I'm working it as hard as I can to find it for you," Carston reassured him.

Carston ended the call. If an Omaha PD detective was following up leads, it was only a matter of time until Carston lost his bonus. They had more resources, more connections and a wider net than Carston did. He was going to have to make something happen quick if he was going to find the hearse before they did. He had to think.

Coming to terms

Xavier picked Gimp's ringing phone up off the passenger's seat and answered it. It was Zee.

"Hello," he said in a jovial tone.

"What's going on?" Zee asked pointedly.

"Right now, I'm sitting in a parking lot in a shitty part of Council Bluffs, watching some private detective sitting in his car across the street and not moving," Xavier replied.

"Why are you watching a private detective?" Zee asked.

"George told me to," Xavier replied off-handedly.

There was a pause. "Who is George?"

"The local guy who was feeding Gimp his leads," Xavier explained.

"You talked to him?"

"Yep," Xavier replied.

"And his name is George?"

"That's the name he made up when I pressed him on it," Xavier explained.

There was another pause. "What about the plan that after you talk to George, you call me up before you do anything?"

"I wanted to see what's up with this private detective first," Xavier explained. "Gimp found out about him last night and we did a drive-by his office. We didn't follow up, though. You know, Gimp getting himself shot and all. So George told me that I should follow this detective because he is looking for the hearse too, so I am. Let him do the legwork."

"Why do you trust this George all of a sudden?" Zee asked. "You don't think he's setting you up too?"

"Fuck no, I don't trust him," Xavier exclaimed. "I don't trust anyone. But he doesn't know that."

"But you are following the private detective like he told you to do?" Zee asked.

"It's the best lead I have right now," Xavier replied.

There was a long pause.

"I know you are running the show here," Xavier said after a moment of silence. "But I'm not stupid. I can think. I'm not trying to fuck with you. Just the opposite, I want to do a good job for you."

"I don't want you to end up like Gimp. One, I don't want another dead Hell Fighter to explain, and two, I don't know who would take your place if you get yourself killed."

"We are on the same page there," Xavier said. "I assure you, anything at all substantial comes up, I'll call you and let you know. But right now I'm following this private detective and it appears to me that he's looking for the same thing we are. Hopefully he knows what he's doing, because I don't have anything else. I'm winging it."

"Nobody knows what's going on right now," Zee confided. "It wasn't supposed to go down like this."

"I figured that," Xavier replied.

"Listen, try this," Zee said. "I want you to call George. Just ask him if he knows Glenn Thompson. See what he says. Don't say anything, don't explain anything. If he asks, just tell him the name came up in your travels. Don't hurry him, see what he says. Then call me back and tell me exactly what he says."

"Okay," Xavier said with some expectation in his voice. "You want to tell me who Glenn Thompson is?"

"I'll tell you what it's all about when you call me back. I don't want you to know when you talk to George. Just say it's a name that came up. Play it just like that. I'm curious what he says, exactly what he says. Ask him and call me back."

"I will do that," Xavier said.

"Do you have a number that I can call you on? Gimp's phone has to be going dead."

"I got a charger; Gimp's phone is fine," Xavier replied. "We might as well keep using it."

The call ended and Xavier found George's number. The phone rang twice.

"X," George answered. "What do you need?"

"Yep," Xavier replied. "Hey, I'm following this detective, have been all morning. He's just making the rounds, it appears to me. You think that I should stay on him, or you got a better idea? I got nothing myself right now, but this guy isn't doing anything."

"Stay on him," George said. "I think he is going to find the hearse sooner than later. Might as well let him do the legwork."

"You're probably right," Xavier agreed. "Say, I got another question: you know a Glenn Thompson?"

There was a long pause. Xavier was smiling and waiting. The name had certainly registered.

"No, I don't think so," George replied a few beats too late.

"Are you sure you never heard of Glenn Thompson? Because the name came up," Xavier said. "I thought that maybe you had heard it before, you being local and all."

"I don't know her," George replied.

"But you heard the name?" Xavier pressed.

"Yeah, I've heard the name, but I don't know her," George answered.

"Okay, probably nothing," Xavier replied. "I'm going to just keep following this detective for now, unless you come up with something else I can work on."

"I'll let you know if I do," George assured him.

"Talk to you later then." As soon as Xavier ended the call, he called the number for Zee. It rang once and he answered.

"What did you find out?"

"George doesn't know her," Xavier reported.

"Bingo," Zee responded.

"I'm guessing that you're guessing that he does know her," Xavier stressed the pronoun.

"I'm guessing that George is working for her," Zee replied.

"You going to tell me who she is then?" Xavier asked.

There was a pause.

"I can go hunt her down and ask her myself if you want," Xavier suggested.

"No," Zee replied quickly. "Glenda Thompson, she runs some businesses in Omaha."

"What kind of businesses?" Xavier asked pointedly.

210

"A sleazy bar, a pawn shop," Zee replied. "She has some real estate, rentals, both commercial and residential."

"Bar owner and real estate mogul," Xavier commented. "I'm assuming her real estate empire is not high rent."

"Nope," Zee replied. "More like slumlord."

"I'm also going to assume she is, let's say, nothing above board," Xavier said.

"Yep," Zee replied.

"So how does Glenda Thompson fit into our missing hearse?" Xavier asked.

There was a pause on the other end.

"Where are you at?" Xavier broke the silence.

"Why?" Zee asked. "What difference does it make?"

"I'm trying to be straight with you," Xavier replied. "You are running the show here. No problem there. But your area code is Montreal. That's a long ways away to micro-manage this fiasco. I want to work with you. I want to prove myself. But I need to know what the fuck it is you are doing."

Here was another pause. Xavier waited this one out.

"Something is hidden inside the casket that is in that hearse that some very powerful people in Omaha want," Zee said. He was realizing that Xavier was a bit smarter than the hired thugs he was used to working. He needed to be careful to stay a step ahead of him.

"What's in the casket?" Xavier asked. "Besides a body, obviously."

"Seriously, that is still above your pay grade. But what is in it is valuable, and it is imperative that it ends up with the right people. The Hell Fighters agreed to help me get it through customs and to Omaha. They came up with the idea for the casket. Putting two and two together, and knowing Glenda Thompson, she got wind of the plan and made her own."

"I thought that Gimp and I were going to jack it," Xavier asked.

"Yes, Gimp was going to jack the hearse, remove the valuable cargo from the casket, and park the hearse somewhere it would be found and the authorities would think that it was just abandoned and wouldn't know why. Then he was going to make sure the cargo got delivered to the right people. He had it all worked out. It was supposed to be smooth going."

"It was never going back to Montreal then, like Gimp said?" Xavier asked.

"Just a little misdirection to keep the plan under wraps," Zee said. "Nothing more."

"In case I blabbed?" Xavier responded.

"Nothing personal," Zee replied.

"You think that Glenda Thompson jacked the hearse out from under us and she has it?" Xavier asked.

"I think that her plan, whatever it was, went haywire too," Zee replied. "Because if it had gone as planned for her, the hearse would have been found by now and that detective wouldn't still be out there looking for it. Something happened."

"What makes you think the detective is still looking for it?" Xavier asked.

"If he wasn't, George wouldn't have you following him," Zee replied.

"And why does he have me following him?" Xavier asked, halfway knowing the answer, but wanting to hear it from Zee.

"He wants to keep track of you both, and he does that by having you follow the detective. Wherever the detective is, you will be," Zee explained. "And then when and if the detective finds the hearse, they have you both."

"What happens then?" Xavier asked.

"Nothing good for you," Zee said. "I don't know about the detective. But the important thing is that we have the upper hand, because we know what is going on and they don't know that we know."

"It's a dangerous game we're playing," Xavier observed. "And it seems I'm the one in the crosshairs."

"You said you were up to it," Zee replied.

"You said there'd be a promotion," Xavier countered.

"If you pull this off, you will be legend," Zee replied.

"I'll keep following the detective," Xavier said.

"You got your gun?" Zee asked.

"I do," Xavier answered.

"Keep it close."

Xavier did not comment.

"Anything else?" Zee asked.

Xavier thought for a moment. "Who's in the casket?" he asked. "Just curious who's guarding the goods."

There was silence on the other end. "Me," Zee finally answered.

"Okay, glad I asked," was all that Xavier could say.

The call ended. The detective was backing out of his parking space. Xavier hunkered down, peering over the dash between the steering wheel. He quickly jotted "Smart Auto Repair" on a notepad on the console and pulled onto the street a judicious distance behind Carston. So far Carston had made two stops since he left his office. The first had been Marzoe's, the bar where Gimp and he had been the night before, less than a half hour before Gimp got himself shot and killed. While he had been waiting across the street for Carston to leave the bar, he had tried to figure out what Marzoe's had to do with the missing hearse. He had ticked off a list of considerations in his notebook. Gimp and he had gone in there asking questions. The bartender had freely given them Carston Hancock's business card and told them that the detective was looking for a missing hearse as well. Was it possible that it was the bartender who set them up, not George? If he did, how and why? Did he tip off the detective, and did the detective set up an ambush at the funeral home? As they made their way south toward Interstate 80, Xavier wondered exactly how much the detective knew about the whole operation. Did he know that Glenn Thompson had the hearse stolen before Gimp could jack it and it didn't go according to plan?

Xavier thought about that for a moment. Did Zee know that this Glenn Thompson stole the hearse before Gimp had the chance, or is that just what Zee presumed? Was anything Zee was telling him even true? This story just had so many holes. Xavier couldn't be sure of anything or anyone.

He followed Carston onto the interstate and across the bridge into Omaha. It was easy to tail him in the traffic, and he stayed close until Carston put on his turn signals to take the 84th street exit. When he did, Xavier backed off. He didn't want to follow Carston into the exit too closely. He hoped that other cars took the same exit so that he could merge in with them unnoticed. Luck was with him, a car and a pickup truck squeezed between him and Carston and took the same exit. Xavier got into line. He caught back up just as Carston pulled into the parking lot at Flingnasties. Xavier recognized the bar. He had been there before a few times. He read the neon sign on the wall beside the door. "Y'all cum on in." Xavier parked in the corner of the lot and watched Carston go inside.

Xavier found his notebook and pen. He wrote "Flingnasties" under Smart Auto Repair with a question mark. How does Flingnasties fit into the equation, he asked himself. This detective likes bars, he thought. Maybe he's just catching a matinee. Maybe he likes to drink. Xavier sat in his truck waiting and watching. He hated waiting. He had been following Hancock for most of the day and waiting. It wasn't getting him anywhere. Xavier decided to take in the matinee as well. He took off his leather jacket and his Hell Fighters colors and stowed them on the floorboard behind the seat. It was warming up anyway, he didn't need a jacket. He got out of his truck, locked the door and headed to the entrance of Flingnasties.

The first person Xavier ran into as soon as he came through the door was a doorman sitting on a stool, his attention on his phone. A sign above his head announced a ten-dollar cover, no exceptions. Xavier attempted to walk past unnoticed.

"Ten bucks," the doorman said, not looking up from his phone.

Xavier stopped. The doorman was even bigger than Xavier, and Xavier was huge. He noted that the doorman's arms stretched the fabric of his shirtsleeves. He looked like he was all muscle. Xavier got out his billfold and found two five-dollar bills. He held them out to the doorman, who took them from his hand and placed them in a cash box on a table next to the stool and handed him an orange ticket.

"Free drink," he said without looking up. A baseball bat leaned against the wall behind him. Xavier was not easily intimidated, but even he would have hesitated to take on the doorman.

Xavier walked into the bar, tucking his billfold back into his pocket. He did a quick scan of the first room and instantly spotted Hancock sitting at the bar with a woman, and the woman was not one of the strippers. She was dressed stylishly in a pair of tan slacks, boots to her knees and a beige satin blouse. She looked to Xavier almost like one of those equestrian riders he had seen during the summer Olympics one night late after all the good sports were over. She looked his way and he quickly moved to the other side of the stage and took a seat where he could pretend to watch the dancer dry hump a pole and still see Hancock and the woman. He suddenly wondered if he was watching the aforementioned Glenn Thompson talk to the detective.

216

A waitress wearing a bikini and carrying an empty tray came by and asked Xavier what he was drinking. Xavier ordered a Miller Lite and gave her the orange ticket. She left for the bar. The dancer had moved from the pole to a position in front of him, blocking his view of Hancock and the woman. He tried to look between her legs. The dancer thought that he was trying to get a look at her crotch and squatted down, undulating her hips in a seductive manner, working to keep his attention. Xavier tried to look around her. She began to move back and forth, still squatting and still undulating. The vision of Carston leaving revealed itself just as the dancer swung herself to the right and Xavier peered to her left. He got up and went after Hancock, leaving the dancer to seduce an empty chair. The waitress, the tray holding a Miller Lite in her hand, watched him head to the door. She followed him to the doorman and spoke to him for a moment, then shrugged and took the beer back to the bar. Someone would order a Miller Lite.

What's really going on?

Carston pulled into the parking lot at Flingnasties and parked. It was four in the afternoon and the lot was packed for the afternoon matinee. Carston came through the door. Harvey was sitting on a stool looking at his phone.

"Ten bucks," he said, not looking up.

"Fuck you," Carston shot back.

Harvey jerked his head up.

"Checking in with the boss," Carston said.

Harvey tossed his head toward the door and went back to his phone. Carston momentarily toyed with the thought of challenging Harvey over his possible connections to Gavin Barker and David Long but decided that Harvey was too hard a nut to crack there in the entry to the bar. He let it go, turned and walked into the first bar. He spotted Glenda sitting in the same spot she was the last time he had visited her there. She looked up as he approached.

"You find my hearse yet?" she asked him pointedly.

"Nope," Carston replied.

Glenda gave him a look that said she wasn't happy about his progress in the case.

"I'm busting ass on this case," Carston said in his own defense. "Your hearse fell off the face of the earth, but I'm working on it." Carston emphasized the "your hearse."

"You realize that if the cops find it first, you get jack shit," Glenda said.

"I get five bills a day," Carston corrected her.

"You get jack shit," Glenda responded.

"That's not the deal," Carston said tentatively, but like challenging Harvey, he knew when to let it go. He needed the money and he didn't want to push the subject to the point that he might force himself to walk away from it.

"So why are you here?" Glenda asked.

"I've got a few questions," Carston replied. "There's been a couple of things transpire in the last day or so. I'm not sure what to make of them. I thought that I would run them past you and see if you could help me understand them better. Maybe help me get some kind of perspective, help me with the case, if you know what I mean."

"No, I don't know what you mean," Glenda replied. "But fire away."

Carston paused to decide how he wanted to start. "Does the name Gavin Barker mean anything to you?"

"Nope," Glenda replied.

"He's a lawyer. He's a junior partner at Barton Law Offices," Carston said. "He tried to call me yesterday. He wanted to talk to me."

"Maybe your wife hired him." Glenda raised her eyebrows and smiled.

"You know, that was my first thought when my receptionist told me that he was trying to get ahold of me," Carston replied in a seemingly thoughtful manner, testing her reaction. "But I talked to my wife last night, and she said that she didn't hire him." Carston raised his own eyebrows and smiled back.

"Then what does he have to do with anything?" Glenda asked.

"Just that Gavin Barker is the son of Vince Barker, and Vince Barker was driving the hearse that was stolen."

"Well that is interesting," Glenda perked up.

Carston couldn't tell if her interest was genuine or if she was playing his game. "Coincidence?" he asked.

"Why don't you return the call, talk to him and find out?" Glenda suggested slyly.

"I've been trying." Carston was deciding if he should tell her about the appointment Gavin had made and then not showed up for. He decided to not reveal that part of the story for the moment. "He is also the attorney for Harmon and Mott Funeral Home and Crematorium."

"I don't know what to advise you about him then," Glenda shrugged. "I guess you keep trying to call him and ask. Maybe he knows something no one else does. Sounds like a good person to talk to."

"Yep," Carston agreed. "I'm playing phone tag with him. Hopefully we connect here soon."

"Hopefully," Glenda agreed.

The two sat for a moment not saying anything. Carston was watching Glenda. From where she sat she could see every patron who came through the door, and every patron who came through the door got the onceover. At the moment her attention was on one particular patron who had just entered. Carston took a quick glance. He was a big guy, at least six-two or six-three, plaid shirt, long hair and a beard. He looked like a lumberjack. Carston turned his full attention back to Glenda, but she was still watching the lumberjack. The bartender came up and asked

Carston if he could get him anything. Carston ordered a Fat Tire.

"What else?" Glenda asked, returning her attention to Carston.

"Why would the Hell Fighters motorcycle club be looking for your Uncle Thomas?"

Glenda raised her eyebrows at the question and shook her head slowly back and forth. Carston felt like she was attempting to make convincing facial expressions to all of his questions and the exaggerated manner that she was doing it telegraphed to Carston that she knew much more than she was pretending to. It was a one-way conversation so far and he was feeding her information and getting nothing in return.

"I wouldn't know," Glenda replied after a moment. "What brought that up?"

"Yesterday I was in a bar over in Council Bluffs, a bar where the two fellows who were driving the hearse when it got stolen hang out a lot, it seems. They didn't happen to be there at the time, so I was talking to the bartender, asking regular questions that a detective who was looking for a stolen hearse might ask the bartender at the neighborhood bar where the drivers of the hearse that got stolen hang out," Carston said. He paused for effect, then continued. "Later on, I got a call from that very same bartender telling me that two Hell Fighters were in there asking the same questions of him."

"Interesting," Glenda responded. "What do you make of that?"

Carston didn't answer for a moment. He watched Glenda. She knew something and she was wondering how much he knew, he could see it in her face.

"One of them got shot and killed later last night," Carston replied.

"No kidding?" Glenda exclaimed. This time she seemed genuinely surprised.

"Yes," Carston responded. "And the most interesting part of the story is that he was gunned down in the parking lot of the Harmon and Mott Funeral Home and Crematorium."

Glenda did not respond.

"What do you think they were doing there?" Carston inquired.

"You said there were two; what happened to the other one?" Glenda asked, not answering his question.

"No idea," Carston replied.

"This is just the strangest thing," Glenda commented, shaking her head. "Poor Uncle Thomas just wanted to be buried here in Omaha, where he grew up. Now all of this is happening. I just don't know what to make of it. I guess that's why I hired you, to figure it all out."

"I guess so," Carston said. "Who would have thought that it would be so hard and so complicated to find Uncle Thomas? I mean, who in their right mind would want Uncle Thomas that bad, other than you, of course?"

"I know," Glenda said. "It is strange."

"You would think that whoever stole that hearse, when they realized he was in the back, they would want to drop him off on a street corner somewhere. I mean, if they wanted to keep the hearse for some reason," Carston reflected. "And I really can't figure out why they would want to hang on to a hearse. It might be fun to drive around for a little while, but then what? I got some connections that know quite a bit about stolen vehicles, and they seem to think that unloading a hearse wouldn't be that profitable for someone looking to sell it. You would think that whoever took it would have dumped it by now."

"You would think so," Glenda agreed.

Carston stood up. "Well, I was hoping you might shed some light on those two occurrences, but if you can't, then I guess I better go out there and see if I can follow up and figure out what they have to do with anything."

"I guess so," Glenda agreed.

Carston turned and left. The bartender brought his Fat Tire and looked at Glenda, then toward the door where Carston was walking out. Glenda shrugged her shoulders and the bartender took the beer away. Glenda watched the dancer on the stage undulating her hips to an empty chair. She had given up long ago trying to figure out dancers. Half the time they were strung out anyway. She glanced toward the door where Carston had left. One of the waitresses was talking to Harvey, a tray balanced on her hand. Harvey shook his head and got up. The waitress returned to the end of the bar. Harvey went to the door and out of sight. He returned momentarily and glanced around, then came straight to the bar and took up the stool that Carston had just vacated.

"I think some guy is tailing Hancock," Harvey informed her.

"How's that?" Glenda asked.

"Just some guy came in right after he did, then left right behind him," Harvey replied.

Glenda shrugged her shoulders. "So?"

"Waitress said he came in, sat down over on the other side of the stage and ordered a beer. She said that she went to get it and he took off before she could get back. He went out right behind Carston."

"Big guy in a plaid shirt," Glenda commented.

"That's him," Harvey said.

"I noticed him come in. Big boy," Glenda remarked.

"He paid a ten-dollar cover, then left right behind Carston. He didn't stay for a set or his beer or anything," Harvey replied.

"I'm going to my office to make a call," Glenda said. "Maybe he went out to get something and is coming back in. If he does, come tell me."

"Will do," Harvey replied. He got up and went back to his stool inside the door. Glenda went to her office, pulled up a number and dialed her cell phone. It rang six times and went to voicemail. She did not leave a message. She sat, waiting. A few minutes later her phone rang. It was the number she had just called.

"What's up?" the voice on the other end asked.

"Carston Hancock was in here asking questions," Glenda answered. "Wanted to know if I ever heard of Gavin Barker. And he also told me about a biker that got shot and killed over in Council Bluffs last night."

"Okay," the voice on the other end replied thoughtfully.

"What's the deal with that?" she asked.

"Okay, it's all good. The other biker, the one that didn't get shot, he's following Hancock. Now we know where they both are."

"That we do," Glenda said noncommittally.

"The questions about Gavin are a little more troubling."

"I thought so as well," Glenda replied. "Hancock says that Gavin is trying to get ahold of him but he hasn't been able to get ahold of Gavin. He says that they are playing phone tag."

"Just a matter of time."

"Yes, it is," Glenda replied. "And if he does, what then?"

There was a pause.

"What I'm saying is that if Gavin and Carston connect, and Gavin tells Carston that we told him to steal that hearse, then what?" Glenn continued. "Carston is going to want to know why I'm looking for a hearse that I had stolen. He might have some questions along those lines, questions that I really don't want to have to answer."

"You don't think that if Gavin calls him up and tells him where the hearse is, Carston won't just call you up and collect his pay, not ask a lot of questions, just let it go? You don't think that he'll take his money and run?"

"I'm not sure anymore," Glenda replied. "Point is, if Gavin tells him everything, do we want Carston out there knowing it all? Seems like a loose end."

"You're probably right, I guess, when you put it that way."

There was a pause.

"You got a plan in that case?" Glenda asked.

225

"Just one more to player to deal with. If we can get them all together at the same time, I can take care of it."

"Can you do that?" Glenda asked.

"I think so, I can do that," the voice on the other end assured her.

"I'm leaving it with you then, you keep doing what you need to do," Glenda replied. "But one thing: I want to be there when you pick up that hearse. Before anyone sees it or touches it, I want to be there. That means you, too."

"I'm aware of that."

"And I don't want to be involved in any of the dirty work when we do find it. I don't pay people to get my own hands dirty," Glenda replied.

"I'm quite aware of that too."

Glenda ended the call. She was not happy about the way this whole scenario was playing out. It seemed odd to her that Gavin would be looking for Carston while Carston was looking for Gavin. Somewhere along the line, something was going on that she wasn't in control of. There weren't very many ways that Gavin and Carston could have found out about each other. She figured one of two people had gone off script, and she had just gotten off the phone with one of them.

Glenda did not like complications, and this plan was supposed to be cut and dried. Now all of a sudden it was a cluster fuck with three loose cannons: Gavin, Carston and the biker. Maybe four loose cannons if she factored in the man she had just spoken to. She had not ordered any biker shot the night before. Things were not going as planned, and it made her very nervous when the people working for her were winging it, and that was exactly what they were doing.

Carston and Gavin hatch a plan

Carston's phone rang just as he was about to pull out of the Flingnasties parking lot. He threw the car into reverse and parked it. He recognized the number.

"Hey," he said quickly into the phone as he caught the call after the fourth ring.

"Carston, what are you up to?" Megan asked.

"Nothing important," Carston replied.

"Are you working a case?" she asked.

Carston was a bit confused about why he was getting this call. It sounded like Megan was calling just to chat. He was not expecting that.

"Yes, I am," he replied. "I'm trying to locate a stolen hearse, actually."

"You don't get a case like that every day," Megan exclaimed.

"No, I don't," Carston laughed.

"I won't take up too much of your time," Megan started.

"I always have all the time in the world for you," Carston replied.

"Probably not if you are working a case, but it is nice of you to say so," Megan said. "I was just thinking, you know that French restaurant, that one we like in the Old Market?"

"I sure do," Carston replied.

"Why don't we go there Friday night, sit down to a nice supper, and talk?" Megan suggested.

"I would love to do that," Carston replied, his heartbeat speeding up. "What time?"

"What time do you want to pick me up?" Megan asked.

Carston didn't have an immediate answer. He had not thought about picking her up.

"How about seven?" Megan suggested.

"Perfect," Carston replied.

"Listen, Carston," Megan said in a serious voice. "This is a date. We are going on a date, nothing more. We are going back to the starting line. See what happens. Think 'first date' when you come to pick me up."

"I got it," Carston replied enthusiastically.

"Afterwards you take me home, maybe get a goodnight kiss if you are lucky, and you go back to your little one room at the Hotel LeVant."

"First date," Carston assured her that he was in complete understanding. "I'll make a reservation, seven thirty."

"You do that," Megan said sternly. "And you make that reservation yourself, not your secretary."

"Absolutely, I'll make it right now," Carston answered.

"I'll see you tomorrow, then," Megan said. "Good luck with your stolen hearse."

"Tomorrow," Carston said into the phone, but Megan had already ended the call.

Carston went straight to google and found the website for the French restaurant where they had spent many evenings sharing a meal and a bottle of wine while they were dating and for the first year or so after they got married. They hadn't been there for years, though. He was happy to see that it was still in business. He punched the number on the screen and waited while it rang.

It was getting late in the day for February, and the sun was getting near sunset. It got dark early in February. The temp had been unseasonably warm all day, above freezing, but it was already dropping rapidly with the waning light. Still, it felt like the frigid below-zero wind chills they had been suffering for two weeks were gone for the time being, and Gavin was happy for that.

Gavin had been driving around all day, and he was filling the tank of his BMW for the second time. He had driven highway six all the way to Lincoln and back. He had pulled in at the outlet mall in Gretna, just west of Omaha, where he got out to stretch his legs. At the moment Gavin was walking around the Nike store and wondering what to do next. He looked at his phone for the fifth time in ten minutes. He had two calls from Harvey that he had not answered and one text message. He did not listen to the voice mails, but the text simply told him to please call Carston Hancock. He had received it two hours ago. Gavin had gotten his phone out to make the call twice and had second thoughts. The worst thing about it was that he didn't know why he was hesitant to call the private detective.

He cursed himself. His whole life had been one success after another. He was a successful high school student. He was a successful baseball player, he was successful in college and successful with law school. He was successful in his job. On the surface to anyone looking in, Gavin should reek of self confidence. The reality was that all his

life Gavin had been so afraid of not succeeding that
he had developed a phobia about it. Gavin did not
trust himself anymore. He didn't feel successful, he
felt lucky. And as time went on he was becoming
afraid that his luck was going to run out someday.
Under his current circumstances he was double
afraid that someday was going to be now. Gavin
did not know what to do. He was paralyzed. He
had no one to tell him whether to round the base
and keep going, or to hold up.

Gavin pocketed his phone, left the Nike store
and went to his BMW, which was parked out away
from the rest of the cars that were near the stores.
He got in and turned the ignition. The engine was
still semi warm and the air coming from the vent
was comfortable. Gavin looked at his phone again.
He sighed. He had put the number in his contacts
under the letters CH at some point. He pulled it up
and looked at it for a full minute before he punched
the call button. The phone rang twice.

"Carston Hancock," a voice answered.

"Detective Carston Hancock?" Gavin felt
foolish as soon as he asked. Of course it was
detective Carston Hancock.

"Yes."

"My name is Gavin Barker. My secretary said
that you have been trying to get ahold of me,"
Gavin said, trying to keep his voice from going
straight to hysterical.

"I have been trying to get ahold of you,"
Carston replied. "Where are you?"

"Why do you want to know where I am?"
Gavin asked, immediately suspicious.

"Because I would like to meet up with you to talk about a case I'm working on. You might have some information that could help me."

Gavin didn't answer.

"I'm just pulling out of a bar over here by Crossroads, Flingnasties," Carston said. "Can I meet you somewhere? You name it."

At the mention of Flingnasties, Gavin stabbed his finger on the screen and abruptly ended the call. He stared at his phone. It startled him when it started ringing moments later and the letters CH showed up on the screen. Gavin hesitated for a moment, then answered the call.

"I think I lost you there for a moment," Carston said in a friendly manner. Gavin was quite sure that Carston was aware that he had ended the call. "You must have driven through a tunnel."

"Yes," Gavin replied, not knowing what else to say.

"Let me lay it all out right here," Carston began talking rapidly, hoping to keep Gavin on the line. "Here's what I got, just bear with me, please. Yesterday I had a client come in and hire me. Seems her uncle died in Montreal, Canada, and the body was coming into Eppley by plane. The funeral home, Harmon and Mott, sent a hearse over to pick up the body. Just a normal, routine event for them. After they picked up the body the driver and another employee who was helping decided to stop and have lunch at Spaghetti Works in the Old Market district and they left the hearse running outside with the body of my client's uncle in it. Someone stole the hearse while they were in Spaghetti Works eating. My client hired me to find the hearse. I've been all over looking for it and asking about it." Carston took a quick breath and hurried on. "There are three things I'm hoping you can help me with. First off, your father Vince was driving the hearse when it got stolen. I have been having a hell of a time catching up to him. I was hoping that you might help me connect up so that I can talk to him. The second thing, Harmon and Mott is one of your clients. A lot of people seem to think this was just a joy rider taking advantage of a hearse sitting there parked and running, easy pickings. I don't think so. There are just a lot of things that make me think that this theft wasn't random. I was hoping you might be able to think of someone who might want to steal that hearse and for what reason. You are familiar with the place, the business, you are familiar with everyone involved there, you've probably been around there all your life. I thought that you could give me a few names, anyone, just someone that I can look at. I'm not making a lot of progress on this case. I need some direction." He paused.

"What's the third thing?" Gavin asked after a moment.

"Okay, don't hang up on me again, okay?" Carston replied. "There is some guy that you went to high school with who has told me more than a few times in the last couple days that you might be good for the theft. I'm not saying that you are," he continued quickly. "In fact, you look to me like the last person I would suspect, and that is what is working on me. What bothers me is why he keeps bringing up your name."

"Harvey Grant," Gavin exclaimed.

"No," Carston replied, surprised at the answer.

There was a pause. "Who?" Gavin asked.

"A fellow named David Long," Carston replied.

"David Long! Why would he tell you that I would be good for it?" Gavin asked, letting his guard down.

"I'm asking you," Carston said. "I thought that it was strange too, especially when I talked to Henry Mott about you. He holds you in very high regard by the way," Carston added. "Everyone I talk to holds you in high regard except David."

Gavin didn't answer. He had no idea why David Long would be pointing a detective in his direction. "I don't know why he would tell you that I had something to do with stealing that hearse," Gavin finally said. "We were buddies at Abraham Lincoln, we played ball together, ran in the same crowd, but after high school we went our own ways. Until a few months ago, when David called me up at the office. Wanted to have some beers. We went out a couple of times to that bar over there by the funeral home. All we did is have a beer or two and catch up. Honestly, we have nothing in common anymore. When we were in high school I dated the gal he married. He spent most of the time telling me how well they were getting along and how great their marriage was. I got the feeling he was trying to convince me that he won. We went out two or three times after that, and then he quit calling me. I didn't try to get back to him. The friendship just wasn't there anymore. I figured that all he wanted to do was tell me how great his life was, and he did that."

"Okay, like I said, talking to everyone else, and your explanation, I think he just pulled your name out of his craw and wanted to make a little trouble. Maybe convince me that he won too. That what you think?"

"Maybe," Gavin agreed.

"So Gavin, can we touch base here this evening and go over those other things?" Carston asked. "I just want to run this stuff by you and let you see if you can make heads or tails of it."

"Why can't we just do it over the phone?" Gavin asked. "Why do you want to meet me somewhere?"

"Because it would be more personable," Carston replied. "Wouldn't you rather talk over a drink or a dinner than talk on the phone?"

"I'm not sure," Gavin answered.

Carston didn't respond.

"Look, I gotta go," Gavin hurriedly ended the call.

Carston looked at his phone screen and shook his head. He wondered if he should call back again. He didn't believe that Gavin stole the hearse, but he had something he didn't want to talk about. Carston needed to think about it, go over what had been said during their brief conversation that raised his suspicions.

Carston was putting his car into drive when his phone rang. He looked at it and recognized Gavin's number.

"Yes Gavin," Carston answered.

"I stole the hearse," Gavin blurted over the phone.

"You stole the hearse?" Carston repeated. He didn't know what else to say.

"Yes, I did," he replied.

"Do you want to tell me why you stole it?" Carston asked.

"Because Glenda Thompson told me to," Gavin answered.

"Glenda Thompson told you to steal the hearse, then hired me to find it?" Carston was trying to wrap his head around this surprising information. After a beat, he had a thought. "If she told you to steal the hearse for her, the one that I'm looking for, then can I assume that after you stole it you didn't deliver it where you were supposed to deliver it?"

"That is correct," Gavin said.

"Okay, first question: why did she want you to steal it?" Carston asked.

"First answer: I don't know," Gavin replied.

"She just asked you to steal a hearse, so you did," Carston exclaimed.

"There's more to it than that. I've been Glenda's lawyer for a while now. Let's just say that I've compromised myself a few times for her. Just a little bit, but enough. She asked me to get a set of the hearse keys, that's all, but then when I got them, she asked me to use them to steal it between Eppley and the funeral home. She seemed to know where it was going to be and when. Honestly, I didn't ask, and I didn't want to know," Gavin explained.

"So then things went south," Carston replied. "What happened?"

"An old friend from high school works for Glenda. He called me up just after I stole it, when I was on the way to deliver it. He called me up to tell me to be careful, to watch my ass," Gavin continued.

"Harvey?" Carston replied.

"You know him?" Gavin came close to ending the call again.

"I've met him," Carston replied. "I don't know him."

"It was the tone of his voice, you know?" Gavin said. "The way he said it. I freaked. It was just this cryptic message, you know, he didn't explain anything, just 'watch your ass.' I got scared. I took the hearse and hid it until I could figure out what he meant by 'watch your ass.'"

"What then?" Carston said quickly. He had Gavin on a roll, and he didn't want to slow down his momentum.

"Then Harvey kept calling and asking me where the hearse was. Telling me that I had to tell Glenda. The more he called the more scared I got. And then I woke up yesterday morning and there were two bikers parked behind my house poking around in my outbuildings." Gavin took a breath.

"What outbuildings?" Carston asked. "You are losing me with the bikers and the outbuildings."

"I live out in the country, north of Crescent. I have an acreage. The bikers were parked back behind my house, by my machine shed. They were looking in my barn. I mean, why would bikers be poking around my place? I don't know. I think that Glenda sent them. I got dressed, went out to the garage, got in my car, and took off as fast as I could. They tried to chase me, but I got a good head start on them. I've been running ever since."

"Okay," Carston said, putting on the brakes and slowing Gavin down a little. "These bikers, tell me more about the bikers. Slow down and take your time."

Gavin took a deep breath and continued. "I took off in my car and lost them. I drove around all day and I didn't go back home. I didn't want to get caught there. I stayed in a hotel last night. Then this morning I was actually thinking about calling you, and then I saw on the news that a biker was shot and killed in the parking lot of Harmon and Mott. I think it was one of those bikers that was at my place. Who else would it be? I just don't understand why Glenda would have bikers looking for the hearse."

"Maybe she doesn't," Carston said thoughtfully.

"What, then?" Gavin asked. "I got nothing to do with bikers."

"There is something in that coffin that Glenda wants," Carston replied thoughtfully. "Something those bikers want, too, but maybe they don't plan to give it to Glenda. I think maybe we are in a three-way race right now: the bikers, Glenda and the cops. Whoever finds the hearse first wins whatever the jackpot is inside. And I really want Glenda to win."

Gavin didn't speak.

"Where's the hearse?" Carston asked.

"Why do you want Glenda to win?" Gavin didn't answer the question.

"Because if she wins, I get my fee plus a bonus. If either of the other two wins, I get nothing. I got no other skin in the game. Nothing more, nothing less."

"What's in the coffin?" Gavin asked tentatively.

238

"I don't want to know, Gavin, and neither do you," Carston replied. "Where's the hearse?"

There was a long pause. "In a hangar at the Missouri Valley airport," Gavin finally said.

"Missouri Valley has an airport?" Carston responded, surprised.

"On sixth street. L20, just a mile south of town. It's a private strip. I have an old Piper there. I moved the plane out of the hangar and put the hearse in there."

"It is just sitting there in the hangar?" Carston asked. "It is locked? Do I need a key? Is there any other way to get in?"

"Locked up tight," Gavin replied. "Not a lot of security at the Missouri Valley airport."

"I'll need the key to the hangar, then," Carston said.

There was a long pause.

"You don't want to give me the key?" Carston asked.

"I want this over with. I want to go home," Gavin said.

"But you don't want to take any chances with me," Carston remarked.

Again, Gavin didn't reply.

"Do you happen to know the LeVant Hotel in Old Market?"

Gavin sucked in his breath and held it. "Why?" he finally asked.

"I live there. There are people all around there all the time. It is a public place. If you drop the key off at the desk, they will give it to me. I'll stay away, and you can text me after you drop it off. I'll get it and go up to Missouri Valley and take care of this hearse business. When Glenda has the hearse, I'll call you. You take care of things from there on for yourself. But until then, you are out of it. I take it from here. I promise you Gavin, all I want is that hearse. Fair enough?"

"Fair enough," Gavin replied.

"You got the keys to the hearse, or are they still in it?" Carston asked.

"I have them," Gavin replied. "It's locked up, too."

"Leave them at the desk. I don't want any hitches in the giddy-up. The quicker we get this done the better for both of us. You good?"

"I'm good," Gavin replied. "Let's do it."

Carston ended the call.

Gavin felt a load off his shoulders. He could see a way out now, pass the whole business off to Hancock. There was something about the guy that was honest. Gavin trusted him. He felt like they were on the same team. He drove toward downtown Omaha.

The key to the whole thing

Gavin found a parking space on the street outside the Hotel LeVant and walked into the lobby. A glance toward the bar as he went in showed a few of the after-work crowd hanging around in the lounge area. He looked for Sylvia on the off chance that she was sitting at the bar but didn't see her. He didn't know why, but he hoped she would be there. Gavin walked up to the desk. A different young man than the one from the evening before was talking on the desk phone. Gavin waited for him. He noticed that the young man's name tag said Tip. The young man asked whoever it was on the phone if they could hold for a minute and looked up expectantly at Gavin.

"I have a set of keys here for Mr. Carston Hancock. He said I could leave them here at the desk and he will pick them up later." Gavin placed a key ring with three keys on the counter and slid them across. Tip scooped them off and put them behind the counter without a word, then went back to his phone call. Gavin stood for a moment, but the man was obviously busy on the phone. He stepped away from the desk and looked around. He considered leaving, but then he looked over toward the bar. No one was paying any attention to anyone. Gavin surmised that most of the people there were looking for a hookup of some kind, either a business opportunity or a clandestine liaison. For the first time in two days he was feeling somewhat comfortable. Handing off the keys made the hearse someone else's problem. He stepped into the bar and took a stool. None of the half-dozen other people sitting at the bar made any attempt to look at him. Most of the tables were occupied. Gavin breathed freely.

"Sir?" Gavin recognized the bartender from the evening before.

"Could I get a margarita?" Gavin asked.

"On the rocks," the bartender remembered.

"Yes, please," Gavin replied.

"Want to put it on the room?" the bartender asked.

"I've checked out," Gavin replied. "I'm waiting for someone. I'll just pay here."

"I'll start a tab," the bartender walked away.

Gavin pulled his phone out of his pocket and brought up Carston's number. "The package is delivered," he texted and hit send.

A few minutes later the bartender returned with his drink. "If you're waiting for the woman you were having drinks with last night, I can give her a call and tell her you're here," the bartender offered.

"That's okay," Gavin replied. "I'm waiting on someone I met today at work."

The bartender nodded and walked away. Gavin turned and watched the door, sipping his margarita. People were coming in and out of the LeVant, but no one approached the desk. The man behind the counter was still on the phone. The woman who was working the desk the evening before came from somewhere and busied herself. Her name was Mona, if he remembered correctly.

Gavin's attention went to the door. The cowboy was coming in. As soon as he entered he stopped and surveyed his surroundings. His gaze locked with Gavin's for just a split second and then continued around the room. He walked to the desk and stood for a moment. The man on the phone looked up, pulling the phone away from his ear and putting a hand over the receiver. He cowboy said something. Tip reached down behind the desk and tossed the set of keys that Gavin had left onto the counter, then went back to his phone conversation. The cowboy took the keys and put them in his pocket. He looked around again, surveying the room, then walked purposely to the bar and took up the stool right next to Gavin. He was a big man, bigger than he had seemed from across the bar the night before, yet not particularly menacing. The bartender approached.

"Mr. Hancock," he addressed the cowboy.

A wave of anxiety bordering on panic washed over Gavin. He turned and stared down at his drink on the bar, pretending he was not aware of Hancock next to him. He thought that he had rid himself of the entire affair, and now he sat at the bar next to Glenda Thompson's detective. He was wishing he had just dropped off the keys and left.

"A brandy, straight; make it a double," Carston said to the bartender.

The bartender left. Carston turned toward the lounge area and did another survey, not making eye contact with Gavin.

"I don't know what I'm getting myself into here, but before this is all over, I might need a lawyer," Carston said without acknowledging Gavin.

"Okay," Gavin replied barely above a whisper.

243

The bartender arrived and put a brandy snifter on the bar in front of Carston. Carston picked it up and drank half of it down in one gulp.

"Just a heads up," Carston said again, not looking at Gavin. "I'll give you a call if I need you. I'd appreciate if you pick up, because I might be needing you quick."

Gavin did not reply.

Carston downed the rest of his brandy, placed the snifter on the bar, got up and left.

Gavin watched him go. As he got to the door to the street, Carston quickly stepped to the side and held it open. A rough looking fellow in a red plaid shirt came through, stopped, looked at Carston, looked around the lounge area, then walked in. Carston went out. The man in the plaid shirt looked lost, as if he didn't know why he was there. He turned and followed Carston out the door.

Gavin finished his drink, called for the bill, paid up and left the bar. He was shaking. His feeling of relief had been short lived. He was clearly not free of the hearse yet.

Xavier followed Carston from Flingnasties on a roundabout tour of Omaha. Xavier wondered if the detective's route was some kind of maneuver to see if anyone was following him and it made him nervous. He admitted that he might not know all the ins and outs of tailing someone, like a private detective might. He felt very vulnerable and noticeable following behind Carston's Escalade. But he couldn't afford to lose him. If he did, chances were he wouldn't see him again and that would be the end of Xavier's promotion. It was getting dark, and just as Xavier was beginning to think of alternatives to driving in Carston's rearview mirror, the Escalade took off toward downtown as if it were on a mission. Xavier followed behind, leaving as much distance between them as he dared.

Carston pulled into the lot next to the LeVant and parked. Xavier did not pull in behind him, but chose to circle the block. It seemed to take forever to get back around to where he could see the front door to the hotel, but he made it in time to see Carston go through it. He was lucky enough to find a parking space right across the street where he could watch the front door and the lot where Carston's Escalade was parked. He pulled in and waited, wondering who Carston would be meeting at the Hotel LeVant. He knew an eclectic crowd of downtown businessmen, high dollar whores and drug dealers who peddled the latest in boutique drugs frequented the place. A crowd that was a few steps up from what Xavier's wallet could afford. He was familiar with the place though, if only by reputation.

Xavier waited for what seemed like a long time. He was wondering if Carston was done for the night. He imagined Carston in a room right at that moment with some secretary that he had met somewhere, and with no intentions of leaving for a while. He was right across the street, Xavier told himself. He could duck in, take a look and be right back to his truck and never lose sight of the lot entrance. He got out, waited for traffic and crossed the street. He went hurriedly through the front door and nearly ran headlong into Carston coming out. Xavier hesitated for a moment, and Carston held the door for him. Xavier walked past him into the hotel and stopped. Carston went out. Xavier looked around quickly and did an about-face, returning to the street.

Carston walked around to the parking lot and got into his Escalade. He took out his phone and pulled up Glenda's number. The phone rang three times. Carston backed out of his parking space while it was ringing.

"Yes?" Glenda answered curtly.

"I know where the hearse is," Carston announced.

"Where?" she asked, unable to hide her excitement.

"Missouri Valley, locked in a hangar at the airport. I have the keys to the hangar and to the hearse. I'm on my way."

"Wait until we get there," Glenda said.

"No problem, I'll meet you there. If you get there first, I'm on my way."

"Good," Glenda exclaimed.

"COD," Carston said before she could end the call.

"What?" Glenda asked.

"I want to be paid then and there," he said. "Once you get your hands on the hearse, I'm done."

There was a moment's pause. "Sure thing," she said. "But wait for me outside. I don't want anyone else around that hearse until I get there, understand? Not even you."

"You're paying the bill. I'll wait until you get there." Carston almost ended the call as he was pulling onto the street, but thought of something else. "One more thing, are you having me followed? Some big guy, red plaid shirt, beard, red Dodge pickup?"

"No," Glenda said decisively. "Is someone following you?"

"I don't know for sure. I'll figure it out before I get there. If someone is following me, I'll lose them before I head over to the airport," Carston replied and ended the call.

Glenda got off the phone and immediately went through her contacts until she found the number that she was looking for. She stabbed the call button with her finger and waited. The phone rang twice.

"Hello," a voice answered.

"Missouri Valley airport," Glenda said excitedly.

"On my way," the voice on the other end said quickly. "I gotta close up the shop, then I'm going straight up. You want to meet up at the Casey's Store in Crescent and go on up there together? I think that would be a better plan. What do you think?"

"Fine," Glenda said. "I'm bringing Harvey with me. Call your biker and tell him, just in case he gets lost. Hancock spotted him, and he's going to try to shake him before he goes to the airport. I don't want him spooking Hancock, but I want him up there too."

"I'll call him right now."

"Timing is everything, don't diddle around." Glenda ended the call.

Xavier was following Carston over the Aksarben bridge when Gimp's phone rang. He glanced down and found it on the passenger seat. He picked it up and answered it.

"George here," the voice on the other end said.

"What do you need?" Xavier asked.

"You still following that detective?" George asked.

"Yep, just crossed over the bridge to Council Bluffs," Xavier answered.

"Back off a little," George advised. "Pretty sure he's going to the Missouri Valley airport."

"Where did you get that information?" Xavier said dubiously.

"Through the grapevine, where I get all of my information," George said. "I'm just passing it along."

Xavier wondered if it was a setup. He needed to be on guard.

"So why the Missouri Valley airport, what's there?" Xavier asked.

"Look, I don't know. I'm passing on info when I get it. That's all."

"Sounds like a good place to get ambushed," Xavier commented boldly. "I've already been through that once."

"Hey, I'm telling you what I hear. You do with it what you want," George said. "I don't know if it is a setup or not, but not on my end. I got reliable sources. I can tell you something else, I did not set up your friend. I didn't have anything to do with that."

"Okay, if you say so," Xavier responded. "Anything else?"

"Just that the detective is on his way up to Missouri Valley right now. That's it."

Xavier ended the call without commenting. He had backed off, but he could still see Carston's taillights ahead of him. Xavier was trying to find Zee's number while he was driving in the dark. He was swerving all over Broadway. The last thing he needed was to draw the attention of some cop looking for an early evening drunk. He pulled off the street into a parking lot to find the number. He pushed the call button and drove back out onto the street. He had lost Carston, but at least now he knew where he was going.

"Yes," Zee answered.

"I think that we might be in for a little luck," Xavier said with a note of triumph in his voice.

"How's that?" Zee asked.

"I just got a call from George. The detective is on his way to the Missouri Valley airport right now," Xavier said.

There was a long pause. "Sounds fishy to me."

"I was following the detective when I got the call. I've been following him all day. It sure looks to me like that might be where he is heading."

"You think so?"

"I do," Xavier said. "I've been talking to this George all day. Everything he's thrown at me has been straight shit. If someone set up Gimp, I don't think it was him."

"Then who?"

"Not him," Xavier answered.

"You got your gun?"

"Yep," Xavier replied.

Again there was a long pause. "First of all, keep your eyes open for a setup. Don't let yourself fall into a trap."

"I will," Xavier reassured him. "Or I mean, don't worry, I won't."

"If and when the detective locates the hearse and you got eyes on it, you take him out of the game."

"How's that?" Xavier asked, confused.

"Kill him."

Xavier didn't reply.

"You wanted in on this. You're in it up to your neck now. When he finds that hearse you kill him before anyone else shows up. You get in that hearse and drive it somewhere out of there. Then you call me and I'll give you instructions from there."

Xavier still did not reply.

"Are you going to do this?"

"Yes," Xavier finally answered.

"Good, then call me back when you have it. And don't mess around chitchatting and bullshit grandstanding like you're acting in some kind of TV show. He don't need to know why you're killing him. Just shoot him until he quits moving. But most importantly, you get that hearse and you get it out of there, wherever it is, and you take it somewhere else. Because you're not the only one trying to get their hands on it. There no doubt will be someone coming in right behind him and I want them to find nothing but a dead detective. If they show up before you get it out of there, you kill them too. You got that?"

"And my truck?" Xavier answered.

There was a pause. "Park it somewhere and walk in." There was another pause. "I don't know if you are up to this," Zee finally said. "You do whatever you have to do."

"I will," Xavier answered.

The call ended. Xavier was shaking. He had already turned off of Broadway and was headed north out of town toward Crescent, then Missouri Valley beyond that. He sped up. He wasn't quite sure where the airport was. Missouri Valley wasn't a big town, he could probably find it easy enough, but he wanted to get the Escalade back in sight. If he was going to get in and get out, he needed to have a visual on Hancock.

Carston looked in his rearview mirror. He was leaving the city limits of Council Bluffs and driving out into the country. There was nothing behind him but empty road. Whoever it was that he thought was following him was not there anymore. He sped up. He didn't want anyone catching up to him if they were holding back. He would drive into Missouri Valley, then back out to the airport, just to make sure. If anyone was following him he would meet them when he turned around. Carston knew that he was playing a dangerous game. He had to be very careful. Whatever was in that hearse, clearly there was a lot at stake. There was a lot at stake for everybody.

The gathering

Gavin sat at the bar at the LeVant nervously finishing his drink. Hancock was the cause of his nervousness. Not Hancock himself, exactly, but the fact that Hancock was able to spot him sitting at the bar seemingly with no effort. He wondered if Hancock had known who he was all along, even the night before when he was sitting at the bar with Sylvia. Gavin had put his trust in Hancock, thinking he had nowhere else to turn. But now he was not so sure that was the best decision. He wondered if somehow he was being played. He feared that he had just fallen into a trap by giving up the keys to the hearse. Had he handed off his insurance policy? He finished his drink and got up from the stool to walk out.

"Six fifty," the bartender called to him.

Gavin turned quickly. "Sorry, my mind was somewhere else," he said, digging his billfold out of his pocket. He took a ten-dollar bill out and put it on the counter. "We're good," he said.

Gavin walked through the front doors and out onto the street. His phone rang and he pulled it out of his pocket.

"Dad," Gavin answered.

"Gavin," his dad replied. "You know that hearse that got stolen out from under me and Bill over in Omaha? Some private detective has been chasing us around. And then last night some biker was shot dead in the parking lot at the funeral home. And we were over at Marzoe's just a little while ago and Martin said that the detective, a big guy, has been over there asking questions about us a couple of times. And there were two bikers there last night asking the same questions as the detective. Then right after that the biker got shot. You think that detective did it?"

"Did what, Dad?" Gavin asked.

"Do you think that private detective shot and killed that biker?" Vince repeated.

Gavin had not thought about that. "I don't know," he said tentatively.

"Maybe he isn't a private detective at all, maybe he's a mobster," Vince suggested.

Gavin had to think again.

"Bill and I are kind of scared right now. We don't know what's going on. You think we're in danger?" Vince said, taking advantage of the silence.

"I don't think so, Dad," Gavin replied.

"I really wish I knew what was going on," Vince said. "I was pretty sure they would have found that hearse by now. Who steals a hearse? Jesus, Gavin, all we wanted to do is have a bite to eat. We shouldn't have left it running."

"You probably shouldn't have," Gavin agreed.

"But how the hell did they get in? We locked the door. Bill had his set of keys."

"I don't know, Dad," Gavin replied.

"I'm just kicking myself in the ass," Vince said. "Why am I so stupid?"

"You're not stupid, Dad," Gavin assured him.

Gavin heard a big sigh.

"Don't worry, Dad," he said.

"I am worried," Vince replied. "Somehow I think I'm responsible for something bad that's happening and I don't know what the hell it was I did, but I need to make it right. I'm thinking about calling up that detective guy."

"Don't do that," Gavin replied quickly.

"You think he isn't who he says he is?" Vince asked.

"I think by tomorrow this is all going to be over. Just let it go, Dad. It wasn't your fault."

There was a pause on the other end. "What makes you think that?" Vince asked.

"I just do, Dad," Gavin said. "Go home."

"Okay, if you say so," Vince replied.

Gavin thought for a moment. "Dad, I'll come over and we'll watch Netflix."

"That would be nice," Vince replied. "I haven't seen you for a long time."

"I'll be there in a little while."

Vince ended the call. By the time Gavin got to his car he was having second and third thoughts. If he was being watched, if the whole deal with Hancock was a ruse, he could still be in danger. If he went to his dad's place he could put his dad in danger. The last thing he wanted to do was drag his dad into it. But he realized that is exactly what he had done, from the very beginning. Gavin felt sick.

Carston drove past the Missouri Valley airport. He slowed a little to get a look at the lay of the land. It was dark, save a light at each end of the three rows of hangars. At a glance it looked like there were three or four tee hangars in each row. That would make a total of eighteen to twenty of them. Making some quick calculations, that would make number thirteen somewhere in the middle. He continued into town, keeping his eye on the rearview mirror. Headlights behind him had slowly been catching up to him since he had passed through the little town of Crescent. But they were still a long way back. Carston pulled into town, crossed the railroad tracks, pulled into a vacant parking lot and waited.

Xavier had sped through Crescent, and when he finally got back out into the country he could spot the taillights of a car at least a mile ahead of him. The road north of Crescent curved around and ducked through the tree-lined countryside. Xavier recognized the house up in the bluffs on the east side of the road where he and Gimp had visited the morning before. The place was dark except for a yard light. Xavier kept driving, backing off a little, catching glimpses of the car ahead of him, not knowing if it was Hancock's car or not. He wasn't going to take any chances. He knew where they were going. He didn't have to catch up, he just wanted to get close.

Xavier saw the lights of Missouri Valley ahead of him. There was no sign of the car he had been following. He slowed and spotted the airport on the west side of the road. If it hadn't been for the sign, he would have thought it was some rundown agricultural business. It looked like three rows of tin machine sheds that he realized now must be airplane hangars. They were clearly visible and he could see no vehicles parked among them. Either Carston had pulled off somewhere along the way, or he had driven into Missouri Valley for some reason. There was a convenience store in Crescent,

Xavier thought. Maybe he stopped there for gas or something. It didn't make any difference. In fact, being the first one at the airport worked in his favor. Just north of the airport was a drive that turned into a field to the east. Xavier put his Ram into four-wheel drive and drove through what was left of the snow plowed across the drive and drove into the field. Most of it had melted away, and what was left had formed into an icy crust that crunched beneath his wheels. He followed a fence row for a quarter mile, then he stopped and turned off his headlights. The lights from Missouri Valley reflecting off the clouds and back off the snow again gave him enough light to back around and position the Ram facing out toward the road. He got out, slid the forty-five auto into his belt and began walking toward the airport.

David Long got to the Casey's convenience store in Crescent fully expecting to find Glenda already there, even though she was coming from Omaha. It had taken him fifteen minutes to get Kenny out of the shop and get the place locked up. He circled the pumps and parked facing out toward the street where he could drive straight out. He didn't have to wait long. Glenda's Mercedes SUV came into the lot driven by Harvey Grant. Harvey came around, waved and drove back out on the street. David followed.

Harvey sped out of town ten over the forty-five mile per hour speed limit. As soon as he cleared the city limits he took it up to eighty. Eighty was a little faster than David was comfortable driving on a winding two lane blacktop through the Missouri River bottoms with trees on both sides of the highway. A deer coming out into their path would put them both off the road, through the ditch and into a tree. Harvey was hitting ninety on some of the straight stretches.

Carston pulled out onto the highway and drove back toward the airport. The headlights of the vehicle following never came into town. It must have pulled into a driveway somewhere or off on a side road. He was certain that he wasn't being followed. In a few minutes he was at the airport and driving between the hangars looking for number thirteen. Just as he had thought when he drove by, it was in the middle of the second row. He turned his Escalade until the lights illuminated the door and spent a minute or two examining it. Glenda had told him not to go into the hangar until she got there, but he could clearly see the gigantic padlock on the door. He left his vehicle running and got out. In the light of his high beams he fished the keys that Gavin had left for him from his coat pocket and opened the lock. He tuned back the hasp and put the padlock back through the eye, then turned to go back to his car.

"Turn around, hands where I can see them," Carston heard a voice from the darkness. He turned toward the voice and a large man sporting a beard and wearing biker gang colors stepped into the light. He had an ominous looking forty-five automatic in his hand pointed directly at Carston's chest. Carston recognized the red plaid shirt under the jacket and the bearded face that he had met in the doorway of the LeVant.

"What's up?" Carston asked in a friendly manner. "Checking on my friend's airplane for him."

"That a fact? I'm looking for a hearse," Xavier replied. "I heard that you found it for me."

"Don't know what you're talking about," Carston said and smiled. "I'm just here checking on my friend's plane." For a brief moment Carston wondered how hard it would be to get to the Smith and Wesson buried deep under his winter coat and decided that even if he made a quick move to get out of the line of fire while he went for his gun, there wasn't chance in hell that he could reach it before the man with the forty-five put a half dozen rounds into him. He had to stall. If he could keep from getting gunned down like the biker at Harmon and Mott the night before, his best bet was Glenda coming to his rescue.

"Let's open up that hangar then and get a good look at your friend's plane, make sure it's okay," Xavier said, trying to keep his voice calm and authoritative. He knew that he should put a bullet into the detective and be done with it, but he couldn't quite bring himself to it yet.

Carston went to the door. It was on a rail so that it could be slid sideways. He put his weight against it, pushing inward. "Won't move," he said. "Must be froze shut. You wanna give me a hand here?"

"No, I don't want to give you a hand, jackass," Xavier said. "Quit fucking around and open the door."

Carston looked down at the ground, as if he was trying to figure out the door. He saw Gavin's footprints frozen in the mud and the snow where he had opened the door two days earlier when he stashed the hearse there. Carston put his weight against the door again, this time pushing it to the side. It slid on the railings, and as it opened he could see the hearse parked inside by the light of his high beams. When the door was partially open, he stepped back to let the biker see.

"Sweet airplane you got there," Xavier said, motioning Carston away from the door with the pistol and stepping in to get a better look.

Carston thought for a moment that he could make a break for it while the biker looked into the interior of the hangar, but the time it took him to think about it was too long and the opportunity was gone in an instant.

"Step over there, away from the Cadillac," Xavier instructed, using the barrel of the forty-five to motion Carston away from the driver's side of the Escalade where the door stood open and the engine was running.

Carston moved the direction that the biker was indicating. He stumbled and caught his balance, pretending to slip on the ice and snow.

"I said to quit fucking around," Xavier said again, trying to muster the nerve to pull the trigger of the gun in his hand. He knew that the detective was stalling, and Xavier knew he was letting him. He knew what he had to do, but he was stalling too. He had never killed anyone before. He didn't want to kill anyone. But if he wanted to move up in the organization, if he was going to be someone in the Hell Fighters, he had to do it. The first time is the worst, he told himself. It would get easier. Just do it, he told himself.

"What's the deal?" Carston asked. "You gonna kill me, or what do you want? You want the hearse, you can have it. I'm just getting paid to find it. I'm a private detective. Five bills a day and expenses isn't worth dying over. I'm not going to try to stop you. If you want it, take it." Carston tossed the keys at the biker.

Xavier tried to catch the keys with the same hand his gun was in. For a moment he fumbled the keys and they dropped to the ground. He instinctively bent down to pick them up. Carston made his move, dodging past the biker and sprinting toward the end of the row of hangars. He was caught in the middle of a chute with nowhere to maneuver, but it was his only chance.

Xavier whipped around and leveled his gun at Carston's back. He lined up the sights and put pressure on the trigger. The gun didn't fire. He pulled harder. He turned the gun and looked at it in the light of Carston's headlights. The safety was still engaged. He flicked the safety off and leveled the gun at Carston, who was putting distance between them at an incredible rate. It was going to be a long shot now and it was getting longer with each step.

David was trying to take his mind off the speed he was driving. He was glad to see that Harvey was with Glenda. He had known Harvey since they were high school kids. Glenda had hired him on David's recommendation. It would be good to have him there corralling Carston and the biker until they could get their hands on the hearse and make sure that everything was there. The lights of Missouri Valley were coming into view. David let up a bit, giving Harvey a little room between them in case he had to slam on the brakes to make the turn into the airport. His heart was racing as rapidly as Harvey was screaming down the blacktop toward the drive into the airport with no intention of backing off.

In the nick of time

Carston was sprinting as best he could. He was a big man, and sprinting had never been his thing. But adrenaline was on his side and he marveled how quickly he covered the ground. Regardless, he expected a shot to ring out at any moment and tensed his back in anticipation, which slowed his ungainly sprint. As he was nearing the end of the row of hangars where he could duck to safety and no longer be a target, he was almost run down by an SUV followed closely by a Ford Ranger pickup truck careening around the very corner Carston was headed for. He was able to dodge to the left, barely escaping in the sloppy and slick mud and frozen snow. As the vehicles passed him the driver's door of the Ford Ranger flew open and he could see someone getting ready to bail out. The two vehicles slid to a stop.

"Put your fucking hands in the air," Carston heard as he pulled up and turned around. "Drop the fucking gun." He heard a shotgun slide being cycled and the thunk of a shell sliding into the chamber.

"Carston, come back here," a female voice that he recognized called.

Carston walked shakily back toward the vehicles, which were now parked side by side blocking the alley between the hangars. Their headlights, in combination with the high beams from Carston's Escalade, had the biker pinned, his eyes squinting in the brightness and his hand with the gun over his eyes trying to shade them. Carston could only see the backs of the occupants who had just arrived. He recognized the silhouette of Glenda on the right, behind the open passenger door of the SUV, and a large figure that he immediately guessed was Harvey, the doorman at Flingnasties, behind the driver's door. Both of them faced the biker. On the far left a tall, lanky figure was strategically positioned behind the driver's door of the Ford Ranger, holding a pump action shotgun. Carston recognized the truck.

Carston approached Glenda, who was still standing at the passenger door of the SUV. He noticed that the biker had laid his gun on the ground and was being instructed by the lanky guy to step back away from it.

"Am I fucking glad to see you," Carston exclaimed as he came up behind Glenda.

"We saw that you were in need of assistance from the road coming in," Glenda replied matter-of-factly.

"Who is he?" Carston asked, looking at the biker. Glenda did not answer.

Carston looked past Harvey, who was also holding a gun on the biker, toward the man at the Ford Ranger. "David Long?" he spoke in wonderment. "What the hell are you—?" Carston glanced back to Glenda. She was holding a small Walther semi-auto pointed toward the middle of his chest. He cocked his head.

"Don't even twitch." Glenda reached out with her left hand and unbuttoned his coat. She reached in and her hand came out with his Smith & Wesson revolver. Carston felt the weight of it go with her as she deftly unsnapped the holster and pulled the gun from under his coat. "Why don't you step over there with our other guest? In the light, where we can see you," she instructed, slipping the Smith into her coat pocket as he backed away.

David stepped out from behind the door of the Ford and quickly retrieved the forty-five laying on the ground, holding the shotgun one handed, pulled back against his torso and still pointed toward the biker.

"Maybe someone could explain what is going on?" Carston asked as he took up a position next to the biker.

Harvey crossed in front of Glenda, who held the Walther on the two. He went into the hangar and pulled on the rear hatch. It did not move. He went out of sight and Carston heard him pulling on door handles.

"We need the key," he called out from the hangar.

"You got the keys?" Glenda directed the question to Carston.

"I believe he does," Carston nodded toward the biker, keeping his hands up where everyone could see them.

Harvey came out of the hangar. He went to the biker, who was standing next to Carston with his hands up where they could be seen as well. Harvey went through his pockets, starting with the left jacket pocket. He came out immediately with the key ring. The biker did not move or say a thing while Harvey searched him. Harvey went back inside the hangar to the hearse, unlocked the hatch and climbed in. Carston could hear some grunting and out of the corner of his eye he saw the lid of the casket slam up against the headliner of the hearse and close again.

"I gotta get it out of here," Harvey yelled. "There's not enough room to open it up in here."

Glenda looked at Carston. "You're still on the payroll."

"Am I?" Carston asked.

"For now you are." Glenda waved the barrel of her gun toward the hangar door.

Carston put his hands down and went to the hatch of the hearse. Harvey was hunched down inside. "We gotta get this out of here," he said.

"Can we handle it?" Carston asked. "Just the two of us? How heavy is it?"

Carston moved back as Harvey climbed out. Carston wondered where Harvey's gun was and if he could make a grab for it, perhaps put up a fight before he was gunned down. Harvey stepped away from the hearse.

"We'll just drag it out and let it fall," Harvey instructed.

Carston didn't move.

"Grab on and pull," Harvey ordered him.

Carston grabbed the ornate handle along the right side of the casket and pulled. The casket was on rollers and moved easily. Harvey reached in with one hand on the other side and hauled. The two stepped aside as one end of the casket fell onto the dirt floor of the hangar, the other end still hung up in the hearse. As the casket leaned mostly out and partially in, Harvey heaved on the lid and it came open. A body lay in peaceful repose, unfazed by the rough handling.

"Let's get him out of there," Harvey instructed. "Grab an arm."

Carston did as he was told. They both pulled and dragged the body out onto the ground. Harvey dragged it like a rug to the side of the hangar door and stepped over it. Carston stood, watching. "Back outside," Harvey ordered him.

Carston walked back out into the beam of the headlights and toward Glenda.

"Over by your friend," Glenda said, stopping him.

"He's not my friend. I have nothing to do with him and I have no idea what he's doing here," Carston said urgently, wondering if for some reason Glenda thought that he and the biker were in cahoots.

Glenda motioned with her gun barrel.

"You saw it yourself. He was going to shoot me, and I was running for my life trying to get out of his line of fire when you got here. I got nothing to do with him. He just showed up."

Glenda did not answer. Her gun never wavered. Carston took up his position next to the biker, who had not uttered a sound since Carston had made his break for it and stood with his hands in the air, staring at the bright headlights that concealed Glenda and David from his sight.

"Hands up," Glenda said. Carston complied.

"Tell them," Carston turned his head toward the biker. "I don't know what you are doing here. We've never met."

The biker did not say anything and Carston turned back to Glenda and David, just barely visible to him in the bright light. He heard cutting and tearing from the direction of the hangar, but did not look. He heard the whistle of a train engine going through Missouri Valley, then the wheels

266

and the creaking of the cars as they rolled through the town. He wondered if those were going to be some of the last sounds he ever heard.

"Finding anything?" Glenda called out.

"Yep," Harvey called back.

"So, you're not that interested in dear Uncle Thomas," Carston said. The silence from Glenda and David made him nervous. "Something else you're looking for?"

Glenda didn't answer.

Carston turned his attention to David. The lights of his Ford Ranger were not as bright as those of Glenda's SUV, and he could make out his shape behind the open driver's side door.

"David, what the hell?" Carston said. "You were in on this all the time, whatever this is?"

"Yep, I was," David replied. "In on it from the beginning. I'm the one who suggested that Glenn hire you to find the hearse. And you did a good job of it. You didn't let me down."

"So that's why you kept telling me to look at Gavin? You knew he stole it?" Carston asked.

"Yep," David replied.

"Shut up, David," Glenda interrupted their conversation.

"What difference does it make what he knows now?" David replied.

"I said to shut up," Glenda repeated.

"Yes ma'am," David replied. "You're the boss." He paused for a moment. "Can't talk to you anymore, boss says," he said to Carston.

From Glenda's words it was clear to Carston that they did not intend to leave him and the biker alive. Right now his only recourse was to stall for time and he was trying to think of how he was going to get some sort of discourse started again. Anything to take their minds off of killing him and the biker. Harvey came out of the hangar and crossed to Glenda, carrying three small bags that looked like marble sacks. She stepped out from behind the car door and took them from Harvey. She hefted them and nodded. Harvey turned and went back into the hangar. Carston chanced a glance over to see him tearing out the lining of the casket. He pulled a small box the size of a milk carton out from behind the torn lining and put it on the ground.

Carston turned his attention back to Glenda and David.

"Seriously, I just want my two days at five hundred a day and my bonus," Carston said. "I don't care what you are doing. I'm ready to just take my money and leave. I got no problems with this. You do whatever it is you are doing. I don't even want to know. What I don't know won't hurt you. What do you say, how about I just get out of here and leave you to it?"

"Stay where you are and don't move," David answered.

Harvey came out of the hangar carrying the box that Carston had seen him remove from the casket and two more marble bags a bit larger than the ones before. He could see the velour fabric in the dim light. They reminded him of the bags that Crown Royal Canadian whiskey came in. He wondered how Crown Royal whisky could be involved in Glenda's plan. The box looked like it was big enough to hold a bottle of liquor, too. He asked himself if whoever shipped the body and casket from Montreal had put whiskey in the

268

casket for Glenda. The thought itself was surreal. Carston and the biker were standing out in the mud and snow at the Missouri Valley airport, about to get killed because someone was sending Glenda whiskey in a casket.

"I'm going to die over a few bags of marbles and booze," Carston muttered.

"What?" It was the first word Xavier had spoken.

"What do you think are in those bags and that box?" Carston asked.

"What bags and what boxes?" Xavier asked.

"The ones that Harvey has been digging out of that casket," Carston said.

"I haven't been watching," Xavier said.

Carston didn't say anything.

"Sorry," Xavier said.

"How are you involved in all this?" Carston asked.

"Well, I just sort of fell into it," Xavier answered.

"Would you two shut the fuck up?" David shouted.

"David, what the hell?" Carston responded.

"Just shut up, Carston," he replied.

"Are you going to kill me?" Carston asked. "I mean, shit, David. I've known your father-in-law ten years or more. I have coffee with you and him. I come to visit. You're really going to kill me?" Carston was close to pleading.

"Shut up, all of you," Glenda interrupted. "David, you keep your mind on what you're doing. You got a job to do. There is a lot of money involved here. That's all you need to think about."

Harvey came out of the hangar with two more bags. "That's it," he said as he came up to where Glenda was standing. He handed them to her and she deposited them in the passenger seat, closed the door and walked around the front of the SUV to the driver's side door.

"Okay, give me ten minutes to get clear of here and then do your job." She placed Carston's Smith on the hood of David's truck. "Shoot the biker with Carston's gun and then shoot Carston with the biker's gun. Drag them into the hangar and make it look like they surprised each other and shot it out. David, when you're done you take Harvey back to the club and drop him off, then sit tight for a few days. No calls. Nothing happened. You got it?"

"Yep," replied David.

"You don't need to make up alibis or nothing," she reiterated. "Nothing happened. You got off work, went home. Nothing else."

"I got it," David said, turning toward Glenda. "I know what I gotta do."

"Just making sure," Glenda said.

"You got any questions?" she turned her attention toward Harvey.

Harvey was moving back away from the SUV. He reached into his coat and pulled out his gun, glancing toward Carston and the biker.

"I have a few questions," Carston called out.

Glenda turned toward Carston. The biker was watching Harvey. She saw something in his face and turned her attention toward Harvey. He held his gun in his right hand, and his left hand just cleared his front pants pocket. There was something shiny cupped in it.

Saved by the cavalry

At that moment all hell broke loose.

Carston would later try to piece it together. He recalled bits and pieces, assembled them and by the time morning rolled around he had a pretty good idea of what had happened. But for the moment, all hell broke loose.

He remembered calling out to Glenda that he had some questions in a desperate attempt to stall for time. Just as she looked his direction, he saw out of the corner of his eye the biker looking to the left toward Harvey. Glenda's attention followed the biker's, and Carston's attention followed hers. Harvey was slowly backing up, adopting a gunfighter's stance: his left leg planted, his right moving back. As his right hand raised his gun, his left hand came out of his pocket. Carston recognized immediately what was in his hand. It was a badge. Harvey brought the badge up so that it was visible in front of him, then placed his gun hand over the top of his left wrist to steady the gun, aimed directly at David, who was still unaware of the whole maneuver.

All of a sudden a calliope of noise erupted all around them. Hangar doors opened and uniformed soldiers streamed out of them. Men came out of the dark, automatic weapons with laser sights emitted red beams that bounced in all directions and put on a surreal light show in the sky, on the walls of the surrounding hangars and on the endless stream of yelling soldiers running

271

from every direction. Strangely, the thing that resonated with Carston was that each little group of screaming soldiers was dressed uniformly slightly different.

"Hands in the air, hands in the air, hands in the air!" shouted a half dozen soldiers from the right who pointed their guns toward Carston and the biker. Several of the men shouted commands in high voices like women. It was strange, when Carston thought about it later, what he noticed and what he didn't. Carston's hands were already in the air. They had been in the air for at least ten minutes, ever since he had helped Harvey remove the casket from the hearse and the body from the casket. He looked over at the biker. His hands were still in the air as well, and he had been holding them up longer than Carston.

"On the ground, on the ground, on the ground!" three soldiers running in from the other side screamed as they pointed their guns.

Carston bent his knees and put his hands toward the ground to lay down in the mud and snow.

"Hands up, hands up, hands up or we'll shoot!" the six on the right yelled in unison.

Carston squatted, looking back and forth between the two groups of soldiers. The biker was following Carston's lead and was in the same position. Carston was about to break into hysterical laughter at the total absurdity of his situation.

"Hands up!" "On the ground!" "Hands up!" He was getting it from both sides. He squatted down as far as he could, fell on his knees, and then belly flopped his torso into the mud and snow,

272

keeping his hands above his head. It was not a graceful move, but he didn't hear any shooting, so he assumed he was doing it right. He looked toward the two vehicles and saw both Glenda and David on the ground. For the first time he noticed big letters, POLICE, printed in white across the back of one of the soldiers who was kneeling on David's back while another two fought against each other to get his hands behind his back and cuff him. Glenda was laying in the mud, her hands already cuffed, staring straight at Carston. Her expression was pleading, as if she was asking him to help her. He smiled and winked. She turned her head. He couldn't tell if she saw, or if she was just tired of looking his direction. He felt his arms being painfully jerked in several directions. He tried to relax; there was nothing he could do to help them. They were shouting unintelligible orders at him while they jerked him around. He realized that anything he did, they would perceive as fighting and they would get even more aggressive in their dogpile. The cops would figure it out eventually and get his hands behind his back. He could only hope that it happened soon. He grunted in pain as they twisted his right arm in a direction that it could not and would not go.

Carston had no idea how long he lay in the snow and mud, turning his face to one side and then the other as he felt like his ears were going to freeze off his head. After a while it ceased to make a difference. Ice cold water had soaked through the front of his coat and the shirt beneath it. He felt as if he was laying bare chested in freezing water. He felt a presence next to him as someone took his handcuffed arm and lifted.

"Sit up and I'll get those cuffs off of you." The female voice was familiar, but he could not place it at the moment. All he could really think about was whether he was actually suffering from hypothermia or if he was still a ways away from it. He had never died of hypothermia before and he was wondering how much more he could stand before he did.

"Carston, help me a little here." The female person standing over him was pulling.

"Can't you just take them off where I'm at?" he pleaded.

He felt the cuff come off his right hand. His hand was numb. He put it on the ground and could not even feel cold through it. The cuff came off his left hand. He tried to get up but struggled. Someone else came up and took his other arm and helped the female voice lift him into a sitting position. Cold water soaked through the seat of his pants.

"Fuck," Carston said. "Quit it, I feel like I pissed my pants."

The two were lifting him to his feet.

"Fuck me," Carston said as they hoisted him up. "It's too cold for piss. What the fuck?"

"Calm down, Carston." He finally recognized the voice, but he wanted to make sure. The woman wore black military fatigues with an embroidered badge that was almost impossible to make out in the dark. It read Council Bluffs Police. Carston had to get his face almost to her breast to see it.

"What the fuck are you doing?" she asked.

"Reading your fucking badge," Carston replied, looking up at Barbie. "Can you just tell me what is going on?"

"Let's get you in a patrol car where it is warm," Barbie said.

"No," Carston replied vehemently. "Tell me now."

"A big bust," Barbie said. "Lots of agencies involved. "We've been setting it up for a month or more. Local, state, feds, everyone's here."

"Is that why it's such a cluster fuck?" Carston asked indignantly.

"No, it's always a cluster fuck," Barbie answered, one corner of her lip twitching into a smile. She was still holding him by the arm to steady him. The other officer, Carston recognized him as Officer Goss, had left. Carston looked around for the biker and didn't see him.

"He's in a patrol car where it is warm," Barbie said. "Why don't you come along and get in one too?"

"I'm going home," Carston pulled his arm away.

"That's not going to happen," Barbie said. "Come along with me."

She took his arm again and led him to a row of law enforcement vehicles of various and sundry colors, from white vehicles with city markings to black vehicles with no markings at all, that stood in formation at the end of the row of hangars. Carston wondered vaguely where they had come from. Barbie held the back door of a Council Bluffs patrol car open for him.

"I'm not getting in there," Carston said. "Am I under arrest?"

"I won't close the door," Barbie reassured him, pushing him toward the door.

Carston reluctantly got in, leaving one foot outside to make sure the door didn't go closed on him. Barbie left him, went around to the driver's side and got in.

"What the fuck?" Carston said.

"Calm down and quit saying 'what the fuck,'" Barbie said. "Here's what's going on: Tommy Gunn in Montreal wanted to do an end run around his niece Glenda, who's been running the show in Omaha, because he thinks she wants to push him out."

"You mean Tommy Gunn who's laying in that hangar over there?" Carston interrupted.

"No, that's not Tommy Gunn," Barbie replied. "Tommy Gunn was arrested an hour ago by Interpol, the Canadian Mounted Police and the US Customs in Montreal for murder, racketeering, theft and smuggling. We don't know who that guy in the hangar is yet."

"Go on," said Carston.

"We've been working on this operation for a while, looking for a way in. Tommy was keeping his fingers in his Omaha organization from Montreal. And it went fine as long as Jerry Thompson was running things. He was a good soldier. Tommy could count on him. But then he disappeared and Glenda took over running the show. She wasn't so loyal, or at least Tommy didn't think so. He had a feeling she wasn't being forthright with him. So he teamed up with the Montreal chapter of the Hell Fighters. Tommy's plan was to smuggle nine million dollars' worth of blood diamonds, rubies, emeralds, amethyst, whatever, you name it, nine million dollars' worth of jewels into the United States, most of them banned internationally. Jewels are the currency of criminal organizations these days. More so than drugs, because worldwide law enforcement is plowing all their resources into illegal drug trafficking, and probably only a half-dozen agents are tracking illegal jewels. Tommy got a body, stuffed a coffin full of illegal jewels, put the body in there for cover and shipped it to Omaha. The word Glenda got was that Tommy was dead and coming home to be put to rest," Barbie paused. "Are you keeping up with me?"

"Keep going," Carston replied.

Barbie continued. "The Montreal Hell Fighters sent down one of their soldiers on the same flight as the casket to sit on it and make sure it got where it was supposed to go, a guy they called Gimp. He was one bad ass. Tommy used Harmon and Mott to receive the body because David Long knew Gavin Barker, whose dad worked for the funeral home. David had known the Barkers all his life. Nothing more to it than that to start with. Just a referral."

"How did David get involved in all this?" Carston asked.

"Glenda has been dumping cars in Council Bluffs for years," Barbie explained. "So have the Hell Fighters. We could never connect Kenny Smart or David directly to any of the stolen cars, or to Glenda or the Hell Fighters, but Kenny and David were always around. Their names came up every time a car got dumped over here. They are facilitators, if you know what I mean. They don't get their own hands dirty, but they know what the hell is going on, who is looking for what, stuff like that. Like I say, David is a facilitator and an opportunist. Glenda threw lots of opportunities his way. He had connections in the Hell Fighters as well. Evidently everyone talks to David and David plays them all in turn."

"And Kenny?" Carston asked.

"Kenny isn't as ambitious as David," Barbie said. "Kenny passes information, but he doesn't get personally involved in anything illegal. He stays just over the line."

"So what was the plan?" Carston asked.

"Simple plan," Barbie continued. "Gimp recruits this dumb shit Omaha Hell Fighter named Xavier Warner, whose only qualification is that he has a big Dodge Ram four-wheel drive pickup that he can use to ram the hearse. When Vince Barker picks up the body and leaves Eppley, Xavier is going to ram it with the Ram and Gimp plans to jump out, jack it, take it to some garage that David has set up, then the Hell Fighters get the goods and dump the hearse and the body so the police can recover it and no one is the wiser about the smuggled jewels. Then the Hell Fighters use the money from the jewels to usurp Glenda and probably, if the truth be known, kill her. But it was a simple plan, a Hell Fighter plan, no finesse, just ram the hearse, throw Vince out and take it. Vince is not going to put up a fight, he's easy pickings."

"What happened?" Carston asked.

"What happened is that David caught wind of it—like I said, people talk to him—and came up with a plan of his own, which he pitched to Glenda. Glenda is close to Gavin, who steps across the line sometimes for her. He has a lot to lose. David and

Gavin were buddies in high school, although not so much anymore. David got in touch with his old pal Gavin. Just wanted to catch up for old times' sake. Pumped him for whatever intel he could get on Harmon and Mott, his dad, habits, quirks, anything he and Glenda could exploit to get the jump on Tommy. Interestingly enough, Gavin mentioned that his dad and the other guy from the funeral home always eat at the Old Market whenever they pick up a body at Eppley. Conveniently, Gavin also worked for Harmon and Mott on the side. Glenda and David played him, pulled him in little by little, until they talked him into getting copies of the keys to the hearse and, ultimately, they got him to steal the hearse while his own dad was eating at the Spaghetti Works. Gavin Barker is not as reliable as he appears. He has a complex. All his life he has felt that he is some kind of poser, that inside he isn't what he appears to be on the outside. He has a real inferiority complex."

"You're shitting me," Carston said. "Everything I hear about him is that he's super successful at everything he does."

"He doesn't think he is," Barbie said. "He thinks that he is going to be found out. He is scared to death. It is a mental illness," Barbie stressed. "David knows Gavin. They grew up together, so he knows how to push his buttons. David helped Glenda take advantage of him. He stole the hearse, but then he got scared, and rightfully so. Harvey called him up and told him to watch his ass, and that scared Gavin shitless. And that was the second twist in the plan that threw everything out of whack. Harvey also grew up with Gavin and

David, they were apparently best of friends when they were kids, so Harvey was genuinely worried about Gavin. But Harvey isn't as manipulative as David is, and he meant it as just a little warning to watch his ass, and Gavin took it way more seriously. He did not know what he had gotten himself into, but he got scared enough to think his life was in danger, so he hid the hearse as insurance and went on the run."

"Was he in danger?" Carston asked.

"Looking at it from what I know now, yep," Barbie said. "Maybe not to begin with, had he followed orders, but he sealed his fate when he failed to deliver the hearse and hid it."

"And that's why Glenda hired me," Carston said thoughtfully. "To find Gavin. And that's why David kept trying to point me in his direction."

"David recommended you to Glenda," Barbie replied.

"Where does Harvey come in?" Carston asked.

"Harvey is a US Marshalls undercover agent. He is a plant. He used his old pal David to get him into Glenda's organization several months back."

"And David didn't know that he was with the US Marshalls office?" Carston asked.

"They—David, Gavin and Harvey—all went their separate ways after high school. Harvey went to Creighton, flunked out, roamed around confused for a while, then found himself in Missouri, went back to college, got a degree in psychology and got a job with the US Marshalls. They brought him in for this investigation because of his knowledge of the playing field and his past association with the players. He was a shoo-in. It was just incredible luck that he is who he is and was who he was. I don't think it would have worked as smoothly without him."

"So you've been all over this for a long time?" Carston asked. "Before I was hired?"

"Yep," Barbie answered.

"And you knew that Glenda hired me."

"Yes," Barbie replied.

Carston didn't respond.

"We were following you." Barbie smiled sweetly at him through the screen that separated the back seat of the patrol car from the front seat.

Carston still didn't respond.

"And then the bikers were following you, and we were following the bikers following you when you were looking for the hearse," Barbie explained.

"You all knew I was coming here?" Carston asked. "Because you were all hid out here, waiting."

"Harvey tipped us off. He thought things were going to go down tonight, we were all ready to go," Barbie explained. "We got set up here quick when he called, then we were waiting for Harvey to give us the signal. We wanted to catch Glenda red-handed with the jewels in her possession."

"Did you even think that you were leaving me hanging out to dry? What would have happened if this Xavier, the biker guy, had shot me right off, before Glenda and Harvey showed up?"

"Our profilers said that Xavier wouldn't have it in him to shoot you in cold blood. You made us a little nervous though, when you ran."

"Who killed the Gimp guy?" Carston asked.

"David," Barbie replied.

"Why? Did Glenda order it? I thought he was working both sides," Carston exclaimed.

"David isn't right in the head. He has been spooky unpredictable as this whole thing has progressed. We have no idea why he killed the biker," Barbie explained. "Gimp was a real bad ass. David wanted to get him out of the way I guess. Frankly, I think that he just wanted to kill someone. You know, get the first one out of the way."

"But you didn't see it coming?" Carston asked.

"The profiler also said that David didn't have it in him. That one caught us by surprise."

"That makes me feel better," Carston said, exasperated.

"All's well that ends well," Barbie replied. "How much was Glenda supposed to pay you?"

"Why?" Carston responded.

"I'm doing some paperwork here to try to get you some money out of this. The victim reparation fund. They pay back victims for their loss. I'm going to run it through."

"Five hundred a day," Carston replied.

"Five hundred," Barbie was writing.

"And a five grand bonus for finding the hearse before the cops."

Barbie stopped writing and peered through the screen.

"Seriously," Carston said. "She offered a five grand bonus if I found the hearse before you guys did. You knew that. I told you."

"What the hell? Not my money," Barbie said, turning back to her work.

Barbie scribbled some more. She had a pile of forms she was filling out and Carston couldn't see from where he was seated what they all were, but he was feeling quite good after hearing that he might actually get paid for his labors. After all, it was him who broke the case when it got right down to it.

Barbie slipped a sheet of paper on a thin clipboard over the screen. "Sign on the bottom line," she told him.

Carston glanced over the form in the dim light and signed it. He passed it back. Barbie removed the paper from the clipboard and attached another, then passed it over.

"Another signature," she said.

"What's this one?" Carston asked.

"Feds are going to give you a reward for info that led to the apprehension and recovery of illegal contraband smuggled into the country. I don't know how much, one or two percent of the assessed value."

Carston reached up and took the clipboard. He was doing some fast calculations in his head. "How long does it take to get that?" he asked.

"No idea, it's the feds' deal," she replied. "I'm just doing the paperwork."

Carston signed the form and handed the clipboard back over the screen. Barbie took it and removed the paper. She placed a pile of blank forms with a printed heading on the clipboard and handed it over. "Statement forms," she said. "Start to finish, in detail, everything you can think of, then you can get out of here."

"Everything?" Carston asked. "You've been sitting out there watching my every move for two days, what do you want me to add?"

"I don't want you to add anything," Barbie replied. "I want a statement in your own words of everything that took place and your involvement from the moment Glenda came into your office until the moment we saved your ass from extinction. When you've done that, you can leave."

Carston took the clipboard, let out a sigh, and started writing. At the moment all he wanted to do was go home and get out of his wet clothes.

The aftermath

It was an unseasonably warm morning. If Carston hadn't lived his entire life in Omaha, Nebraska, he might be lured into believing that winter was over. He walked to the Hancock building from the Hotel LeVant. It was later than he usually went in, and he was feeling unusually good. The air was fresh, the sounds of the city waking up and getting moving were familiar and comforting, and he was just glad to be alive to enjoy it. He thought about Megan and looked forward to their dinner together. Carston walked up the stairs instead of taking the elevator and found Stephanie at her desk with a cup of coffee and a particularly delicious-looking cinnamon roll in front of her.

"What's up, boss?" she asked, looking up from her computer.

"Any emails?" Carston asked, knowing that although she was on her computer, she wasn't doing anything that had to do with business.

"Did you find the hearse yet?" she asked without answering his question.

"Yes, I did," Carston said triumphantly. "Last night."

"Good for you. Get paid?"

"Not yet, but the check is in the mail, or will be someday, I hope," Carston answered. "Did you happen to get me one of those cinnamon rolls?"

"I didn't think to," Stephanie replied.

"I see you brought in your coffee. I suppose that means you didn't make a pot yet this morning," Carston observed.

"You are such a good detective," she teased. "I'm not your coffee maker. That's so misogynistic."

Carston shrugged his shoulders and walked into his office, shedding his coat and hat. He knew better than to comment. It would go nowhere but down if he did.

"You got a couple of calls this morning. Messages are all on your desk," Steph called out from her desk.

So she had done some work before he got there. That surprised him. He looked at the Post-It notes stuck to his desk. The first one had "Barbie" printed on it in Steph's flowing handwriting, then a number. The second said "call Kenny." The third had the number for the local radio news station. Carston sat down and punched Kenny's number into the phone first. While it rang he wondered whether he should even bother to call the news station or not.

"Hello," Kenny answered on the first ring.

"Kenny, what do you need?" Carston asked, knowing quite well what he needed.

"David's in jail," Kenny blurted. "Federal jail over there in Omaha. Something about illegal contraband and conspiracy to commit federal crimes. Something about murder, too. My daughter called me last night. I don't know what is going on. No bond yet. She wasn't sure what was going on either. She talked to him on the phone last night but she said that he didn't want to say anything more about it over the phone, they might have it bugged and recording the calls."

"Holy shit, man," Carston said in mock wonderment. "That's crazy."

"You got connections," Kenny said. "You do investigations and stuff like that. You want to see if you can find out what's going on and call me back?"

"I'll see what I can find out," Carston assured him. "Does he have a lawyer?"

"Kathy is trying to get ahold of that hot shot lawyer he went to high school with. Works for a big law firm over there. She called his office and they said that he isn't in yet today. She left a message for him to call her."

"I'll see what I can find out," Carston reassured Kenny and ended the call.

He had forgotten about Gavin. He took out his cell and found the lawyer's cell number. He pushed the call button and waited. It rang several times and went to voicemail. "Carston Hancock here," he said into the phone. "Just checking in. I think you are in the clear now. They aren't looking for you anymore. Glenda and her whole crew got arrested last night. Long story, if you want to call me back, I'll fill you in. Hope you are alright." He almost ended the call, but put the phone back up to his head. "If your friend Harvey calls, go ahead and answer it. Harvey has your back on this. He's not what you think."

Carston ended the call and immediately punched in the number that Barbie had left.

"Officer Rimes," she answered.

"You called?" Carston responded.

"I did," she answered.

287

"Did you work all night?" he asked.

"Most of it," Barbie replied. "I was in meetings with the county attorney, the state attorney and some federal attorney, and sundry other big shots. I thought you might want to know what is going on."

"That would be nice for a change," Carston replied. "Letting me know what's going on, I mean."

Barbie laughed. "First of all, they decided not to file any charges on you, provided you cooperate with the investigation."

"Whoa!" Carston interrupted. "What charges aren't they going to file?"

"I don't know, they're good at finding charges to file," Barbie replied. "The good news is that they are not going to file any charges on you."

Carston didn't respond.

"David Long and Glenda Thompson are in the federal lockup right now, no bond yet. They are having a bond hearing later today, but no one thinks that they'll get out. The feds filed a load of charges on both of them. We have murder charges on David and conspiracy to commit murder charges on Glenda here in Pottawatomie County, so if for some unforeseen reason they get bond set on the federal charges, we'll bring them over here. No bond for murder over here."

"What about Gavin Barker, you heard anything about him?" Carston asked. "I tried to call him just before I called you."

"He's in talking to the feds right now," Barbie replied. "He's cooperating. Harvey's talking to him. They're getting a lot of good intel on Glenda and Tommy Gunn. I'm pretty sure Gavin is going to slide out of this one. Harmon and Mott got their hearse back and they don't want to file any charges on him. He did say that if anybody files any charges on you, that he's representing you."

"Jesus, he's the one who stole the hearse and you're talking about charging me," Carston was a little exasperated.

"I told you that they aren't going to file any charges on you," Barbie said.

"What about the biker?" Carston asked.

"Xavier Warner?" Barbie said.

"If that's the biker, then yes. I don't think I ever knew his name."

"They talked to him and then cut him loose last night."

"He was going to kill me!" Carston said in disbelief.

"Was he?" Barbie asked.

"Yes, he was, that's why I ran," Carston replied. "He was about to shoot me."

"Well, we can't prove that he was going to kill you," Barbie replied. "Really, all we got on him is that he was following you around. I suppose we could file stalking charges on him, but they probably wouldn't stick."

"He was with that Gimp guy, they were planning to ram the hearse and steal it," Carston said.

"Well, that was Gimp's plan, Warner was along for the ride," Barbie replied. "They hadn't really conspired together to do anything at that point."

"And you are talking about filing charges on me," Carston exclaimed again in disbelief.

The Hearse

"Again, I said that they decided not to file charges on you," Barbie reminded him. "Thing is, Harvey pushed not to hold the biker. I don't know what he has in mind."

Carston didn't say anything.

"You should be happier to hear that I filed that paperwork to get your victim reparation and your reward from the feds," Barbie said. "It should come fairly fast. I handed the paperwork directly over to them at the meeting. That should circumvent some of the bureaucracy."

"That's nice," Carston replied curtly.

"Wanna hear something crazy?" Barbie asked. "After Gimp got killed, Warner stepped in and started following you around, and Tommy Gunn himself was giving him the orders and telling him what to do. At the same time, David was feeding him information, posing as a local connection so that he and Glenda could get him and you together and kill you both. Two birds with one stone."

"They were going to shoot us both with one bullet?" Carston said sarcastically.

"Don't be that way, Carston," Barbie replied. "You know what I'm saying, everyone was counting on you to find the hearse. Even Tommy Gunn was counting on you to find it. That's something."

"That makes me feel pretty important," Carston replied.

"Well, I can see you're in a pissy mood this morning, so I'll let you go," Barbie said.

"I wasn't in a pissy mood until you started talking about filing charges on me," Carston replied.

"I gotta go," Barbie said. "I'll call you later and let you know what's happening."

"Hey, if you see my lawyer floating around there, tell him to call me," Carston said.

"Will do." Barbie ended the call.

Carston threw the two post it notes with Barbie's and Kenny's names on them in the trash. He looked at the one from the radio station, wondering if he should call. There was only one reason that he could think they would want to talk to him, and it had to be about the Glenda Thompson case, and he didn't want to talk about it.

"State Farm called while you were on the phone," Steph said from the door. She placed a form on his desk. "They want you to find a 1966 Ford Mustang that was stolen sometime this winter out of a rented garage over in west Omaha. Collector car. Owner went to get it out to take advantage of the warm spell and it was gone. State Farm had a rider on it. I guess it is like new. Thirty-something original miles. It's all there."

Carston gave the form the once-over. It was the form that he and Megan had designed when he first started the business. He thought again about how excited he was to have dinner with her.

He stood up and took his coat off the tree behind his chair. "I'm going over to Kenny's to see if he has any ideas where to start looking on this Mustang," Carston said, taking his cowboy hat from the tree and putting it on his head. He took the form, folded it into quarters and put it in his coat pocket. "He needs to talk to me about David, anyway. David got himself in a little trouble last night."

"You didn't tell me what happened with you last night, with the hearse," Stephanie remarked, leaning forward and looking up at him expectantly.

Carston had purposely not said anything to Stephanie about the case. He had too much to think about today to stay and banter with her, but he was going to have to have a talk with her eventually. Maybe after he finished this Mustang case.

"I'll tell you about it later," he said as he walked past her toward the door. "We need to talk about some other things anyway."

"Whatever you say," Steph said merrily as he went toward the door. She was back on her computer surfing the online shopping site before the door shut behind him.

Dinner

Carston sat in the familiar driveway of his own home waiting for Megan to come out. He had dressed in his best for the occasion. He felt like he would make a good first impression. He had texted her that he was there and she had not answered. He texted her again and waited.

His phone chimed immediately with an answer. She must not have seen the first text. "Come to the door, stupid, like a proper date would," it said with a smiley face emoji.

Carston hastily got out of the Escalade and walked up to the door. He tried the knob and it was locked. He rang the doorbell and waited. It was starting to get cold again and a light wind was buffeting the landing where he stood, cutting through his sports coat. The door finally opened and Megan stood in the doorway, elegantly dressed for their evening. She was a knockout. Carston could barely breathe at the sight of her.

"Ready?" he asked.

Megan didn't reply but stepped out on the stoop and closed the door behind her. Carston led the way to the car and held the door open for her. He was starting to figure out how this was going to go.

"Thank you," Megan said with a smile as she got in.

Carston shut the door and went around to the driver's side to get in.

"Where are you taking me tonight?" Megan asked.

"It's a surprise," Carston replied, playing her game and getting into it. He was pretty impressed with himself.

"I'm excited," Megan exclaimed. "How did your case go? Did you find your stolen hearse?"

"Yes I did," Carston answered. "Tied it all up in a neat package and put a bow on it. I'm looking for a stolen 1966 Mustang right now. Real collector's car. Thirty thousand original miles."

"Do you have any leads?"

"A few. Kenny is asking around for me." Carston turned onto the main four-lane going south toward Dodge Street. A few blocks later he put on his blinkers and tuned into the B-Bops. "Here we are," he said jovially. "Nothing but the best."

"Real funny," Megan said in mock disgust.

Carston drove through the parking lot and back onto the street.

"What happened with the hearse, who stole it?" Megan asked.

"A guy named Gavin Barker," Carston replied.

"My so-called divorce lawyer?" Megan exclaimed.

"Actually, he's my lawyer now," Carston responded.

"You got yourself a divorce lawyer?" This time there was genuine concern in her voice that was not lost on Carston.

"No, absolutely not," he replied quickly. "It's a long story. Anyway, the whole hearse case became so convoluted that I wasn't sure where it was coming from and where it was going and how involved I was going to get pulled into it. Things got just a little dicey. I sort of unofficially retained him along the way, just in case."

"If he stole the hearse, exactly how does it work that he represents you?" she asked.

"Have you ever heard of a guy named Tommy Gunn and some woman named Glenda Thompson?" Carston asked.

"Tommy Gunn the gangster?" Megan inquired.

"That's the one," Carston replied.

Megan thought for a moment. "I think I met this Glenda at some muckity-muck event out at the country club before we got married. I might have been still in college. My dad and mom used to take me out there with them once in a while. I kind of had a thing for the bartender out there. I wonder where he's at and what he's doing now," Megan teased. Carston didn't respond, at least visibly. "As I remember, Tommy Gunn was always out there. Glenda was always there too, hanging on him and not letting him out of her sight. Everyone said she was his niece," Megan continued. "But sometimes I wondered."

"That's her, and it's a long story," Carston said. "I'll start with Glenda Thompson coming into the office the day before yesterday," he began.

Carston finished his story and answered Megan's questions as they finished their last course at the restaurant. It was very nice telling Megan about his case and her listening and asking questions. She was always interested in his cases. Sometimes, after a good one, he couldn't wait to get out of the office, go home and tell her about it over supper. He could tell that she was a little disturbed by the danger that he had found himself in, and he may have played it up a little more than he would have usually done, trying to get some sympathy points. He was careful not to take it too far and unduly concern her.

"So that's it, start to finish," Carston said.

"That has to be the craziest case that you have ever worked," Megan exclaimed. "It's a good one."

"No doubt about that," Carston agreed.

"The biker just walked away?" Megan remarked.

"Appears so," Carston replied. "I don't know exactly what is going on with that."

"They couldn't have at least filed assault charges on him for pointing a gun at you, even if he didn't actually shoot you?"

"I don't know," Carston replied. "Barbie just said that the US Marshalls let him walk."

"How is Barbie?" Megan asked.

"She's looking real good," Carston replied.

Megan looked at him askance and narrowed her eyes.

"Getting you back for the country club bartender remark," Carston smiled slyly. "Looking good, happily married, two kids, happy with her job," he quickly continued.

"I used to be happily married," Megan said absently.

Carston lowered his head in shame.

"Do you feel like desert?" she asked. "Want to share something?"

"Sure," Carston perked up.

"Crème brûlée?" she asked, waving to get the waiter's attention.

"Sounds good," Carston said. "We haven't shared a crème brûlée here for a long time."

"No, we haven't," Megan replied.

The waiter came to the table and Megan ordered the dessert with two spoons. "We'll share," she told him.

"How bad do you want to get back together?" Megan asked when the waiter left with the order.

"It is the only thing I want in the world," Carston replied earnestly. "If I could go back in time and change things, I would. I screwed everything up. I don't know what I was thinking, how I could do it. I am so ashamed of myself. I'm so sorry. If we can get back together again, I'll make it just like it used to be. I'll apologize every morning when I get up and every night before I go to bed for the rest of our lives."

Megan interrupted him. "Apologies aren't going to get it, Carston. I'm sick of apologies. I'm sick of talking about it. Apologies don't change a thing. I don't want to hear it anymore."

Carston took a big breath. "What do I need to do? You tell me. I don't know. There has to be something I can do. I can't live with the way things are between you and me."

"I've been thinking about it a lot the last couple of days," Megan continued. "And you keep saying that if you could go back and do it over. Well, I'm willing to let you go back and do it over again."

Carston started to say something, but she held her finger up to stop him.

"I think if we are going to save our marriage, our relationship, we have to start all over again," she continued. "This right here is our first date.

297

From here on, you need to make me love you. You
gotta treat me like I'm the girl you spotted in the
bar with her friends at the Universtiy of Nebraska
and asked out on a date. You need to be my friend
first. And if that works, then maybe I'll be your
friend with benefits. Maybe you can move out of
that hotel room you're living in and move in with
me at some point. We will have to see. Then maybe
we find out we love each other, get engaged, plan
a wedding, and hopefully it works out and no one
comes along better looking, smarter, more fun and
takes me away from you. That's the way it is going
to work."

"I'll make you love me again," Carston said
eagerly.

"Not 'again,' Carston," Megan replied. "This
is the first date. We are not picking up where we
left off. There is not going to be an 'again.'"

"I got it," Carston said.

"Another thing," Megan said.

"Anything," Carston answered.

"You need a new office manager."

"You are right," Carston said. "I've been
planning on getting rid of Steph, but the timing has
to be right. I can't just fire her. I need to give her
some notice. I need to give her some time to find
something else."

"You're stalling, Carston," Megan replied.
"You've been giving me that same song and dance
for two months. You're just stalling. You're a
coward."

"I know," Carston agreed somberly.

"The time is now." Megan continued. "I don't
want to hear any more excuses. I do not want to

hear her name. I don't want her to exist. I want her out of there Monday morning."

"I'll need to get someone in to take her place before I let her go," Carston said. "It will take time."

"Time's up, Carston, I'm coming in Monday morning to take her place."

"What?" Carston said.

"I said that I'm your new office manager. You want to have an office romance, you have it with me. I'm coming in Monday morning to start work. I don't want her there. I don't want any of her stuff there, I don't want her coming in to pick up her paycheck or anything else that she might leave behind. I don't want her fingerprints on my desk, I don't want some scarf that she left behind hanging in the closet or a strand of her blond hair on the carpet. She no longer exists. Any sign of her or any mention of her from this moment on, and the deal is off. We're done. I don't know how I can make that any clearer."

"I think it is clear enough," Carston said seriously.

The waiter arrived with the crème brûlée.

"This looks really good," Megan commented as if their intense conversation had never occurred. She placed the plate between them and handed him a spoon. "Beat you to the middle," she challenged.

The new beginning

Carston walked into his office in the Hancock building at ten to nine, a full ten minutes before he usually came in. The moment he walked through the door he felt an energy. Megan was sitting at the desk and looked up at him, then at the wall clock.

"I usually get in at nine. I work late most days, so I come in a little later," Carston defended himself.

"That's fine," Megan replied. "I just came in early to get myself acclimatized to my new job before you showed up."

"Good," Carston replied. "Everything okay? You get settled in?"

"I was looking at this paperwork about the stolen Mustang and there wasn't much to work on," Megan started, getting right down to business. Carston could see that small talk was not going to be the routine with her. She continued. "I was able to talk to the agent herself and got some info. Nice gal. We're going to get together for lunch someday. Anyway, she got ahold of the owner and he got back to me. It is a Shelby Mustang, and not one of those production Shelby Mustangs they were manufacturing for a while, this is the real thing. Carroll Shelby himself built this one."

"Who's Carroll Shelby?" Carston asked.

"Some racing muscle car guru from the sixties. Anyway, this car is valued at fifty-five grand, so the insurance company wants it found, bad. The owner sent me a bunch of pictures. You really need to know what you are looking for on this one."

Carston looked at her expectantly.

"Pictures are on your desk, a vintage white race car with a blue stripe," she said in answer to his expression. "Another thing," she continued without losing momentum. "Same agent had a brand-new Tahoe stolen from Westroads. Three months old, lime green. Honestly, it is the ugliest color you've ever seen," she commented. "She gave that case to us, too, so when you talk to Kenny about the Mustang today, give him the skinny on the Tahoe too. I pulled up some pictures off the internet, same year, same model, same ugly lime green, and they are on your desk with whatever information I could get from the agent and the owner as well. I called the owner of the Tahoe too, after I talked to the agent. It's all there. If you have questions let me know and I'll run down the answers."

"You have been very busy," Carston observed.

"These collectable cars, like the Shelby Mustang," Megan continued without acknowledging his compliment. "The parts aren't worth much on their own and the cars are hard to move. Most of the ones that get stolen are shipped out of the country. A lot of them go to the Middle East. Did you know that?"

"No," Carston admitted.

"Yeah, I was talking to the agent and did a little research. You might want to look at that angle. If that's the case, and the car is long gone, I don't know what we do. Check it out and if you decide that might be the case, I'll call the agent back and ask them what they want to do. The owner wants his car back, but if it isn't recoverable, he wants a payout so he can get something to replace it. He takes his old cars all around to car shows during the summer. He doesn't want to be left high and dry this spring. Nice guy, I enjoyed talking to him."

"Sounds like you are keeping me busy," Carston noted.

"Gotta make money, that's what a business is all about. This is not a hobby, Carston," Megan lectured.

"You are absolutely right," Carston replied, nodding his head. "You didn't happen to make a pot of coffee this morning, did you?"

"I picked up a cappuccino on the way in," she replied. "If you want coffee, you'll have to make it yourself."

"Yep, I'll do that. I was just asking," Carston replied.

Carston went to his office, shed his coat and hat, then sat down at his desk and started going through the two piles of forms and pictures Megan had placed on it earlier. If she was anything, Megan was thorough.

"Hello, this is Megan Hancock, Carston Hancock Investigations,' Carston heard Megan on the phone. "We're a private investigation agency that specializes in stolen motor vehicles. We do a lot of work for State Farm, Farmers and Allstate. We would like to add Farm Bureau to that list. We have a very high closure rate and we are quick." There was a pause in the conversation.

"Stolen livestock?" Megan said. "We sure do investigate stolen livestock. The fact is, Detective Hancock is quite the cowboy himself. Just looking at him you can tell he just came off the range. We would most definitely be interested." There was another pause. "They were stolen this weekend," she commented and there was another pause. Carston could tell she was taking notes. "Five hundred a day plus expenses," Megan continued. "Yes sir, we'll take it. I'll need to get some info from you right now over the phone, and then I'll email you a form to fill out to start the investigation."

Carston leaned over his desk to look through the door at Megan. She tuned and was looking back at him nodding with a smile on her face. "We're all over it. Thank you, we look forward to working with you." Megan ended the call.

"Farm Bureau Insurance company. Stolen cattle. A dozen head of Angus from a farm up by Blair. We're expanding our base," she remarked. "Nice guy. I would like to do a good job on this, maybe pick up some more cases in the future."

"Livestock?" Carston replied.

"Yep," Megan grinned. "We're expanding."

"'Detective Hancock looks like he just come off the range'?"

"It's called a hook," Megan replied, still grinning.

"And I suppose by the time I go through these two stolen vehicle reports you'll have googled 'cattle rustling' and have a handle on being a range detective so that I can get going on it. History and all, right down to Tom Horn."

"As soon as you quit talking," Megan replied. "The sooner you find that Mustang and that Tahoe the sooner you can go looking for those cattle."

"Don't let me hold you up," Carston shook his head and went back to the stolen Shelby Mustang and the lime green Tahoe.

"I'm looking up Tom Horn," Megan called back. "He was a range detective in the eighteen hundreds. Looks like they ended up hanging him for murder."

"Great," Carston replied under his breath.

More books from G&B Publishing

G&B Detective Agency: Case of the Missing Tucker
By R. L. Link

G&B Detective Agency: Case of the lonelyfarmer.com
By R. L. Link

G&B Detective Agency: Where the Hell is Angie?
By R. L. Link

G&B Detective Agency: The Welch Avenue Wizards
By R. L. Link

G&B Detective Agency: Case of the Cold Case
By R. L. Link

G&B Detective Agency: Case of the Femme Fatale
By R. L. Link

Made in the USA
Monee, IL
08 December 2023